FAITHLESS

ABOUT THE AUTHOR

One of the fathers of the Nordic Noir genre, Kjell Ola Dahl was born in 1958 in Gjøvik, Norway. He made his debut in 1993 and has since published fifteen novels, the most prominent of which is a series of police procedurals cum psychological thrillers featuring investigators Gunnarstranda and Frølich. In 2000 he won the Riverton Prize for *The Last Fix* and he has also been awarded both the prestigious Brage and Riverton Prizes for *The Courier* in 2015. His work has been published in fourteen countries. He lives in Oslo.

ABOUT THE TRANSLATOR

Don Bartlett lives with his family in a village in Norfolk. He completed an MA in Literary Translation at the University of East Anglia in 2000 and has since worked with a wide variety of Danish and Norwegian authors, including Jo Nesbø and Karl Ove Knausgård. He has previously translated *The Consorts of Death, Cold Hearts, We Shall Inherit the Wind* and *Where Roses Never Die* in Gunnar Staalesen's Varg Veum series.

PRAISE FOR KJELL OLA DAHL

Winner of the Riverton Award
Shortlisted for the Glass Key Award
Shortlisted for the Martin Beck Award
Winner of the Brage Literary Award

'A formidable talent' *Booklist*

'An absorbing study of sexual enthrallment, dogged police work and a harrowing twist or two: Fans of procedurals … will snap this one up' *Kirkus*

'As in previous books by Dahl, we are presented (in a subtly nuanced translation by Don Bartlett) with a dexterous synthesis of classic police procedural and social novel. The details of life in modern Norway are more than added value. Such texture is as pleasurable as the whodunnit elements, particularly as the detectives' caustic observations on the absurdities and irritations of Norwegian society are so sardonically entertaining. If there is a discernible influence on Dahl, it's the matchless Swedish detective novels of Maj Sjöwall and Per Wahlöö. *The Last Fix* has all the skilfully orchestrated tension of that duo's Martin Beck series' Barry Forshaw, *Independent*

'I have read many clever and thrilling crime novels through my life, but often they have nothing to do with real life. If I don't believe in them, they don't impress me. But when Kjell Ola Dahl tells his stories, I believe every single word' Karin Fossum

'Little is as it seems in Norwegian author Dahl's debut, which features a tangled web of art theft, blackmail, torrid sex and double crosses … an exciting read' *Publishers Weekly*

'If you want your worst fears about what goes on inside a cop's mind confirmed, meet KO Dahl's Oslo sleuths, Gunnarstranda and Frølich … this is a book that's hard to put down' Cathi Unsworth, *Guardian*

'*The Fourth Man* begins feverishly, intensely, and unexpectedly, with the affair which whips up between Frank and Elisabeth. From the quick rush of the first chapters, it soon turns into a dark psychological thriller where Frank is left reeling, wandering whether the things he thinks are true really are. From there it morphs into a complex and involved police investigation into fire, theft and death. It's a mix, really, of the noirish and the psychological, almost a blend of the European and American schools, and it works very well. The characters and plot are compelling, the case-shifting events seemingly never-ending to keep the reader and police permanently on their toes … well-worth reading, another excellent translated crime novel. I recommend it very highly, especially as it's ever-so-slightly different from those we've seen recently. Another author to add to the list, then' Eurocrime

'Very realistic and convincing dialogue, which together with an intelligent plot, divided into short chapters, contributes to a very enjoyable and, certainly, entertaining reading. I look forward to reading the rest of the series which falls well within the most rigorous canons of good detective fiction. K. O. Dahl has been an interesting finding for me this year' A Crime is Afoot

'The plot of the book is quite complex, but completely engaging … Each of the possible suspects seems to be hiding something, and virtually no one tells the truth. It's a difficult job for the police in that there are very few leads. Dahl excels at upping the psychological suspense; it is almost impossible to determine who the murderer is' Reviewing the Evidence

'A well written and evocative crime novel … As literary fiction it plays in a higher league than most crime novels' *Dagbladet* (Norway)

'Kjell Ola Dahl has written a captivating detective story with plenty of nuances, and there is no reason for him to hide in the shadow of Mankell' *Zillo* (Germany)

FAITHLESS

KJELL OLA DAHL

Translated from the Norwegian by Don Bartlett

**ORENDA
BOOKS**

Orenda Books
16 Carson Road
West Dulwich
London SE21 8HU
www.orendabooks.co.uk

First published in Norwegian as *Kvinnen i plast* in 2010 by Gyldendal, Norway
First published in the United Kingdom by Orenda Books 2017

ISBN 978-1-910633-27-4
eISBN 978-1-910633-28-1

Typeset in Arno by MacGuru Ltd
Printed and bound by CPI Group (UK) Ltd, Croydon CR0 4YY

This publication of this translation has been made possible through the
financial support of NORLA, Norwegian Literature Abroad.

NORLA
NORWEGIAN LITERATURE ABROAD

SALES & DISTRIBUTION

In the UK and elsewhere in Europe:
Turnaround Publisher Services
Unit 3, Olympia Trading Estate
Coburg Road, Wood Green
London N22 6TZ
www.turnaround-uk.com

In the USA and Canada:
Trafalgar Square Publishing
Independent Publishers Group
814 North Franklin Street
Chicago, IL 60610
USA
www.ipgbook.com

In Australia and New Zealand:
Affirm Press
28 Thistlethwaite Street
South Melbourne VIC 3205
Australia
www.affirmpress.com.au

For details of other territories, please contact *info@orendabooks.co.uk*

1

He had to inhale some fresh air, but to buzz down the electric windows he would first have to switch on the ignition. If he switched on the ignition, the headlamps would come on automatically and most probably ruin everything.

He raised his arm and placed the back of his hand against the car window. Rested his head on it. Shot a look at his watch. Still not two o'clock. Studied the detached house at the end of the street for the nth time. The windows shone yellow. No sign of activity.

The phone in his breast pocket vibrated.

He straightened up. Heard the sound of heels clicking on tarmac. In the wing mirror a woman appeared. She was wearing a short jacket and tight jeans. Carrying a shoulder bag. Her shadow shrank as she passed under the street lamp. She was focused on her bag, lifted it to her chest and opened it while walking.

With his eyes fixed on his mirror he sank down in the seat. Trying to make himself small.

When she was level with the car, she stopped.

He slumped down further.

She took something from her bag.

He leaned back so as not to be caught in the mirror.

She crouched down. Looked at her reflection in the mirror. Ran a lipstick over her lips, pressed them together and checked the result. Raised her little finger and removed a smudge in the corner. Stood up.

An eternity passed.

At long last she set off for the house at the end of the street.

She stopped in front of it. Looked around. There was a clang of metal on metal as she opened the wrought-iron gate. The hinges screamed as she closed it behind her.

Slowly, the figure moved towards the front door, which opened as she reached the steps.

Frank Frølich checked his watch. 02.08.

Immediately the door closed behind her, Rindal's voice was in his earpiece.

'What was that?'

'Don't ask me.'

'Did she see you?'

'No idea.'

'If she saw you, he knows we're here.'

'He's known all the time.'

Silence. Frølich quietly counted to ten.

'It can't be a coincidence that she stopped right by your car.'

'It could be. She checked her appearance and put on lipstick.'

'Did you get an ID?'

'Only saw her from the side. Fringe, red hair, thirty plus.'

'Stay where you are. We'll contact you.'

The earpiece died. The night was silent again, and the ache in his body returned. All he could do was find a more comfortable position.

*

He woke up to his phone vibrating. It was light outside. His watch showed six o'clock. He had slept for about four hours.

Rindal was in a good mood. The voice in his ear was singing 'Frère Jacques'.

'Sorry,' Frølich yawned, 'I fell asleep.'

'We gathered that.'

'Have I missed anything?'

'Not a scooby, but things are happening now. You can atone for your sins.'

Offside mirror. A taxi. The car passed, drove to the turnaround, did a U-turn and came back and stopped outside the end house. A white Mercedes. Diesel engine ticking over. The front door opened. The woman rushed towards the car.

The voice in his ear said: 'Ready, steady, go!'

Frank Frølich waited until the Mercedes had driven away before starting up. Tyres screamed as he swept into the turnaround and did the same U-turn as the taxi. He glanced to the right as he passed the house. A familiar silhouette stood in the window following events. It was Zahid.

He caught up with the taxi and stayed a few metres behind. There was hardly any traffic so early in the morning. The odd lorry, occasional taxis, a few vans.

They went onto the E6, down towards Oslo Centre. The taxi was doing a hundred and twenty.

The phone vibrated again. 'What's happening?'

He straightened the mike as he headed into Vålerenga Tunnel. 'I'm behind him.'

'Find out who she is and where she lives. No reason to keep a low profile if Zahid saw you.'

Frølich pressed *Off*. The taxi took the exit in the gap between the two tunnels. He followed suit. As the cars raced side by side in the hairpin bend he could see her profile. Attractive woman. She was chewing gum.

The taxi turned off again, heading up into the tunnel towards Ryenberg and Simensbråten.

It slowed as it entered a residential district, but not by much. A sprightly jogger crossed the road. A girl with wet hair from a morning shower was sauntering along the pavement.

The taxi braked before the speed bumps.

When it finally pulled into the kerb Frølich activated the blue light on the grille of the car. The driver sat stiffly staring in the rearview mirror, panic-stricken. This guy knew he had broken the speed limit.

Frølich let him suffer in uncertainty while the woman paid for the ride. When she opened the door he also got out.

'Would you mind coming with me?'

She stared at him in bemusement.

She was shorter than he had at first thought. An oval face, regular features. Full lips, eyebrows like two brackets resting face down, a little kink a third of the way along. Her expression, because of the gum-chewing, was provocative. She looked from the unmarked car with the blue light to him and back to the car. He opened the rear door. The taxi driver was quick on the uptake and had gone before she reached it.

Her jacket had no pockets and her jeans were so tight that she certainly didn't have anything in them.

She got in, shoes, no socks. Slim ankles.

Frølich held out an authoritative hand. She looked up at him, still questioningly. 'Bag,' he said.

She hesitated at first, as though considering a discussion. She seemed calm, no noticeable nerves. In the end, she took the bag from her shoulder and passed it to him.

He got in behind the wheel. A scent of perfume mixed with chewing gum filled the car.

'Would you mind showing me some ID?' Her voice was deep, a little husky.

He flashed the card he had hanging around his neck. 'Frank Frølich, Violent Crime and Sexual Offences.'

He opened her bag.

'Would you mind switching off the blue light?'

'Would you mind being silent until you're spoken to?' he retorted.

'As this is where I live,' she continued, warily.

He left the light on. The blue flashes rebounded off the brick walls. He emptied the bag's contents onto the seat beside him. There was mascara and a lipstick, a packet of cigarettes, Kent. A gold lighter.

He found a wallet. Gold Euro card and silver Visa card. They told him she was Veronika Undset, born in 1973. In the photo she had staring eyes and a perm. Her present hairstyle suited her better, unruly with a fringe. Otherwise, the wallet contained a customer loyalty card, a gym membership, two hundred-krone notes and one two-hundred note. No driving licence.

'What do you do, Veronika?'

'This and that. Sit in police cars, as you can see.'

He met her eyes in the rearview mirror. Colour: green. She blinked.

'What do you do for a living?'

'Businesswoman.'

'What's the business?'

'I run a home-help service.'

'At night?'

She sighed heavily and looked away. 'During the day. I've been visiting an old friend.'

He tried to catch her eye again, but she wasn't playing ball.

Two brown pills wrapped in cellophane were under a bunch of keys. 'What's this, Veronika?'

'Voltaren, for muscle pain. I bought it on prescription. I pulled a muscle in the dance class a few weeks ago.'

On prescription. She hadn't needed to say that.

A bottle of perfume, orange, Lancôme; a packet of chewing gum, recently opened. Extra. On top of a flat restaurant matchbook. The last object was a packet of panty liners – unopened. Once again they exchanged glances in the mirror, and he put the packet back. 'Sorry,' she said with a feisty smile. The gooseberry irises flashed beneath the dishevelled fringe.

He flicked up the cover of the matches; several were used. He opened the packet of cigarettes. She had smoked three. If she used matches, why did she walk around with a lighter in her bag?

It was a Zippo. He opened the lid. Flicked it. The flint wheel didn't spark at all. He smelled the lighter. Not a drop of petrol in it.

But Veronika had stopped chewing. Frølich thought, *Getting warmer*.

The felt pad that was supposed to cover the petrol case was missing. The cotton that should have been under the pad was also missing. Instead there was crumpled-up greaseproof paper.

Veronika swallowed.

He took his time. Turned around slowly. The glint in her green eyes was gone. She seemed confused.

'Would you like to tell me what you've concealed in the lighter?'

'No idea.' She looked away, through the window.

He pressed the switch that locked the doors and there was a dull click. She gave a start and looked up: 'Please,' she said with a heavy sigh. 'I'm tired and want to go home. It's not my lighter.'

'Not your lighter?' He raised both eyebrows.

She was silent.

'Whose is it?'

Another resigned sigh.

He repeated the question.

'Would you believe me if I told you? Would you open the door, let me get out and go home? Would you then go to the house of the relevant person and do the same as you've done to me?' She shook her head in desperation. 'You're playing a game I don't understand, but there's nothing I can do anyway.'

He coaxed out the greaseproof paper and carefully opened it. It contained several doses.

'Where did you buy this, Veronika?'

She was silent. Sat with her face averted, her eyes on the street. She didn't even react when he turned the ignition key.

*

It was ten in the morning when Veronika was summoned once again from her cell. Frølich was standing beside Rindal and watching the TV screen in the interview room. She had been through the mill now: no previous convictions, but thoroughly humiliated anyway. Stand on the line, off with your shoes, list personal possessions and hand them over. Afterwards: sit on the floor of the cell for a few hours, answer questions in the interview room and go back. A minor hell for someone who had been up all night. She must have been absolutely exhausted.

Frølich took a deep breath and strode towards the interview room. He entered.

She was saying nothing. Her face drawn, she stared at the wall.

'It's five minutes past ten and Frank Frølich is continuing to interview Veronika Undset,' he said to the recorder.

Slowly, she lifted her head and met his gaze.

'You were arrested because you were in possession of several doses of cocaine after leaving Kadir Zahid's house at 0550 hours. You were observed as you arrived at Zahid's house at 0208 hours. Did you buy the drugs off Zahid?'

She shook her head.

He raised both eyebrows.

She cleared her throat and said, 'No'.

'Who did you buy them off?'

She took a deep breath and grimaced at the very idea that he could even ask the question.

'The witness didn't answer the question. You left Zahid's house at 05.50—'

'I've never bought drugs from anyone,' she interrupted him angrily. 'The lighter isn't mine. I have no idea how it got into my bag and I've told you this many times.'

'Do you really believe this story yourself, deep down?'

'Why are you tormenting me with this? I haven't slept for twenty-four hours. I'm worn out. If it's illegal to walk around with a line of cocaine in your bag, then fine me. You can have the money right now. Just let me go. What you're doing is utterly out of proportion.'

'What were you doing at Zahid's last night?'

She pinched her mouth shut. Made an impatient movement with her body. A lock of hair fell forward creating a dramatic line across her face. He found her good looks unsettling.

'The witness didn't answer the question. Veronika Undset, aren't you going to tell us what you were doing at Zahid's?'

'We were talking.'

'Who was in the house?'

'Kadir and I.'

'How long have you known Kadir Zahid?'

'Many years. We went to school together.'

'Kadir Zahid usually has a couple of bodyguards around. Weren't they there?'

She shook her head.

He tilted his head again to provoke a response.

She said: 'No, we were alone.'

'Why was he alone, without any bodyguards?'

'You'll have to ask him. I have no idea.'

'But you must have wondered yourself?'

'No, I didn't, not then and not now. He and I chatted.'

'Chatted about what?'

'That's private.'

'Private? You're aware you're being questioned by the police, aren't you?'

'It was a confidential conversation, and I won't say a word about it, however much pressure you apply.'

'You went to see him for a chat at two in the morning?'

'That's what I said.'

'Did you and Zahid go to bed together?'

Her full lips stretched in a caustic smile.

'Are you going to answer the question?'

'It's my business who I go – or don't go – to bed with.'

'Could Zahid have put the lighter in your bag without your knowledge?'

She sat looking at him without saying a word.

'Would you please answer.'

'The answer's no. Kadir's fanatical about drugs and alcohol. He doesn't even drink beer.'

'Did you intend to sell on the drugs?'

She bristled with annoyance. 'No. Can't you make this easy and say what it is you want? Why are we here?'

'You were in possession of five grams of cocaine. That's illegal.'

'You must have more urgent cases to spend your time on. Go online and you'll see what the police should be doing now.'

She shifted position and crossed her legs. 'Have we finished if I admit to having the drugs?'

He trod water. They exchanged glances, and he knew she knew. She sent him a wry smile, and he couldn't help but admire her style.

The door opened. Emil Yttergjerde poked his head in.

Frølich said: 'It's 10.14 and Frølich's leaving the interview room.'

He walked out.

'It's true what she says,' Yttergjerde said. 'She runs a firm called Undset AS. Something to do with cleaning. The manager's called Veronika Undset. Registered in Brønnøysund. She keeps tidy accounts, pays tax, nothing dodgy there.'

'What the heck's she doing at Zahid's in the middle of the night, then?'

Rindal came out of the TV room.

Frølich heaved another sigh and said aloud what they were all thinking: 'I can't see the point of this. She knows we're going to let her go any moment. She's just biding her time.'

The three of them looked at each other. Yttergjerde said: 'So what are we going to do?'

Rindal, hands upturned, smiled and said: 'Let her go.'

2

Frank Frølich stopped in the corridor and yawned. A whole night on his backside in the car had made him stiff and sore. He started at the sight of Lena Stigersand. She had a nasty swelling under her left eye.

'New missing-persons case,' she said, passing him a report.

He flicked through the papers. 'And what about you?' he said. 'Fall off your bike or have you got a new boyfriend?'

'Girl gone missing,' she continued undeterred, 'or to be more precise, a young woman from Uganda, the university in Kampala, Makerere. Her name's Rosalind M'Taya. That's an M followed by a T, like in Mt Everest. A student at the university's international summer school. So, smart. It's probably hard to get in. She checked into the student hall of residence on Wednesday and stayed there two nights. But when her room-mate arrived yesterday, a girl from Pakistan, sorry, young woman, she wasn't there and she hasn't been seen since.'

Frank Frølich studied her in silence. 'Lena,' he said.

'The point is she's missed loads of events on the programme without informing anyone. What I did find out was that she arrived on Tuesday morning on a flight from London, which coincided with a flight from Kampala.'

'You look dreadful. What happened to your eye?'

'Eye?' Lena said in the same casual tone. 'There's nothing wrong with my eye. Perhaps you need to go to the optician? You're the right age.'

Frølich carried on walking to his door. Here he met Emil Yttergjerde. Frankie nodded in the direction of Lena's erect back. 'Seen her black eye?'

Emil nodded.

'She doesn't want to talk about it.'

Emil grinned. 'Spanking overload, maybe?'

Frølich mounted a doubtful expression. 'Lena?'

'Haven't you heard? Last Friday. She and Ståle Sender left the pub – together. According to the rumour mill, it's "absolutely true".'

'Lena and Ståle?' Frølich found that hard to believe, at first anyway.

'Steely Ståle, you know. Probably warmed up with *Blue Velvet*. With or without laughing gas.' Emil grinned and walked on.

Frølich went to his desk. Lena and Ståle Sender? Ståle had been moved – how many times? Now he was checking passports at Gardermoen Airport when he wasn't harassing asylum-seekers.

An odd couple: Lena was an only child and a Bærum girl who would return bottles of wine at a restaurant if they weren't the right temperature. Lena spoke refined Norwegian; she was 'exhausted' when others were 'knackered'. Ståle was a working-class boy from Furuset with three interests: cars, watches and cognac – in that order. In his wallet he had a photo of the seventies' Ford Mustang he kept under a tarpaulin every winter. Twice Ståle had been investigated for violence by the special unit, not including the many other cases that had been hushed up or conveniently forgotten.

Frølich looked down at the report. It was stapled to a pile of photocopies. The missing woman's application papers to ISS – the international summer school. Rosalind M'Taya studied sciences at the University of Makerere and – as far as he could see – had received impressive grades. Glowing character references from two professors. Letters of invitation from the University of Oslo to a six-week stay at the international school, which boasted extremely competent lecturers. The photo revealed that Rosalind M'Taya was very attractive. She had her hair pinned up on the crown and stylish Afro braids across her scalp. Full lips. Her eyes were doe-like, lashes curled upwards.

A couple of days in Norway and then gone? This was *not* trafficking. Rosalind was a serious student, not brought in by dubious Eastern Europeans to serve men from a flat in Bygdøy allé.

She lands at Gardermoen. She goes through passport control and customs. Takes either the express train or the airport bus. Definitely not a taxi. She must have received instructions from the summer school. The train is the easiest option. Then she changes to the Metro at the National Theatre and carries on to Blindern. Nice-looking girl and most likely poor, rewarded with an overseas stay. Unsure of herself, maybe abroad for the first time. Clever – no doubt careful too, thorough. What sort of people would she trust? Other Africans? Students on the course?

Rosalind M'Taya disappeared two days after she checked into her hall of residence.

In Oslo there are plenty of Norwegians who have worked in East Africa with Norad and the UN. Perhaps Rosalind had an address with her from home, perhaps she visited someone. Perhaps she was still with them. Perhaps a former missionary was driving her around, showing her the Viking boats or the Vigeland Sculpture Park right now. Perhaps these speculations were simply a waste of time.

Lena with Ståle Sender!

Could that be possible? The posh girl from Bærum in bed with the missing link, a primitive, racist street urchin who got an erection from using live ammo on jobs?

It had been a long night. *Should go home*, Frølich thought.

*

An hour and a half later he was in Rosalind M'Taya's student room. Her Pakistani roommate reached up to his chest. Her plait was a work of art, thick and long and black and with a pattern like the climbing rope in the gym. When she smiled she revealed long and irregular teeth. She told him she had never met Rosalind, but the things in the suitcase were hers.

Frølich opened the suitcase. And had his assumptions about her background confirmed. She was poor. Most of the clothes seemed to be home-made. Right at the bottom: some kangas and batik materials. Her jewellery was typically African: big shapes and bright colours.

He could feel the Pakistani woman was ill at ease. 'Don't worry,' he said. 'I can manage on my own.'

She left.

He emptied the contents of the suitcase onto the bed. And two objects gave him cause for alarm. A full billfold wallet and a well-equipped toiletry bag. She had gone without taking toiletries or hiding her money. The suitcase was full. It was unlikely she had taken a change of clothing with her. The possibility that Rosalind had disappeared of her own free will had shrunk considerably.

He stood by the window. Looking out on the paths and grass between the tall trees in the park. Saw groups of students of various nationalities. One large group sat in a circle on the grass. An open-air class.

Suddenly a chill went down his spine and he turned back to the room. It was as though someone had touched his shoulder. There was a loud whining noise. The next second it was gone, and the room filled with sound again: someone was cooking in the student kitchen. A man called something from far away behind a wall and pipes gurgled.

He shook off the feeling he'd had.

Outside, he admired the beautiful gardens. When he was a student it was generally assumed that people in the hall of residence had got their rooms by underhand means. Those who lived in what resembled a manor house only a stone's throw from the university complex were extremely lucky.

The problem is, he mused, Rosalind M'Taya could have bumped into anyone at all when she went out on Friday. Perhaps she caught the tram to the centre. It was more likely though that she stuck together with students she *barely* knew – colleagues. So they would have to go around with a photo asking in shops and cafés…

He wasn't up to that now. He had to go home and sleep.

3

It was five o'clock in the afternoon when his phone woke him. He lay in bed, slightly uncertain as to why he had set the alarm. Then he remembered the party.

Frankie hadn't had any contact with Karl Anders Fransgård for several years and was therefore somewhat surprised when he received an invitation to his fortieth birthday party. As teenagers they had been almost inseparable, but they hadn't seen a great deal of each other since.

They met at school, brought together by a common interest in model aeroplanes and mechanics. For Christmas Frankie had received a little propeller engine which he filled with naphtha, fixed to his desk and started up with his index finger. Starting a combustion engine like that, adjusting the mix of petrol and air and then letting it run was the height of happiness in those boyhood days. But his friend's interest in planes went much further than models. He was obsessed with the technical wizardry behind jet engines and propeller power. His bedroom was full of books about model planes, pioneers' lives and achievements and the history of flying. He also collected old film clips: Roald Amundsen in sealskin clothes waving in front of the Latham flying boat before boarding to search for Umberto Nobile, the Hindenburg airship that caught fire over New York, Charles Lindbergh in his plane, a Curtiss 'Jenny' – already in those days Karl Anders's room was a mini aviation museum.

Everyone thought Karl Anders would become a pilot, but colour blindness put paid to his dreams.

The two of them chose different paths. Frankie felt a clammy unease spread down his back whenever thoughts strayed to the incident. *But it's a long time ago*, he told himself and got up. He started pacing the room, the way he did when similar thoughts struck him. He walked off his unease.

On the grapevine he had heard that Karl Anders had trained as an engineer. They bumped into each other a year ago. Karl Anders, wearing a hi-vis vest and a helmet, was inspecting some pipes that had been dug deep in Oslo Centre.

Frankie had made a witticism out of it: seeing his friend again under the ground and not in the air. They hit the right tone, joked and reminisced for a few minutes, exchanged telephone numbers and concluded, what the hell, they should have a beer one day.

Neither of them had actually rung. The times Frølich had happened to think about his friend he presumed they both felt the same way.

But four weeks ago an invitation landed in his post box.

Twenty years is a long time. Things get overgrown with moss, disintegrate and disappear. The unease he felt now was because he had been single for too long. It was a strange feeling to turn up at this kind of party alone when he had been invited to 'bring a partner'. The invitation was printed on exquisite paper and there was even a reference to dress code. Most of the guests would be married couples or living together, and conversations would inevitably revolve around these people's lives. Children, all the jokes and the linguistic nuggets the little ones came up with, the parents' problems getting child care, the incompetence of nurseries and the lack of after-school care. Those couples that didn't have children yet would talk about their trendy holidays and house-renovation plans. The women would blithely chatter away about their partners' less salubrious sides, snoring, salmon-fishing mania, elk-hunting or football, all put in such a way that Frankie Frølich – because he was a single man – had no chance of making any kind of contribution. On the other hand, it was always fun to meet people from the old days. After a couple of glasses most were good for a few reminiscences.

The choice was either to sacrifice an evening for the sake of an old friendship or to sacrifice his dignity. Better to sacrifice a free evening and retain his honour, he had reflected, and fetched the charcoal-grey suit from his wardrobe.

The present was already wrapped and the best possible if it had been for himself: the collected works of Genesis on CD with Peter Gabriel on lead vocals. *From Genesis to Revolution, Nursery Cryme, Trespass, Foxtrot, Selling England by the Pound,* the live recording from 1973, topped by the double album of all albums: *The Lamb Lies Down on Broadway.* Nearly eight hours of recorded meditative brain massage.

*

The party was held in a place in Eiksmarka, just outside Oslo.

He pushed the boat out and took a taxi from Oslo Station. The taxi driver was an Iraqi Kurd whose knowledge of the roads to Bærum was as good as his spoken Norwegian. He couldn't use satnav either. The man would happily have driven to Drammen or Hønefoss if Frølich hadn't given him directions from the rear seat. It was as light as day as they turned into the drive where lit torches indicated the location of the party. Couples were making their way in through the door as he clambered out of the car.

Ten minutes later he was standing with a glass of Cava in his hand looking for familiar faces while exchanging platitudes with people he had never met.

'Karl Anders and I studied together in Trondheim,' explained a tall, roguish-looking man with a sensitive mouth and combed-back hair. 'Now we're almost neighbours!'

A sweet girl with black ringlets said she had worked with Karl Anders before he started at the council. Frølich followed her gaze and spotted his friend at the back of the room. Karl Anders was, as always, dressed in shabby chic, black jeans and suit jacket over a black T-shirt with a profound slogan across his chest.

'And there we have the main man,' said the girl with the ringlets, and she beamed as Karl Anders tore himself away and strode towards them.

'Frankie,' exclaimed Karl Anders with a smile. 'Great you could make it. This guy here,' he said, putting an arm around Frankie's shoulder, giving him a friendly punch in the side and a pally grin, 'this is the guy I've known longest of everyone here!'

'Are you the one who had a darkroom in the cellar of the block where you lived?' asked Ringlets. When Frølich nodded, she added: 'I've heard *so many stories* about you and that darkroom. Is it true you had a mattress on the floor in case there was a party?'

Frølich sent her a forced smile. He never felt at ease when he was the centre of attention.

'Sorry,' said Karl Anders, a little the worse for wear. 'I have to steal the star.' With which he pulled Frølich away. He grabbed his old friend around the neck and hugged him.

'Happy birthday, Karl Anders.' Finally, he got to read the quote on his friend's T-shirt: *The worst crime is faking it – Kurt Cobain.*

'You're the *only* one of the old boys here, Frankie.'

Frølich didn't answer. He had been counting on his old pals to get through the evening.

'I didn't invite any of the others,' said Karl Anders, his eyes glassy. 'None of them. Only you. This day's special for me.'

'Of course,' Frølich answered, deflated.

'This is the start of my new life,' Karl Anders said. 'I'm getting rid of the person I don't want to be. Look,' he whispered and pointed to a group of women with their backs to them. 'Women are lovely, Frankie. Women are bloody lovely! But not for me any more,' he beamed. 'I'm engaged!'

He stumbled towards the women with his arm around Frølich's waist.

A woman dressed in a short, tight-fitting black dress turned. Her eyes glinted green in the dim lighting.

'Veronika,' Karl Anders said. 'Say hello to Frankie – my old pal Frank Frølich.'

Frølich shook Veronika Undset's slim hand.

In a fraction of a second her face underwent a transformation. Her eyes dilated and shone with fear until once again she appeared totally relaxed, with the same knowing gaze he had seen that very morning in the car.

He was so surprised he wasn't sure his voice would carry.

'Haven't we met before?' she asked in a drawl.

He hesitated for a few seconds. Registered from a distance that her pinned-up hair revealed a wonderful arched neck.

'You'd better remind me where and when, if so,' he said, looking into her eyes, and letting go of her hand. 'But I think I would've remembered,' he added.

She was silent, holding her glass with both hands now and studying the floor.

Karl Anders grabbed her around the waist and drew her to him. They were a good match. A rock-'n'-roll guy and his elegant squeeze.

'Veronika and I are getting married in April,' he said. 'In Rome, and do you know what, Frankie?'

Frølich shook his head.

'I want you to be our best man.'

Frankie smiled at them. It might have been the Cava or maybe the pressure in the room, but his ears were ringing. He swallowed the rest of the bubbly. Karl Anders produced another glass straight away.

'Ahem,' came a loud voice.

Frølich turned. Beside Veronika Undset stood a woman with a corn-blonde page cut. 'Hi,' she said, holding out a hand. 'My name's Janne and we're sitting next to each other!' At which she burst into laughter and gave him the feeling the evening was saved.

*

The dining table stretched over two rooms through a wide doorway, splitting the gathering into two halves. Fortunately, Janne and he had seats in the half without the hosts and the toastmaster. Tapas were served from a large buffet and conversation around the table and in the queue was lively. He sat waiting until most people had served themselves. As did Janne, who told him that she was a single mother with a boy of almost nineteen. 'Got knocked up,' she grinned when his eyes widened. 'I was sixteen.'

'You're joking.'

She pursed her lips and shook her head.

'Do you read gossip magazines? That part of my life was like a bad film based on an even worse book. I was working as an au pair in France. He was ten years older than me, had a cool tattoo on his arm and so on. He worked behind a bar in Montpellier – but did a runner when I got pregnant. No, I'm not joking. My story and Kristoffer's is full of clichés, but we turned out OK.'

They clinked glasses. Her grey eyes shone as her full lips broke into a smile, which revealed a slightly irregular left canine and beguiled him.

'Kristoffer's my son.'

They just managed to serve themselves before the toastmaster at the other end of the table stood up and reeled off a few well-prepared quips that sent waves of chuckles through the guests. Frankie had entertained the thought for a few seconds that he ought to pluck up courage and say a few words as none of his peers was present. However, he reasoned, if Karl Anders chose to ignore a large section of his past it would be impolite of him to protest. *Had he wanted me to talk about the old days he would have asked.* So he decided to let it go. After the toastmaster had finished welcoming them the buzz of conversation resumed.

'Aren't you going to ask what I do?' she asked.

'I was thinking of starting at the other end,' he said deftly, 'by asking you what your favourite meal was.'

'Waffles and champagne,' she grinned. 'The first thing you learn about wines in France is that champagne goes with everything.' She blinked. 'Champagne is to women what milk is to babies. Next question.'

'Would you miss your job if you were on a desert island?'

'Depends what there was to do on the island,' she parried. 'Where is it?'

'If I was allowed to choose, in the Caribbean,' he replied.

'Is this where I say I love going on holiday to Greece?'

'If that's true, yes.'

The toastmaster rose to his feet and tapped a fork against his glass.

'Khao Lak,' she whispered quickly. 'My dream destination in Thailand. By the way, I'm an accountant. But I'm not as dry or as rigid as the myths suggest.'

Frankie hardly noticed time pass. Janne said she knew Veronika from school, in Nadderud. Veronika had moved to Bærum from somewhere in the East End of Oslo. Janne had lost a few years in her education because of her son and finished upper secondary at the age of twenty-four. She and Veronika were the same age and had found common ground in their frustration with the childishness of the other students. Since then they had stuck together and now it was Janne who took care of her friend's accounts.

'Why did Veronika go to school several years after the others? You had to struggle with bringing up a child, but…'

'Don't we all have something *to struggle with*?' she rejoined. 'What about you and the darkroom I've heard so much about? I'm dying to hear the *real* story.'

The real story, he thought, and fell into a reverie.

'What is it?'

'Nothing.'

'I can *see* there's *something*.'

'Do you remember the Chinese Politburo once blamed the cultural revolution on the so-called Gang of Four?' Frølich asked. 'They as good as rewrote history, airbrushed them off photos and so on. You saw a long row of prominent politicians and holes where the four had been standing.'

'What's that got to do with your darkroom? Were you airbrushing photos?'

Frankie took his glass. 'I'm just not sure how comfortable it is to be the sole witness of Birthday Boy's younger days.'

It was midnight by the time the dinner was over. He and Janne sat on a sofa drinking liqueur coffees. Gradually there was more liqueur than coffee. The music got louder, but no one was dancing. People sat around in groups chatting. It was only when some started leaving that

Frankie realised he had spent the whole evening with Janne and had barely exchanged a word with anyone else.

She blinked when he said as much. 'Bit late to do anything about that now,' she said. 'People are leaving.'

'I should ring for a taxi too,' he said.

'We can split it.'

They behaved like a married couple. When she kicked off her party shoes for boots he stood holding her bag. They said goodbye to the hosts together. Veronika Undset hugged her friend, turned to Frølich and gave him a hug too.

It was three in the morning when he held open the rear door of the taxi. 'I knew it,' she said, climbing in. He closed the door, walked around the car and got in on the opposite side. 'I knew you were a gentleman,' she said, and giggled as they exchanged glances. 'Or is that your seduction move – opening doors for women?'

'Høvik,' he said to the driver, who started the engine. 'Høvik first,' he added guiltily.

Frankie leaned back. Breathed out. It was over. It had been a nice evening. Now he was in a taxi with an attractive woman.

The driver didn't spare the horses. When the taxi made a sudden turn, Janne moved with the centrifugal force into the crook of Frankie's arm. 'Oh, dear,' she whispered, laughing at herself and glancing up. He tentatively tasted her lips.

Silence fell over the subdued half-light on the rear seat. When they finally decided to come up for air, she withdrew to her corner.

The taxi approached Høvik Church.

She grabbed his hand. 'I don't want things to go too fast,' she said when he found her grey eyes in the semi-darkness.

She cleared her throat. 'Besides, Kristoffer's at home.'

'You don't need to make excuses,' he said. 'I can invite you out.'

She slipped back into his arms. 'Will you?'

'I get off here,' she said to the driver, later.

'What about—?'

She shook her head. 'Can't you ring me?'

The taxi stopped. They had arrived. Frankie looked out at a wire fence around an older detached property.

'So this is where you live,' he said, looking at her.

She leaned forward and kissed him lightly. Seconds later she was outside and ran in without a backward glance.

'Ryen,' he said to the driver, who put the car into gear. 'Back the same way and then right through the town.'

4

Sunday was setting out to be another boiling hot day. The sun would bake down from a blue sky, animals would doze in the shade, too lethargic to stand up and graze. The gravel road was already dusty. It was so quiet you could actually hear the sun burning and sweat running – a silence that was only broken by occasional words stealing between the tree trunks, fragments of conversations between people who couldn't be bothered to do any more than talk.

Gunnarstranda had another week left of his holiday. It was ten o'clock and he was strolling between the post box and his cabin. He had the *Aftenposten* tucked under his arm and was enjoying the start of a new day.

He hadn't lit a cigarette for two whole months. Instead he had worked his way through an impressive pile of nicotine gum. He started the day with one piece, continued at a steady rate and consumed several packets a week. Tove thought he looked weird when he chewed, so he would put the chewing gum under his lip like a nicotine pouch.

They had been at the cabin for two weeks. Gunnarstranda had lived his life with Guinness and gardening without giving work a single thought. But once the thought struck him, that was it. Work filled his consciousness the way a sponge absorbs water in a bathtub.

He went into the cabin, lifted the cellar lid, took a can of Guinness and hurried on to the stoop with a glass in his hand.

Tove found him there with the cool glass pressed against his forehead.

'What are you thinking about?'

'Mustafa Rindal,' he said. 'Tomorrow's Monday and there's only a week left.'

'Don't call him Mustafa. It's so patronising.' She showed him the bunch of flowers she had picked. Red sticky catchfly, white lady's bedstraw and meadow buttercups.

'But that's his name.'

She went inside looking for a vase, without answering. On her return she put the bunch in and rearranged a flower here and there.

'They got married,' he said, sipping the beer.

'Who did?'

'Rindal and the engineer who works for Kripos. Leyla. Long, dark hair, much younger.' When Tove nodded, he continued: 'She's from Syria. As she's a Muslim they did it Muslim-style, but he had to become a Muslim as well. He converted in the mosque in Åkebergveien. When you convert you have to take a Muslim name, and he chose Mustafa, so he's called Mustafa Rindal.'

'But you don't need to call him that.'

'He received that name at the conversion, upon his encounter with Allah.'

'Upon his encounter with Allah? Remember you have colleagues who are Muslims from birth. They don't think this is comical. We both know you don't like Rindal and you think it's humorous that you have a Muslim boss, but the conversion he went through was because he loves this woman. And in your heart of hearts you know that's a wonderful act of devotion. Rindal knows, of course, that you're all grinning behind his back. He knew that before he converted too. Rindal sacrificed himself for love. What are you laughing at?'

Gunnarstranda whinnied, and repeated: 'Sacrificed himself for love? Hel-lo? This is Rindal we're talking about.'

She was about to answer when he got up suddenly.

'What is it?'

Gunnarstranda raised a finger to his mouth. 'Listen,' he whispered.

Tove pricked up her ears. After a while she arched her eyebrows.

'The buzzing noise.' Gunnarstranda pointed under the terrace roof.

A handful of bees were whizzing around.

They exchanged glances. She opened her eyes wide and hurried in.

Gunnarstranda stood watching the bees. He knew the buzz. This was scouts looking for a new house and they had chosen the terrace roof of the cabin. He couldn't allow that.

Scouts on the lookout for a house meant a swarm of bees.

He strode down to the hives. Where was the swarm? It was always close to the hives. He gave a start of alarm when he saw it. This was the queen on her travels. The fat old lady had managed to fly to the closest tree, the ancient oak. But she hadn't chosen a branch. No, she had clung to the bark, making the swarm long and large, like an excrescence of the tree trunk, a tumour. He walked back to fetch his straw hat, a bee smoker and a white sheet.

Tove stayed in safety behind the windows. She didn't like bees. She didn't like insects in general. Some education was required, but it would have fallen on deaf ears anyway. Bees in a swarm don't sting. They are preoccupied with very different things. He must have said that at least fifty times. She hadn't taken it in, however.

He spread the sheet in front of the tree. Then he held the straw hat under the fattest part of the swarm and swept them in, turning it as quick as a flash. Face down. Tens of thousands of bees flew into the air, but they were harmless enough. They just wanted to be with their queen. Gunnarstranda found a stick and lifted the hat he had placed on the sheet. One by one the bees crawled in under it. He stood watching the swarm. So he had caught the queen. He lit the bee smoker and used a broom and the smoke to hurry the stragglers. When they were all with the old lady, he tied the sheet around the hat and put it in the shade. It was important to find a new home for the swarm now. He would have to knock together a new hive.

5

Yes, the woman behind the bar was pretty certain. You couldn't be mistaken. She was such a good-looking woman. Black, wasn't she; and her hair: It was braided and pinned up and in place. She must have spent hours on her hairstyle. 'She was just *so* attractive!'

A bite, Frølich thought contentedly. *A bite on his first attempt. This is my day. Lady Luck is smiling on me.*

The student pub hadn't opened yet; the woman was getting things ready for the evening. She was from the north and wearing a black dress with a narrow neck and ruffles on the sleeves, as though she were appearing in a dancing show. She had been at work on Friday too. And it had been impossible not to notice the girl with the Afro.

'It must have been quite late because there were *so* many people; in Oslo you don't go out before midnight.'

'Was she with someone?'

'I haven't the foggiest.'

'Was she standing at the bar or—'

'No, she was sitting at a table.'

'Alone?'

The woman behind the bar pressed her lips together as she considered the question. 'There were some Tiggers around.'

'Tiggers?'

'Tomcats.'

'Any you knew?'

She shook her head.

'Can you describe any of them?'

She hesitated. This kind of description wasn't easy. 'Students, usual kind, you know. It's dark in here.'

As if on command, a door opened and sunlight flooded in. A man with a shaven head, tattooed upper arms and white calves made his entrance. He was dressed in summer shorts and a T-shirt which was nearly bursting around his stomach. A Coke in one hand, a DVD in the other, and in his mouth he had a newspaper, like a dog. 'What's up?' The newspaper fell on the counter. *Verdens Gang*.

Frølich showed him the photo of Rosalind M'Taya. It was obvious that this guy remembered her, too.

'Did you see who she was sitting with?'

'Mr Cool,' came the quick response.

The woman behind the counter gave a start. The two of them exchanged glances.

'Who's Mr Cool?'

They exchanged glances again.

'Come on,' Frølich urged.

'He makes films. That's all I know.' He nodded towards the woman behind the bar. 'You know him better than me.'

'But I don't know his name,' she said. 'And I didn't *see* who she was sitting with.'

'He makes films, you said.'

'Ads,' she informed him.

'Full of himself,' the man added, starting to put away the glasses. 'Tall and dark, soul patch and probably a six-pack. A little scar at the side of his mouth.' He took a sip of Coke and smiled at the woman behind the bar. 'Women like that. It makes him look a bit *brutal*.' He grinned.

Her index finger found some grains of dust on the counter. She pulled them towards her, one by one.

'Do you know where I can find him?'

'He's the type to go to the Business School or the Music Academy.'

'Westerdal Advertising School,' she corrected him. 'He teaches there.'

The guy with the Coke winked at Frølich.

'He's cute. Nothing wrong with that, is there?'

He ducked as she threw the duster at him.

*

When Frank Frølich got in his car and checked his phone he saw there were two calls from Rindal. He ought to ring back at once.

Actually he had been planning to call Janne Smith. Had been thinking about it all yesterday and didn't want to let the intimacy that had grown between them slip away. OK, they had only spent one evening together; they had been pushed together by others. But that was irrelevant. They shared the same sense of humour, liked the same music, read the same books and had similar attitudes. He couldn't remember the last time he had communicated with a woman so easily. Sitting beside her at the party had been the perfect jam session. No dodgy notes, barely a break of rhythm. Her laughter and eyes, he thought. She seemed like a happy woman. He liked the easy laugh, her maturity. She'd been through tricky times, but she had landed on her feet. A teenage pregnancy, abroad what was more – yet she'd chosen to keep the child, bringing up a son alone. Doing that showed determination, caring, strength, self-sacrifice, optimism and, last but not least, self-belief. And, if he concentrated, he could still feel the brush of her lips on his the second before she jumped out of the taxi.

He started the engine to activate the air-conditioning. Took his phone and chose duty before pleasure. He called Rindal.

Another break-in. The case of Kadir Zahid.

Frølich could feel the twin claws of fear and trepidation taking hold. 'What do you want me to do?' he asked.

'Follow up on the woman we let go before the weekend. The one running the home-help services.' Frølich opened the door and got out of the car while Rindal brought him up to speed on the case.

'Go there now,' Rindal ordered. 'Question her.'

Frølich hesitated. Should he ask Rindal to send someone else?

'What's the problem?'

Frølich hesitated a little while longer. 'Nothing', he said, and hung up.

Afterwards he stood thinking about the party. He had felt his stomach churn when his boyhood friend's fiancée turned and he saw who she was. On the other hand, the evening had taken a very pleasant turn.

Then I'm back on the job, he thought. *I receive a call and have to look at Veronika Undset through a policeman's eyes again.*

He got back into the car, but still hesitated.

The invitation to the fortieth birthday party had landed in his post box four whole weeks ago. What happened in the early hours of Saturday, him having to arrest Veronika, was a coincidence.

Anyone could have been sitting in the car outside Zahid's house on that night. If he hadn't gone to the party, he would never have guessed the woman he arrested was engaged to Karl Anders. There would hardly have been a relationship between Karl Anders and himself. It had been years since they last saw each other.

The only event of interest on the night of the birthday celebration was that he'd met Janne. The party *hadn't* brought him any closer to Veronika Undset, he thought, repeating it to himself without feeling any real conviction: not at all.

He stared at the wheel and the gearstick through distant eyes.

OK, he said to himself. Veronika Undset may not be at home now. If she is, and the conversation becomes too awkward, I will have to ask to be released from this case. That's how it will have to be. Definitely.

With that, he blinked left and pulled away from the kerb.

*

On the door hung a scrappy sign: UNDSET AS. He tried the handle.

Locked.

Relieved, he backed onto the tarmac area beyond the entrance. Through the window that covered nearly all the wall on the ground floor he glimpsed office furniture. The house seemed abandoned and somewhat in disrepair. The ground floor must have been a grocery shop once, presumably in the Sixties, when there were local shops like this.

His watch showed five past three. Two young girls came walking along the pavement. He wondered whether to ask them if they knew the house. They looked at him, exchanged glances, giggled and walked on.

Then a taxi pulled into the kerb. The driver turned to the rear seat and took some money from the passenger. It was Veronika.

'Nice to see you again,' he said, as she opened the door and stepped out.

Her answer was drowned in the noise of the taxi accelerating away. She walked past him, fumbling with keys.

'Did you enjoy it?' she asked, holding the door open.

'Yes, I had … a brilliant time.'

They went into an office, which was a mess – full of cardboard boxes containing cleaning products and piles of plastic buckets. A collection of mops resembling a wigwam stood in the corner behind the desk.

'I had a bit of a shock,' she said. 'Karl Anders has talked about you, of course, but I had no idea it was *you*.'

Shock, he reflected, and said: 'I'm here professionally.'

She fell quiet.

He took a breath. Yet she spoke first.

'I thought the fine cleared up that matter. I paid it today – even though I've never touched cocaine before or since.'

'It's about something else.'

She tilted her head.

'Regine Haraldsen.'

She said nothing. Went to the desk. Fiddled with the phone, pressed a key and read the display.

'Has he rung?' Frølich asked.

She looked up. 'Hm?'

'I was joking. You seem to be expecting a call.'

She straightened her back. 'Regine Haraldsen, right?' she said with a disarming smile. 'Would you have asked me if she *hadn't* been one of my clients?'

'Her house's been burgled.'

Veronika Undset stopped smiling. 'Oh, tell me more.'

Frølich took his time. Leaned against the wall. 'Now we have to play our roles properly,' he said, trying not to seem too dispassionate or arrogant. 'I'm a policeman. *You* have to tell me.'

She looked down. 'But I have no idea what you're talking about.'

The silence was awkward. She broke it. 'How is Regine? I hope she hasn't been hurt.'

'Physiologically speaking, she's unhurt. She wasn't at home when it happened. She was at her son's in Fredrikstad for the weekend. But when she returned home the house was as empty as an eggshell. I'm sure you can imagine how distraught she is.'

'I'd better ring her,' she said.

'Do you know this client well?'

Veronika shook her head.

'Think carefully before you ring. This is a woman who's lived a long life and has scrimped and scraped to get by. She's lost everything. Strangers forced their way into her house and helped themselves. The shock after such a violation would be bad enough for most people. On top of that, she's lost everything she possesses, everything she's accumulated in the course of eighty-four years, things she was going to leave to her children.'

They stood gazing at each other in silence. There was something defiant and introspective in her eyes. This face with its clean, classical features suddenly seemed stiff and stylised, like a porcelain mask.

'Regine Haraldsen is old, but not stupid,' Frølich continued. 'Neither she nor the police consider it a coincidence that the burglars struck the night before last. Whoever did it must have known she was away and that the house was worth a visit.'

'So?' she retorted.

'So?'

'What are you actually saying?'

'Regine Haraldsen's circle is small and diminishing. She has no home visits from nurses …'

'You think one of my staff is involved?'

He shook his head.

Veronika gesticulated and smiled like a blonde in a high-school comedy: 'Do you think *I'm* involved? I can tell you here and now – I have *nothing* to do with this. But of course I'll ask the employees who were at Regine's. You can talk to them; you can have the numbers of all the firm's employees. I can't have rumours like this hanging over me.'

'Let me be perfectly honest,' Frank replied. 'The police wouldn't be investing resources into following up this case so meticulously unless we could see a connection with another case. These people were *not* junkies on the lookout for money and dope. The people who did it worked like a removal firm. They knew the old lady would be away at the weekend, they've had their people inside her house, people who knew exactly what items of value there were. The burglars didn't break anything. They didn't go on the rampage searching for valuables. We in the police are also fairly sure who's behind this – your old friend Kadir Zahid. You may have known all along why I'm here, but now finally I've got to the point: we believe we know why you visited Kadir on Friday night. We believe you are the missing link in this case. You don't only organise home-help services for the likes of fru Haraldsen.' He waved his notepad. 'In four of the six burglaries like this one your firm was responsible for cleaning the house in question. That's a score of around seventy per cent!'

Veronika sat down on the swivel chair behind the desk with a distant gaze.

Frølich shoved the notepad towards her. 'Aren't you curious about your clients?'

She looked at the pad without saying a word. The chair creaked as she swung from side to side. A car passed on the road. The room was warm. Her face really did resemble a mask, a carnival mask of the Italian *donna*, a high forehead above deep-set eyes, heart-shaped lips.

'I didn't want to be the officer to conduct this interview,' he said.

'But I'm doing it because I like you, Veronika, however odd that might sound. You and Karl Anders are getting married. I wish you well, so I won't be coming back here again. I know Karl Anders, and I can't get to know you so long as Zahid is under investigation. I came here to tell you this: this case is watertight. Kadir Zahid's finished, believe me. With all the resources we've invested it's just a question of time before we arrest him. I don't know what hold he has on you, but I can promise you one thing: when Kadir goes down, he'll take you with him – if you don't do something hellishly quick to save yourself. You can still avoid being charged if you co-operate with the police. You don't have to do that now – wait!' he said when she tried to interrupt: 'I don't want you to talk to me, but talk to *someone*. I can help you find an officer to talk to. If you lay your cards on the table, you could end up with a fine or the case might be dropped. If not—'

'Don't waste your breath,' she interrupted with a raised chin. 'I have nothing to do with this business,' she continued, overwrought. 'Listen to what I'm telling you. I don't know what you're talking about. If there's nothing else, I'd like you to go.'

He was silent.

'I have work to do,' she added.

'If Zahid's pressurising you, has a hold on someone you know, we'll ensure no one comes to any harm.'

She smiled with downcast eyes and slowly shook her head.

He tried to interpret what this gesture meant, but gave up. 'The longer you sit on the fence, the less credible you become,' he pointed out.

Her eyes flashed again. 'Less credible? You stand there and accuse me of exploiting my own customers. That's a mistake. I'm not a thief and I have nothing to do with this business.'

'Nevertheless I have to ask you: did you speak to Kadir Zahid about Regine Haraldsen?'

'No.'

'Not in any connection?'

'No, I said!'

'What about Harder Skaare?'

'No.'

'What about Solfrid and Henrik Gravdal?'

'No, and you don't need to mention any more names. I don't discuss my clients with anyone! Now listen, Frankie, as Karl Anders calls you. I know you have a job to do. I want you to respect me and *my* job. I have nothing more to say. If you're not happy you'll …' She searched for words. 'You'll have to arrest me again. So please go, will you?'

Frølich was very uncomfortable with the role he had assumed. But there was little he could do about it, except turn and go.

Once outside, he glanced in through the large window. Veronika had the phone to her ear. When she saw him she swung the chair around. *Wonder if that's Kadir Zahid*, Frølich thought, getting into his car.

6

The train rattled along. He was sitting in an old-fashioned compartment with curtains in front of the windows. When he looked out he saw green countryside, a golf course with hollows and dips broken by lines of deciduous trees. Behind the greenery, the blue sea gleamed and on the horizon the azure merged into the light-blue sky. He stood up and leaned out. The wind caressed his face. The locomotive whistled. It was a black steam train – the sort with a thick, grey billow of smoke from the chimney stack trailing after it. The locomotive whistled again, a lighter note this time. Gunnarstranda turned his face to the sun and closed his eyes. There was another sound, but this time it wasn't a train whistle. The locomotive was playing a strangely mechanical version of Mozart's 40th symphony. And someone was digging him in the side. At that moment he realised he wasn't sitting on the train but lying in bed. The sound came from his bloody phone and the hand shaking him was Tove's.

'Your phone,' she whispered.

He opened his eyes. 'Leave it. I'll call them back tomorrow.'

The phone finally fell silent.

There was bluish-grey light in the bedroom, so it must have been early, very early, before the sun had risen properly. With great difficulty, he sat up. He checked his watch. Ten to four in the morning.

'You don't know who it was, do you?' Tove said.

Gunnarstranda yawned. 'Yes, I do. I know who it was.'

His phone beeped as it received a message.

'Such a short time for Adam in Paradise,' he sighed, and got out of bed. 'You sleep some more. Or…' he added upon reflection. 'Actually we ought to discuss this.'

'Discuss what?'

She was sitting up too now, naked. Her hair in a mess. Eyes blinking. This was a sight that made him understand the meaning of life.

'Whether you'd like to continue the holiday here alone or do something else?'

'Stay here on my own? Are you out of your mind?'

He nodded towards the phone on the bedside table. 'I have to work.'

'How do you know?'

'If I say no, they'll tell me it's an order.'

They gazed at each other. Minutes passed. In the end she swung her legs onto the floor. 'Well, we've had two fantastic weeks,' she said. 'Fancy some coffee?'

He nodded, and took the phone.

7

At last somewhere to pull in. A gap in the line of vehicles parked alongside the blocks of flats in Bjerregaards gate. It was boiling hot and there was no shade for the car. Frølich left the windows open and strolled down Damstredet and Telthusbakken.

A film crew was at work. The camera was placed on a little cart with four bike wheels. A young woman with a microphone on a mount in front of her mouth ran bent double towards three actors. On the cart was a man wearing drop-crotch trousers and a pirate's kerchief – the cameraman. He was receiving instructions from a skinny guy with a back-to-front cap.

Two of the actors were men in clothes that reminded Frølich of Ludvig Holberg's dramas: top hats, breeches and jackets with tails. The woman was dressed in a long, loose-fitting dress and had a bonnet on her head. She looked like someone from Elsa Beskow's children's books – Aunt Green. The three of them merged into the surroundings of small timber houses and narrow alleys. Only the tarmac spoiled the scene. *They couldn't have had tarmac in Holberg's day, could they*, Frølich wondered. But perhaps it didn't matter, there are so many weird and wonderful things you can do with films. He studied the guy with the cap. Good-looking man with sunglasses and a little soul patch. The colleague at Westerdal's had said the man's name was Mattis Langeland.

Ten to fifteen curious onlookers sat on the grass watching what was going on. Mattis Langeland shouted: 'Action!' The three actors walked towards the camera while two guys pushed the cart. 'Cut!' yelled

Langeland. This was repeated a couple of times, then it was all over. The film crew packed up their equipment while Langeland sat with the cameraman viewing the recording on a screen.

Frølich headed for them.

Neither turned away from the screen. Langeland waved an arm and said: 'Please, I'm busy.'

Frølich stood his ground.

'Are you hard of hearing?'

That was the cameraman with the pirate's kerchief.

Frølich brandished his ID. 'Police.'

The cameraman said nothing and at length Langeland turned around. 'What's the problem?' The scar by his mouth was unmistakeable.

'Mattis Langeland?'

Langeland nodded.

'Apparently you were in the student pub in Blindern on Friday,' Frølich said.

Langeland considered this statement. 'That's possible.'

'Well,' said Frølich in a measured tone. 'This is a police matter. Were you there or not?'

'I popped in, yes.'

The cameraman stayed seated.

Frølich showed him the copy he had of Rosalind M'Taya's passport photo. 'Apparently you were talking to her.'

Langeland studied the picture. The cameraman looked over his shoulder. Langeland nodded. 'Chick from Africa. Just arrived in Norway.' He passed back the photocopy. 'Why?'

'Tell me about it.'

Langeland shrugged. 'Not much to say. I go there from time to time for a beer and a chat with people. That's about it.'

'See if there's any talent?'

Langeland smiled wanly.

'Did you pull?'

Langeland recoiled and threw out his arms theatrically as he said loudly: 'OK, why don't you tell me what this is all about.'

'You're the last person to have seen her alive,' Frølich said coldly. It annoyed him that the cameraman didn't have the wit to withdraw. He turned to the man and put out a hand. 'I don't think we've introduced ourselves.'

The cameraman warily shook his hand. 'Andreas.'

'Andreas, I'm talking to Mattis Langeland with regard to an investigation. Would you mind leaving us to it?'

The man shuffled off, like the wannabe film extra in *The Wire* or the star of an American rap video: kerchief tied tightly around his head, rings in his ears and eyebrows, T-shirt that was at least five sizes too big, ditto pirate pants.

Frølich turned back to Langeland, who said: 'Andreas is my younger brother, you know.' Then continued with, 'Well, she was a real babe, right, but lost, kind of serious, not focused on having fun. We just exchanged a few words. Hi, what's your name? Rosa or something like that and stuff about Africa and well … I had a couple of beers and hit the town.'

'Did you notice her talking to anyone?'

Langeland shook his head.

'Was she there when you arrived?'

'No idea.'

'When and how did you notice her?'

'I suppose she must have come in after me. Yes, I think she did, or else she was in the toilet when I arrived.'

'Was she alone when you saw her?'

Langeland nodded. 'That was why I went over and chatted to her. She was alone.' He nodded to himself. 'That's how it was.'

'What did you talk about?'

'Eh?'

'You went over and chatted to her. What did you say?'

Mattis Langeland gave an embarrassed smile. 'Bit corny. I said she was very beautiful and asked her if she'd like to be in a film.'

'And?'

'It was bollocks, of course. Terrible pick-up line. She didn't take me seriously, so I slung my hook.'

'Did you leave before or after her?'

'Before.'

'So she was on her own when you left?'

Langeland nodded.

'The staff at the pub only mentioned you when we asked who she talked to.'

Langeland grinned. 'That girl? Alone on the town?' He opened his palms again. 'Well, I left on my own…'

'Where did you go afterwards?'

'Into town. Lots of places. Hell's Kitchen, Robinet. Where there were people.' Langeland was suddenly cautious. 'Hey, what is all this?'

'Just answer the questions. Is there anyone who can confirm that they were with you after you left Rosalind M'Taya that evening?'

'Of course.'

'Then I'd like you to give me some names and addresses.'

*

It was early afternoon by the time he was back at the police station.

Frølich heard a phone ringing as he removed the headset to his iPod on the way down the corridor. He turned towards the coat hooks and hung up his jacket. Emil Yttergjerde was sitting next to the telephone, but ignored it as he studied the pictures in the latest edition of *Autocar*.

'Aren't you going to answer it?'

Yttergjerde glanced up. 'It's for you.'

'How d' you know?'

'Because he's rung three times already.'

Frølich and Yttergjerde exchanged looks. Frankie put on a deep frown. 'Him?'

Emil Yttergjerde nodded with a grin.

'I thought he was on holiday.'

'It's been cut short.'

Frølich lifted the receiver. 'Station, Frølich.'

'It's me. Now you listen here. On Saturday morning you arrested a woman – Veronika Undset. Is that correct?'

'Nice to talk to you again too,' said Frølich, winking at Yttergjerde who peered up from his magazine with a grin.

'Seen today's *Verdens Gang*?'

'Nope.'

'Front page. The dead woman.'

Frølich's insides froze.

Gunnarstranda's voice was still formal and concise: 'We've matched the prints. It's her, definitely. Can you come and ID her at pathology?'

Frank Frølich looked at his watch. He swallowed, but that didn't help. The dreadful unease and heaviness in his stomach wouldn't go. 'Give me half an hour,' he said, and rang off.

8

After parting company with Gunnarstranda at the pathology lab, Frølich needed to be alone and used the missing-person case as an excuse. He drove off without any real aim and ended up at the old seamen's school in Ekeberg. He parked and sat for a few seconds in the car.

He had already tried once, but called Karl Anders on his phone again. No answer. He tried again. The voicemail answered. He switched off without saying a word, stuffed the phone in his pocket and got out of the car.

He ambled towards the park around Ekeberg Restaurant. Perfectly formed sculptures of women gazed at him with their unseeing eyes through the foliage and undergrowth. He found a bench with a view of the harbour and the mountain ridges to the north and the west. The Frederikshavn and Kiel ferries had docked. One of the Nesodden boats was on its way and the low drone of the motorway was somewhere beneath him.

It had shocked him to see Veronika Undset's white, lifeless face. The state of her body, where it had been found. He could barely think about it. For the first time in many years he didn't know how he would be able to cope with his job. He recited to himself: '… all the king's horses and all the king's men couldn't put Humpty Dumpty together again.'

This wasn't only about murder. This was about Karl Anders and himself – whether he liked it or not.

It was typical that he got landed with a job like this just when he had some steam up in the Rosalind M'Taya case and a plethora of leads.

That was where he ought to be putting his energy, checking statements, putting the skids under that conceited I'm-so-cool film director wanker, smashing his alibis. Some shithead in affluent Norway – possibly Mattis Langeland – had committed a crime against a poor girl who was alone and miles from home. It was offensive, galling, and had kindled a passion for the job he hadn't experienced for years – until the encounter with the mortal remains of Veronika Undset.

His phone rang.

He fumbled for it with trembling hands. Read the display. Discovered to his disappointment that it wasn't Karl Anders's number.

'Yes?'

'Lena here. Thought I should tell you that we've had an alibi confirmed. A guy called Mattis Langeland was in Bar Robinet until it closed on Saturday morning.'

'Alone?'

'Alone.'

'Who says so?'

'A guy who works in the bar. Mattis Langeland contacted him and told him to ring the police.'

Frølich put the phone back in his pocket. This was not his day. Not at all.

He leaned back on the bench with his eyes closed. The sun baked down and he was already sweating. He mentally shelved the missing-person case. Couldn't get Veronika Undset out of his head. Went back over what happened that morning: she opened the rear door of the taxi and stepped out. The glance she sent him, calm, knowing. He had sensed it then – and now he was absolutely sure. She had known someone was tailing the taxi she took from Kadir Zahid's. It was so obvious. Kadir had told her: the cops are keeping me under surveillance. Be prepared. They might approach you when you leave here.

That was exactly what they had done. He could visualise the little smile on her lips as she got onto the rear seat of the police car. Two images, he thought. Spot the difference.

The difference was that he found something in her bag.

Could she have been telling the truth?

She *must* have been telling the truth. She would have been clean if she knew she was risking an encounter with the police after leaving Kadir. She wouldn't have had drugs on her. Her reaction when he found the lighter was genuine.

But why didn't these thoughts give him any peace?

Karl Anders and he had history. They had a shared past. Was that why he was so clammy and restless?

No. It couldn't be. What happened took place more than twenty years ago. This was about Veronika Undset – a woman with many layers to her personality. She had been streetwise, had managed to retain her composure in tricky situations. She wasn't given to outbursts; she waited, she examined the circumstances …

He weighed the phone in his hand. He had rung twice without getting an answer. Karl Anders should ring back of his own accord.

He put the phone in his pocket. His shirt was sticking to his body in the heat. The ground was dry; the trees in the park had absorbed all the moisture and left the grass looking yellow and scorched. He longed for a shower. Glanced at his watch. It was time to pick up old sourpuss.

*

Frølich was driving and the Dandy Warhols were on the radio as they went down Sognsveien. 'You Were the Last High'. They passed the tram on the bend by the entrance to the university. They had to stop at the lights by Ringveien and the tram swept past again. Gunnarstranda, who had been sitting lost in thought, turned the volume down and said:

'Let me get this straight. You arrested her as she was leaving Zahid's at the crack of dawn, you found some cocaine on her and threw her in a cell – and you did that to your pal's fiancée?'

'I didn't know about their relationship then. I only found out in the evening. Karl Anders was celebrating his fortieth. We hadn't seen each other for many years, but I was invited – I received an invitation several weeks ago. I went into the party and who did I see? Her! She was as shocked as I was, but we managed to keep our masks on, both of us.'

'But she visits Kadir Zahid alone, at night, when she's engaged to someone else? What sort of person is this Karl Anders? Is he jealous?'

The lights turned to green. Frølich put the car in gear. He gave the question some consideration and chose his words with care:

'Once I knew Karl Anders well. Very well. But when we were young and artless, straightforward; we knew everything about each other, right, the way boys are. That was many years ago, though.'

'You don't know him any more?'

'We haven't been in contact for a long time.'

'Why not?'

Frølich buzzed down the window. He had been expecting the question, but he wasn't ready to tackle it. Instead he concentrated on the traffic, exaggeratedly. The lights on the Adamstuen crossing went amber. Aggressive motorists surged forward. He sat waiting for a gap in the stream of cars. It took time. Another tram approached. The car behind hooted. Frølich set off and shook a fist at a driver who only just managed to brake.

He continued down Theresesgate. Glanced at Gunnarstranda who was still waiting for an answer. Frølich said nothing.

'When I haul in this Karl Anders for an interview, we'll use the TV room. I want you to watch,' Gunnarstranda said at length.

Frølich cast an involuntary glance at the rear-view mirror. Remembered again Veronika's slightly condescending smile from the rear seat on the Saturday morning. Now he was onto her. She couldn't bluff any more, she couldn't hide. He had the authority to explore all her secrets, read private letters, diaries if she had any, go through her medicine cabinet and find out any little ailments she may have had, acquaint himself with her vices and bad habits, he could even nose through her rubbish. He felt a quiver of power run through his body. He knew he should feel sullied, but he didn't. He felt strong and focused, as though she were lying beneath him in the sunshine, naked, right now.

Frølich blinked and breathed in. This couldn't go on. He pulled in suddenly to the bus lay-by at Bislett.

'What's up, Frølich? Aren't you well?'

'Perhaps I shouldn't be on this case,' he answered. It was so hot and he was about to undo the top button of his shirt when he realised it was already open.

'Why not?'

'I might be too close to the people involved.'

'You've investigated Veronika Undset. You know about Kadir Zahid's relationship with her. Of course you should be on the case!' Gunnarstranda snorted. 'What do you mean close?'

'I'm not impartial.'

'As far as your friend's concerned, yes, but you can still do a job on the investigation.'

Frølich took his phone. Keyed in the number. The phone rang and rang. Until the dialling tone returned. Frølich sighed. 'He's not answering.'

'Who isn't?'

'Karl Anders.'

'Something tells me you've been trying all day,' Gunnarstranda said.

Frølich texted him: *Hi KA, we must talk. Ring me on this number. FF*

He sent the message, left the phone on the console in the middle and checked his mirror before driving off. Waited for a gap in the traffic. He asked: 'Could she have been attacked out of the blue and raped?'

Gunnarstranda shook his head. 'Then we would have found the body at the crime scene. She was killed somewhere else, rolled up in plastic, transported – presumably by car – and thrown into a refuse container. Clothes? We haven't got them. All we have is a diamond earring in her left ear. You probably didn't see, but there were burn marks on her stomach and between her thighs – and so on. The pathologist thinks someone washed her with boiling-hot water *post mortem* – probably to remove any biological clues.'

Both men went quiet.

'As after a rape,' Gunnarstranda added.

The silence persisted. Frølich thought about Karl Anders, thought about Veronika being killed, now, right now.

'Friends,' Gunnarstranda said after a while.

'Hm?' Frølich replied, pretending not to understand.

'Your friend's playing hide-and-seek with us. But you were at his party. Where there must have been some friends of theirs, friends of the couple. People who knew her. That's the place to start.'

Frølich nodded. 'I've got a missing-person case as well,' he said. 'The African girl who disappeared. There's a possibility she might have been killed too…'

Gunnarstranda angled his head. 'And so?'

'It's difficult to do both, two murders…'

'Rosalind M'Taya's status is *missing*. You don't know if she's been killed.'

'The point is—'

Gunnarstranda interrupted him: 'Veronika's friends, Frølich. Names of the people at the fortieth birthday party who can help us to find out what she was doing yesterday. Veronika Undset *was* killed, patently.'

'I hadn't seen Karl Anders for many years. I was the only one of our old pals to be invited. He has a completely new circle of friends.'

'But you spoke to some of them, I suppose?'

'I had a woman sitting next to me who knew Veronika well. Janne Smith. I can start there.'

Gunnarstranda nodded with satisfaction. 'I'll talk to Veronika's family, then.'

*

Back at the police station, the first thing Frølich did was to ring the home number of Janne Smith. She didn't answer. Instead he was put through to an answerphone. He hesitated, but in the end didn't leave a message. He rang her mobile, but it was switched off. The same voice-mail. At that moment the door opened and he put down the receiver. It was Lena Stigersand.

'Am I disturbing you?'

He shook his head.

'I'm going through some surveillance videos from Gardermoen Airport,' Lena said, 'with regard to Rosalind M'Taya. The ones I've checked I've marked with a yellow sticker.' She showed him a DVD with a Post-it on. 'It'd be good if you did the same. There are so many bloody films.' She placed a pile on the desk.

'What are you going to do?' he asked.

'Have lunch,' Lena said cheerily. 'And afterwards both Rindal and Gunnarstranda consider the Veronika case more important than this.'

With that she was gone.

Frølich sat looking from the door to the pile of DVDs to the phone. He opened his laptop and inserted the first film.

9

The others couldn't fathom how she had the energy to run in such heat. But they knew nothing. They knew only about Ståle, believing they knew everything. What Lena herself thought, they had no idea. This couldn't go on, she realised that. Ståle probably agreed. Deep down, he also wanted an end to the relationship. Perhaps that was why they were continuing the way they were. Everything was about sex, which escalated every time they met.

She liked his self-assurance, but hated his brutality. She didn't want to think about their last meeting. She preferred to attempt an analysis. As passion was all that bound them, all their energy was channelled into a sexuality whereby both pushed the boundaries every time.

Like now, she thought ironically. His free day and she jumped at his idea of having lunch. Role play.

She put on her tracksuit and trainers and ran off with a small rucksack on her back. Jogged down the path in Grønland Park and then up towards Åkebergveien. She loved running, feeling her knees, thighs and calves absorbing the weight of her body with ease. Breathing correctly. Not letting her imagination run wild. Not thinking about what would happen. Running across the roundabout in Galgeberg. Not warm yet. Listening.

There. She heard the roar of the V8 as he braked behind her. She didn't turn. Kept jogging. Thinking that he was watching her now, fantasising. Soon he would be alongside her. Rolling down the window as she approached the bus stop. She thought: *He'll do it there, at the bus stop.*

She braced herself. No one around at the bus stop. She sprinted. For a short distance. The car pulled in and forced her off the road. She had to stop, stand, gasping for breath. The window was open. Sunglasses hid his eyes. He ordered her into the car. She asked why.

'Jump in,' he repeated peremptorily. An elderly lady came towards them. The car was in her way. Annoyed, the woman stopped.

'Do as I say,' Ståle said.

She obeyed. He put the car into gear. Silent. It was wonderfully cool in the car. Cold air streamed towards her face.

He drove along Ringveien, turned off up Maridalsveien. She had her breath back now. The air-conditioning was cooling her body, but not enough. He ordered her to get undressed, and she obeyed until she didn't have a stitch of clothing on.

He told her what to do to herself. Again, she obeyed.

At length he parked under the deciduous trees. Told her what to do to him. She did as she was told. She didn't think, she just reacted and enjoyed doing so. Going with the flow, like a kayak down a rushing stream, concentrating on the pleasure of controlling the forces and the boundless power she had. She did feel dirty afterwards sometimes. Sometimes she wondered about her own powers of judgement.

No one knew better than Lena that this was theatre. She was the daydream. She fulfilled the fantasies Ståle couldn't realise with his wife, who was going through the change and suffered from osteoporosis. He always complained about his wife and she let him. This woman was mere words. *She* was his dream about the source of youth, and she didn't give a damn while she was in the middle of it. No amount of self-contempt could outweigh the intoxication and the power she experienced as he surrendered totally.

Afterwards, however, she was the equally dominated slave of her super-ego: as sure as rain follows the sun, condemnation and self-mockery took the place of desire in her consciousness. Then he was nothing. Then he was as dirty as she felt.

His member died inside her however little she wanted it to. Soon he would push her away, throw the condom out of the window without realising that such an act was vulgar and offensive and illustrated with total clarity the absence of genuine feeling in their relationship. He was a child. A child with a chest that rose and fell like after a long sprint. His sweat made the silvery hairs on his chest glitter. He was sated. She raised her head and kissed him on the chin although she didn't really want to do that. Her fingers stroked his hard abdomen and pecs. Astonished now that this was what lit her desire. The flesh under the suntanned skin. 'Get dressed,' she whispered.

'I might want you to do it again,' he replied.

His words increased her sense of unease, and she kissed him on the neck to avoid any further talk that might ruin any remaining tenderness.

She nimbly sat up and turned to the side. Picked up her clothes and dressed. Collected her rucksack from the rear seat.

He inhaled to say something.

'I have to ask you a favour,' she broke in. 'Now.'

'What's that?'

'I need transport. And you're free.'

*

Half an hour later he swung his Mustang into the empty forecourt in front of Dekkmekk. She sat for a few seconds looking out before saying: 'Despite almost non-existent activity he manages to support his mother, his father, his sisters and his brothers with this business. None of the sisters has paid work. They sleep during the day and go on the town at night. The four brothers have at least two cars each. All of them have wardrobes a footballer would envy. The parents live in Peshwar for six months, where they own one of the town's most attractive houses.'

'You have the choice,' Ståle said. 'If you drive a Rolls or a Ferrari, it's thirty litres to a hundred kilometres. If you drive a Micra, five.'

She glanced at him with a smile. 'And what do you mean by that?'

He grinned back. They looked into each other's eyes. 'I think you'll have to squeeze into your Lycra again soon.'

She quickly opened the door and put one foot on the ground. The heat from outside entered the car. The draught derailed his thoughts.

'What sort of place is this if there's no one around in the middle of the day?' he asked.

'There are people here only twice a year,' she explained. 'That's at the transition between autumn and winter and winter and spring. Then his brothers are here changing tyres for the customers who stray here by chance. But this lot aren't cheap, so the customers never come back. This activity only keeps invoices and accounts alive for VAT and tax-return purposes.'

'My wife says even couples who have no children drive five-seaters. They don't drive a two-seater. That's the way it is.'

Lena stared at him. 'Don't think so much, Ståle,' she said in a low voice.

That wasn't nice. She could see he was furious and as she read his reaction she wondered why she was so nasty.

He was about to say something, but she put a finger in front of his mouth. Then she leaned forward and brushed his coarse mouth with her lips.

A dark blue Audi A6 drove past them and onto the forecourt.

'Who's that?'

'The owner,' Lena said. 'He keeps the place under surveillance 24/7. It took him less than five minutes. Not bad when we arrive in an unmarked car.'

She got out of the car. 'Wait for me,' she said.

The Audi had stopped by the garage entrance. A man in shorts and a polo shirt stepped out.

Lena showed him her ID. 'Kadir Zahid?'

'Lena,' Kadir grinned. 'We've met several times. Why so formal?' He glanced at Ståle's blue Mustang. 'You've come here in a fancy car, Lena. Is that your boyfriend?'

'That's Ståle Sender, a police officer. He's my back-up, as we in the profession call it.'

'Shame he's a cop. I like to talk cars with men who know one end of a car from the other.'

'I'm here to ask you about Veronika Undset,' Lena said.

'What about her?'

'She's dead. Veronika's the woman they're talking about on the news. The one who was found in a refuse container, murdered.'

Kadir Zahid turned on his heel and pulled open the shutters. A few seconds later he was standing with his back to her. As she was about to speak he walked between piles of tyres, past lifting equipment and machines, towards an office with glass walls.

Lena glanced over her shoulder.

Ståle Sender opened the car door and got out. She waved to him and mouthed: *Back soon.* He crossed his muscular arms and leaned against the bonnet of the Mustang. Sunglasses in front of his eyes, the V-shape of his upper torso and his pose made him the cliché he wanted to be.

She followed Zahid, past the tyres, the jacks and hydraulic machines.

Inside the office the air was stale and reeked of old dust. Zahid sat down. He was plump, she could see now. His stomach rested against the desk. He seemed exhausted. The manicured beard and the combed-back hair no longer exuded the playboy look. A Rolex with a loose bracelet slipped down his forearm and met a gold chain with a barely audible clink.

'Can you tell me about her?' Lena asked.

On the wall hung a tyre-company calendar. It was still on February, five months out of date. A naked blonde with plaited hair and rouged cheeks was holding an aluminium wheel rim under her breasts. The lollipop in her mouth said it all.

Kadir breathed in and straightened up. 'We were in the same class at school from the first to the ninth year.' His eyes were shiny and his lips trembled when he spoke.

Lena didn't buy the performance, but she said nothing.

'Veronika was my idealised Norway, Lena. A friend, but not only a friend. She was my Bond girl. Imagine it yourself: the eighties, I was a foreigner, you know, a Paki. But Veronika was the most attractive girl in the school, and she was my best friend.'

'Veronika was arrested and placed in custody after visiting you on Friday night. Why did she go and see you that night?'

'I asked her to come over.'

'Why?'

'I needed some company.'

'What did you talk about?'

'You.'

'Me?'

'Or the police, you're there all the time, you don't leave me in peace, don't leave my family in peace. It's impossible for me, this, you're making my life a misery, mine, my mother's and father's, my sisters' and my brothers'. You even hauled in Veronika. A guest. What was the point of that?'

Lena didn't answer.

'When we were younger it was Veronika I turned to when things got too much for me.' Zahid's face softened, as though he were remembering an amusing incident. 'We used to sit together drinking tea in her room. We could sit there talking and laughing for hours. She made me see the comical side of everything.' Zahid's face darkened again. 'That night I longed for that. So I rang her and she came over. As always,' he added before Lena could say anything.

Again his eyes were shiny.

'When she was arrested she was fined for possession of cocaine.'

He raised his head and eyed her suspiciously. 'You know very well that I neither deal in nor use drugs. I'm a Muslim, Lena. I don't drink wine, don't drink beer, don't drink spirits, I don't smoke hash, I don't mess my head up with clouds of intoxicating substances.'

'What about Veronika?'

Kadir Zahid looked up at her. 'Will you believe me if I answer your question?'

'Why wouldn't I?'

'Because the answer's no. I knew Veronika. She might have had the odd glass of Campari or some trendy drink with a parasol at a party, but that was the extent of it. She never took any drugs. Do you believe me?'

'You asked her to come to your place for a chat at half-past one at night. Couldn't you have had a chat during the day?'

'At work?'

'You work, do you?' Lena said sarcastically. 'Here?'

She walked out of the office and did a round of the workshop. He followed her. She paused and studied the blockwork wall where more tyres were stacked high. She raised her arm and looked at her watch. 'It's pretty quiet here today. Have you given the boys the day off?'

'You're not listening,' he countered. 'I rang Veronika to have a chat at a difficult moment. It wasn't a bloody consultation.'

He walked past her and through the entrance. There, in the sunshine, he stood looking at her. She walked towards him, but stopped in the doorway.

'Were you in a relationship with Veronika?'

Zahid shook his head. 'She was engaged to a guy who works for the council. She wanted to invite me to her wedding – even though the date hadn't been set.'

'So her fiancé knew about you?'

'Naturally.'

'What did you do last night?'

'What do you think? I was at home. You shadow me all the time, Lena. I can't walk a metre without having a cop on my tail. Check their reports and you'll see I was at home.'

'Alone?'

Kadir shook his head. 'Two of my brothers were there.'

Standing in the doorway and watching Kadir, Lena had a sense he was play-acting. He hadn't moved after he left the workshop, so they almost had to shout to each other. Why had he gone out? Did he want to lead her out? What had unsettled him? To provoke him, she took a couple of steps back into the workshop. Then she made a discovery, turned back to him and realised she was onto something. He was wary. Followed her movements with his eyes, like a fox from its lair. She smiled at him, but Kadir didn't return the smile. Lena came out of the workshop. Pretended to be mulling over a smart question as she took some slow steps. Used her eyes and confirmed what she had seen inside. The workshop was narrower than the whole building. The building might have been twenty metres wide, but the workshop was fifteen, maximum. There were a few extra metres in the building, but there were no windows. And where were the gates and the forecourt to that part? Presumably at the back.

It didn't have to mean anything, but there was something in the man's body language that had alerted her. She spread an arm across the forecourt. 'Looks like there must be lots of customers here during the day. Hard work, eh?'

'You know as well as I do that the tyre business is seasonal. In the summer we might change a wheel for an occasional tourist with a puncture. Come here in October. The place is heaving then!'

No, she thought. He wasn't as relaxed as he had been a few minutes before.

'When did you last see Veronika?'

'Saturday morning, when she left my place and you followed her taxi.'

'Spoken to her since?'

Kadir shook his head.

'Did you talk to her about any of her clients?'

'What do you mean by that?'

She had to smile at his innocent expression. 'You know what I mean. You know why we keep an eye on you. You're a thief, Kadir. We believe you use people to find victims for your activities. We believe, for example, that you robbed an elderly lady in Malmøya last weekend, someone called Regine Haraldsen.'

'It's dishonourable stealing from old ladies,' Zahid answered.

'Regine Haraldsen was one of Veronika's customers.'

Kadir Zahid said nothing.

'Sure you didn't speak to Veronika on the phone after she left on the Saturday?'

Kadir sighed. 'Give up, Lena. I've neither seen nor spoken to Veronika since then. Tell me, does her mother know this? I'd like to offer her my condolences.'

'Do you know her mother?'

'Of course.'

'She knows her daughter's dead.'

Kadir rolled down the shutters with a clatter. He locked them and turned to her.

'Anything else I can help you with, Lena?'

She walked towards Ståle and the car. Thinking: *he's still play-acting.*

Once inside the Mustang, she noticed Zahid had put on sunglasses. The garish logo of Dolce & Gabbana flashed at the side of his head. He waved to her.

She waved back.

'Don't have time for this,' Ståle said grumpily and started up the car.

She raised her hand and stroked his arm.

'Stop that,' he responded, tetchily.

She realised he felt humiliated by being an extra on this assignment. But she couldn't do anything about his feelings. 'A tiny favour,' she begged. 'When you get onto the road please go right instead of left.'

He put the car into gear and obeyed.

She studied the building as they left. Correct: there was a shutter at the back, closed with a robust padlock.

'Great,' she said, sitting up. 'Now you can drive back to town.'

10

It was past eleven in the evening when the Metro doors opened. Frank Frølich stumbled out. Fellow passengers hurried past him, with determined strides, eyes glued to the ground, their feet longing for home. The cool breeze in the evening air drove the temperature down to under twenty. At last it was pleasant to be outdoors.

He strolled down the street. As he cut across by the Esso petrol pumps a car hooted. There was someone sat behind the wheel in a parked black Volvo. A door opened. It was Karl Anders.

Frølich's joy at seeing his friend again was muted by the state of him: listless eyes and a half-open mouth with the corners saliva-flecked. Karl Anders was good and drunk and making life difficult for himself.

'I've been waiting for you to ring,' Frølich said in a measured tone.

'Have you got time for a chat?'

'As long as you leave your car there.'

They walked side by side along Havreveien in silence. Nor in the lift on the way up did they say anything. Karl Anders avoided eye contact. His breath was sweet, sated with beer and sugary spirits.

The lift stopped. Frølich held it open for his friend, took out his keys and unlocked the front door.

The air in the flat was close after a long day's baking sunshine through closed windows. He opened the terrace door to freshen the place. 'Coffee?' he asked with his back to Karl Anders.

'Haven't you got a beer?'

Frølich always had beer. There were two six-packs in the fridge.

Lysholmer Ice – the cans stood in soldierly lines watching over the brown goat's cheese, which reigned over the fridge, with no royal court or subjects.

He put the cans and two glasses on the table and slumped down onto the sofa. 'I've tried to call you many times, texted you and asked you to ring me without any response. You weren't at work either.'

Karl Anders didn't answer. His eyes were swimming.

'They had no idea where you were – the people at your workplace.'

Karl Anders drank and put down his can, still as silent.

'First and foremost I'd like to offer my condolences,' Frølich said, thinking that it was still an unpleasant word, but it was right to say it. The word brought them to the essence of this visit.

Karl Anders looked down at the floor. When he raised his head it was clear he had been struggling with himself. 'Frankie … did you lock Veronika up for possession of cocaine?'

'Who said that?'

'Veronika.'

So she had confessed to her fiancé. Frølich sat for a few seconds deliberating how to carry on. 'Karl Anders,' he said.

Who reached out for the can again.

'I'm working in a team trying to find out what happened to Veronika. I'm completely open to everyone in the group. I have to be. Several of the others know that you and I are pals. Everyone knows I was at your party. I'm completely open because murder feeds wild speculation, with everyone.'

Karl Anders said nothing.

'Norway's a little country in this world,' Frølich went on. 'If you go on a package trip to Kos or Cyprus, there's a good chance you'll meet a neighbour or his family. That's how small the world is, and that's how small Norway is. Veronika turned up in a case I was working on. I had no idea who she was when we met. I couldn't have known that she was with you. I realised that only when I saw her at your party. I was shocked, but I had to be discreet.'

Karl Anders interrupted him: 'What about the drugs?'

Frølich stared at him. In the end he said:

'Veronika was fined for being in possession of drugs. After paying the fine the matter was done and dusted. No one else but Veronika needed to know about the case, so I've kept quiet about what happened.'

Frølich wasn't sure if his friend was listening. He was still sitting in the same position, his expression vacant.

'I can't stop being a cop just because I know you.'

Karl Anders raised his head. They exchanged glances. Suddenly he didn't seem to be drunk. 'What do you mean by that?' he asked in a sharp tone.

They held eye contact. Frølich didn't know for sure, but he had a feeling they both had the same thought. *It's such a sore point*, he thought, *neither of us wants to say it straight out. Twenty years have passed and we are no further on.*

Or was that really how it was? Wasn't the situation completely different now? He represented officialdom while Karl Anders … he didn't have the energy to complete the thought. Instead he said: 'The police need to hear what you have to say. We have to know where you were when Veronika was killed, but you were nowhere to be found today. No problem – so long as no one else managed to locate you. People have been ringing you all day, on your mobile, at home, at work. As I said, Karl Anders – you're a central figure in this case. Where have you been?'

'I thought you'd got over it,' Karl Anders said.

Frølich didn't answer.

'But you're just the same. Just the fucking same.'

Frølich regarded his friend without speaking.

'My bad luck that Veronika happened to bump into you on precisely that morning.'

Frølich looked down at his hands. They weren't shaking. He told himself: *He's drunk, he's lost the woman he loved – that's why.* He cleared his throat and repeated his original question: 'Where have you been all day?'

Karl Anders smiled coolly. 'You think it was me, don't you.'

Frølich opened his can of beer and poured it into the glass. Glanced up. Same chilly smile on his friend's face. Cold smile and staring eyes. There was nothing Frankie wanted more than to tear down the veil over the past and recall the moment. Confront his friend with what he *actually* thought, deep down.

Nevertheless, he refrained. He sipped his beer with his eyes trained on his friend. He had been longing to drop his shoulders this evening, sit in a heap and watch a bad film with lots of shooting, car chases and crazy dialogue. But Karl Anders had prolonged his working day and brought it home to his flat. He didn't like the job of following him around.

He put down his glass.

'Our relationship wasn't as hot as you think,' Karl Anders started. 'I've got an ex,' he continued, gazing into the air dreamily.

'Who hasn't?' Frølich said, to keep the conversation moving.

'I was with her.'

'When?'

'All the time.'

Frølich leaned back and realised that friends you had as a child stay in your mind the way they always were – even when you see them after an absence of many years. When he met Karl Anders at the party it was the teenager he had rediscovered: unconsciously he had thought his old friend was hiding in in a shell. He had seen inside it and thought he had found the mannerisms, the body language and the old glint in his friend's eyes. But now he saw Karl Anders as he was, as an adult: an anonymous-looking man bordering on skinny. Short hair without a suggestion of grey. Hollow cheeks which, in his drunken state, gave the impression of a skull. A little gold ring in one ear, an attempt at a Mr Cool signature. Karl Anders even had a ring on his left thumb. And when he drank from the can his sleeve slipped down and revealed the end of a blue tattoo.

Frølich cleared his throat again and said:

'Veronika was killed at some time between eleven and a little after midnight. Where were you?'

'At home.'

'Alone?'

'She was with me.'

'Who?'

'The ex.'

Frølich could feel himself getting annoyed at the leaden pace of the conversation and deliberated. He said: 'Well, the police will have to have a chat with her.'

Karl Anders turned his face towards him. Now the smile was crooked and sneering. 'And you don't think I killed Veronika?'

When he spoke, Frølich had to exert himself not to lose his temper: 'I don't think anything. The police don't think anything. We're setting out the jigsaw, finding out what happened. Charting what Veronika did in the time before she was killed – hour by hour, minute by minute. The person who killed Veronika was in the same place as her. Those who were elsewhere are not under suspicion. Simple as that. If you say you were with your ex, you weren't with Veronika. But for the police to believe you, they will need her to confirm your alibi.'

'Veronika and I had a row – well, about the cocaine. She told me after all the guests had left the party. It was five o'clock in the morning when she told me. We'd never rowed like that before. You don't need to ask. I didn't hit her. I didn't touch her. All that happened was that suddenly I understood things. There were sides of Veronika I didn't know, do you see, Frankie? You realise your girlfriend plays games! I thought, what the hell. Are we going to get married? Am *I* going to get married to a woman *I don't know*?'

'What kind of games?'

Karl Anders took another sip of his beer. 'Don't know. Game is perhaps the wrong word, but what you see is a different person standing there. You wonder what's going on. The following day I dreaded talking to her. I thought that if she isn't at home when I call, if she doesn't answer the phone, what the hell is she doing? And if I ask, she'll probably lie to my face again!'

'Again?'

'Hm?'

'You said lie to your face *again*. Has she lied before?'

Karl Anders didn't answer. The silence continued, and Frølich said:

'She insisted it wasn't her cocaine and she didn't know how it had ended up in her bag. And you know what,' Frølich said, trying to make eye contact with his friend, 'I believed her. I think the surprise she showed when I found the cocaine in her bag was genuine. But it wasn't me who took the decision. My bosses concluded she'd broken the law. She was fined, and that was that as far as she was concerned.'

Karl Anders was unmoved. He looked away, silent.

'How did you find out about the murder?' Frølich asked.

Karl Anders took his time to answer. 'Her mother,' he said at length. 'She rang me at work.'

'So you *were* at work? I also tried to ring you at work.'

'I had to get out. Couldn't stand being there.'

Karl Anders shook his head, then leaned back and closed his eyes. 'I've thought a lot about this,' he said, 'and I know a lot of people will probably despise me for doing something like this. Her mother rang to tell me that Veronika was dead – and she wanted me to go there, to talk about it. But I couldn't. Couldn't sit with Veronika's mother crying. I was … it was as if I was too charged. All I had in my head – all I could do was go back to another woman and have sex. But we talked about it afterwards. Having sex in that situation made me feel I was alive, Frankie. I needed it, and I think she did too.' Karl Anders opened his eyes and took a deep breath. 'After the party, when Veronika said she'd been arrested—'

'The name, Karl Anders. What's your ex's name?'

'Janne Smith, you know her. She sat next to you on Saturday.'

Frølich couldn't stay seated. He got up. Stood staring through the open terrace door. There was only one thing he needed. To be alone. He leaned against the door frame and let the cool breeze waft over his face.

'Janne and I have decided to keep a low profile,' Karl Anders went on. 'As Veronika's dead and all that.'

Frølich turned back to his friend. 'It's late,' he said, 'it's been a long day.'

Karl Anders nodded, but didn't move. The silence was long and awkward. Eventually he got up and stood, swaying. His eyes were downcast and he seemed to brace himself before asking: 'Was she raped?'

Frølich began to sweat. He could feel his friend's presence like a clammy, heavy blanket of unease over his shoulders. He wanted to get him out. He said: 'I can't discuss the investigation with you, Karl Anders.'

'It says in *Verdens Gang* she was raped.'

Frankie made for the front door, wordless and distant.

Karl Anders grabbed his arm.

Frankie looked down at his hand.

Karl Anders let go. 'I'd like to ask you a favour,' he said. 'I'd prefer it if you kept this – what I've told you – to yourself.'

'What?'

'The stuff about Janne and me. That I was with her while Veronika was being raped and murdered. It won't sound good.'

Frølich stared at his friend with a weary expression. 'As I said, it's been a long day.'

'For the sake of old friends,' Karl Anders begged. 'I'm struggling with this, Frankie. Blaming myself. What could I have done? What would have happened if I hadn't been with Janne on Monday evening?'

'Do you know if Veronika had any specific plans that evening?' Frølich asked.

Karl Anders shook his head. 'I didn't speak to Veronika from the moment we parted company on Sunday morning. It's not comforting to know, Frankie, that we parted on bad terms.'

They stood looking at each other, not speaking, as though these last words were having an effect on both of them: *on bad terms*.

It was Karl Anders who broke the silence. 'I'll have to be off then. I'm not planning to go home. I—'

'I'd ring for a taxi if I were you.'

They held eye contact for a few long seconds. Once again Karl Anders seemed stone-cold sober.

'I know what you're thinking,' he said suddenly – in a clear voice. Took his phone from his trouser pocket and tapped in a number.

'What am I thinking?' Frølich asked in a harsh tone.

Karl Anders smiled coldly. Turned his back on him, went outside and slammed the door behind him.

Frølich stood staring at the closed door for some time.

At length he turned, fell on the sofa and leaned his head back thinking actually he should have put on some music. But he was exhausted. Even the idea of music seemed off-putting now.

He studied the can of beer his friend had drunk from. He took it. There was a bit left. Frølich placed the can on the mantelpiece above the fire. *A nearly-empty can of beer*, he thought dejectedly. *I wonder if this is a monument to a past friendship.*

11

When he awoke, his thoughts were immediately with his friend Karl Anders, Veronika and Janne.

This business had become too personal. He couldn't allow that to happen. Karl Anders's words had etched themselves in his brain. *Having sex in that situation made me feel I was alive.*

Frølich tried to recall an image of Janne Smith. It had become a tiny bit blurred. She had kindled a spark in him. There had been something, *something or other*, between them. He couldn't allow his friend's assertions and pompous babble about life and death to extinguish that spark. He wanted to hear her version of events. Talk to her first of all, he reasoned – afterwards decide what step to take next.

*

He parked more or less where the taxi had stopped the night they drove here after the party. When he finally got out of the car he hardly knew where he was. Daylight filled in the details the night had obscured. The contours of the house were the same. The crown of a tree arched over the roof. The little garden was screened by a tall hedge. Many years ago an occupant had laid some flowerbeds which were now overgrown. *Gunnarstranda would know the names of the flowers*, he thought, studying an old climbing plant clinging to the thick trunk of the maple tree. A black and yellow lawnmower stood by the house. In the middle of the lawn there was a battered, greasy and rusty grill. Frølich looked up. A face was hidden behind a curtain. It wasn't her, so it had to be her son. He rang the bell, stepped back and examined the house front. It could have done with a lick of paint.

The door was opened by a thin, pale boy with long, black hair and the first signs of a beard carefully accumulated and groomed into a point on his chin. His T-shirt bore the logo of a heavy-metal band and his bare arms were as pale as his face.

'Are you Kristoffer?'

'Who are you?'

'I'd like to talk to your mother.'

'But who are you?' the boy insisted, cautiously.

'Tell Janne this is Frank Frølich here, a police officer. She knows me.'

The boy stood looking at him.

From indoors came the sound of footsteps on the stairs. 'Kristoffer?' A hand pushed him aside.

Silence descended as they exchanged glances. 'It's you, is it?' she said in a tone that hit him in the solar plexus.

'I'm off,' Kristoffer said, walking down the steps. His shorts reached below his knees. He grabbed a skateboard, jumped on it and pushed off. The head of black hair glided along the hedge. After a few metres he glanced back over his shoulder. Frølich met his look, uncertain what it meant.

He turned to Janne, who was still standing in the same place, in sandals, jeans and a pale yellow top. She was holding a basket of laundry under her arm.

'Nice boy.' He could hear how stupid his comment sounded.

Fortunately, she ignored it and said: 'I was in the cellar. Let me hang this up.'

She walked past him, down the steps and across the gravel path. He followed her. Behind the house there was a clothes line. The ground sloped. A wall of granite ran along the bottom of the slope. He sat down on the wall. Every time she stretched to hang an item of clothing on the line, her belly button appeared.

'You've come to talk about Veronika, haven't you?'

'That too.'

'That too?' She stopped hanging up the clothes. Her hair fluttered in the breeze. The sun shone on her greyish-blue eyes and made them glitter like two jewels.

'That was stupid. I've come to talk about Veronika.'

Triangular panties of various colours flapped like small pennants on the line. 'Yes?' she asked suddenly, still hanging up the clothes, without turning.

'Did you have any contact with Veronika in the days before she was killed?'

Slowly, she bent down and picked up a red bra, fastened it to the line carefully with three pegs. 'No,' she said at length. 'In fact I didn't. The last time I spoke to her you and I were leaving the party, when we caught the taxi.'

'Don't you do her accounts?'

'Yes, but I don't talk to her every day,' she said. Then repeated 'don't', disconcerted. 'Didn't, I mean. It's so difficult to get used to her...' She wiped the back of her hand across her face and looked away.

'We're trying to work out what she did in the time before she was killed. Do you know if she had any plans for that day, if she was meeting anyone?'

She shook her head.

'The guests at the party, were they Veronika's friends as well?'

She nodded. 'Most of them, anyway.'

She cleared her throat.

'Could you write down a list of the friends you know, of people who can help us to find out what specific plans she had for that day?'

She nodded. 'Have you got an email address?'

He dug down in his pocket and passed her his card. She quickly stuffed it into her back pocket without looking at it. 'Some time during the day,' she said.

Her tone and body language were cold, a brush-off.

'What do you think?' he asked.

The basket was empty. She took it and turned to him. 'Think about what?'

'What do you think about this murder?'

'Nothing. It's just dreadful.'

He didn't want to, but he had to ask the next question. He braced himself: 'Have you had any contact with Karl Anders since?'

She nodded. 'He came here. He'd talked to her mother on the phone and was done in. He almost lives here now; he can't be on his own.'

'Is he here now?'

She shook her head. 'He went to work.' She looked at her watch. 'An hour ago.'

'You say Karl Anders came here *after* Veronika was found murdered?'

She nodded.

'What about the evening before?'

She smiled: 'Why?'

'Karl Anders says he was with you the night it happened.'

She glanced up warily.

He cleared his throat and asked the unavoidable question. 'Were you together that night or not?'

'He came here the day after. He'd received the phone call from Veronika's mother, saying that Veronika was dead.'

'You were at home?'

'I felt it was right to be there for Karl Anders on that day.'

They stood looking at each other. He had to clear his throat several times to make his voice carry:

'Karl Anders popped by last night. He told me not to tell anyone that you two…'

When he failed to finish the sentence she raised her face and studied him as though searching for a barb in his eyes. 'You're different now,' she said.

He hesitated.

'From last time.'

He looked away, past the house. Behind the hedge a bit further away there were some kids jumping on a trampoline. Their upper bodies rose and sank behind the foliage. They were squealing with joy and laughing.

'Karl Anders said you used to be a couple,' he said.

She nodded. 'We were together for three years.'

'Why did it finish?'

She looked down, rapt in thought. 'What's the classic excuse? I wanted a break. I was unsure and felt life had been reduced to routines and boring TV nights. Besides, Kristoffer was in the worst phase and needed a lot of attention. I didn't want to have rows with a man because of my child.' She took a deep breath and carried on: 'A lot happened at once. My mother died, the house here became empty. Karl Anders and I were struggling. I felt I had to choose between several roles and chose to be a mother. Kristoffer and I moved here.'

'And now?' he asked.

'What do you mean?'

'Now you've started up again?'

Now it was her turn to let her gaze wander over to the children jumping on the trampoline. She said nothing.

He wished they could have had this conversation under quite different circumstances. But forced himself to ask: 'Where were you when Veronika was killed?'

'Here.'

'Alone?'

She shook her head. 'Kristoffer was here. It was a normal evening. TV and other 'highlights' – like a glass of wine from a box. I went to bed at around midnight. Kristoffer went a bit before me. Which he still does sometimes – surprisingly enough.'

'Has your son got a mobile phone?'

'Of course, why?'

He refrained from answering. Instead he asked. 'Has Karl Anders told you where he was that evening?'

She shook her head.

Frankie rose to his feet. 'Then I won't bother you any more.' He walked past her.

'Hey!'

He stopped and turned. 'Yes?'

She looked at the ground and shook her head. 'Nothing.'

He hesitated for a few seconds. If there was anything she wanted to say, he wanted to hear it. 'What?' he repeated, without eliciting any reaction. Then he decided to go the whole hog. 'As a matter of form,' he said, 'why do you think Karl Anders says he was with you all evening?'

Eye contact again. 'No idea.'

Suddenly she recoiled as though she understood a hidden suggestion in the question. Her eyes narrowed. 'He would never have hurt Veronika,' she said in a low, controlled voice. 'You know him. You know that too. If you're the friend you say you are.'

Frankie had nothing else to say. He wished it were possible to press a button, rewind the whole meeting and start again.

Janne came towards him with the basket under her arm. When she stopped in front of him her eyes were still narrow slits. 'Has it ever struck you that you could drop what you're doing now?'

Her words stung. Nevertheless, he asked: 'What do you mean?'

'You said yourself, he asked you not to drag us through the mud.'

She walked past him and up the steps without a backward glance, her neck and back erect. The door slammed shut behind her, and the only thing he was sure of was that he wasn't going to ask to be released from this case, not yet.

As he walked back to the car he rang Directory Enquiries and got her son's mobile number. Seconds later Kristoffer Smith's high-pitched voice answered.

Frølich opened the car door. 'This is Frank Frølich, the police officer you just spoke to,' he said, and got in.

12

The corridor was as good as empty. Emil Yttergjerde stood in the TV-room doorway. 'Do you know who has voluntarily contributed to the case of the African babe?' he asked with a grin.

'The man in Lena Stigersand's life, the asylum-seeker killer himself, in person – Ståle Sender. He dropped by today. It struck me that he might have his finger on the pulse, so I asked him a few questions about Rosalind M'Taya. Strange, I thought, that Lena hadn't asked him, but they've probably had other things on their minds than police work, ha ha ha. Anyway. Ståle rang up Gardermoen and talked to the woman who was at passport control when the passengers from London landed. And, sure enough, she had taken Rosalind M'Taya aside. But our girl had both a visa and a letter of invitation from the university and the whole deal, so after a little check with customs she was let through. But that means we have the precise time of when she left the arrivals hall. So I was able to check the CCTV and looked for a black girl. It was so easy that being a cop was fun. Run the film,' Emil said.

The picture on the screen showed the arrivals hall with the escalator down to the train platforms. 'Had a bit of luck,' he continued. 'There are about six hundred cameras in Gardermoen. But we've got our girl … here!' He freeze-framed the picture.

On the TV was a curvy woman with wonderful hair. Short jacket that reached to her waist, tight trousers and high heels. Emil started the film. The woman was manoeuvring her suitcase and carrier bags down the stairs.

'Her? How do you know that's Rosalind? All we can see is her back!'

'Just wait,' Emil grinned.

The woman went down the stairs. Emil fast-forwarded. People jigged up and down. 'Now,' he said, and ran the film again. 'Escalator on the left.'

A black woman was on her way up the escalator. When her top half was visible Emil freeze-framed the picture again. Zoomed in. The quality was poor, but not that poor. This was Rosalind M'Taya. No doubt about it.

'On her way up? She *doesn't* catch the train?'

'She walks out of the terminal, through the car parks. The interesting bit though is that someone helps her with the suitcase.'

Emil fast-forwarded the film. Rosalind M'Taya flew up the escalator. Behind her was a young man. As he left the escalator you could see he was carrying her suitcase.

'This is seven minutes later,' Emil continued. 'She's been down to the platform for normal trains, which are cheaper than the Airport Express, but she arrives between two departures. The train from Lillehammer to Skien via Oslo has just left. It's half an hour to the next, the local train to Kongsberg. My guess is she went down to the platform, got into conversation with this guy who informed her, advised her, to take the airport bus or offered to drive her. What do you think?'

'He drove her,' Frølich said.

'Why do you think that?'

'I know him.'

*

Less than an hour later Frølich was on the Airport Express train. The air-conditioning ensured a cool breeze. He stared out at the mown fields where the tractors were pulling machines that rolled the grass into white bales shaped like eggs or packed it into squares. Bare chests under the baking sun. His mind went to Janne Smith and Karl Anders. The hypocritical request from friend to friend was exposed: *don't tell anyone.* What did Karl Anders expect? Was he supposed to keep quiet about his friend establishing a false alibi? For Christ's sake, he was a policeman.

He sighed and rubbed his face hard with his hands. Sooner or later he would have to take this further. Or would he? Were his colleagues entitled to know about the past? Well, anyway – he had to say something: Karl Anders lied about his alibi for the evening Veronika was murdered. Nevertheless, Frølich didn't want to be the one running to Gunnarstranda with his friend's head on a platter. Sourpuss could work it out on his own.

He grabbed his phone and texted:

G! Hope it's OK if you deal with Karl Anders Fransgård before 16.00. Available on this number. F

Half an hour later he was given a yellow vest and ear defenders by Ståle Sender.

If it became necessary to play good cop/bad cop, Ståle was the perfect foil: cast in the same mould as Chinese gymnasts and with the same sharp crease in his trousers. Cold, blue eyes above narrow lips. Bristles on his chin as short as his hair, uniform shirt open at the neck where a chunky gold chain rested on suntanned clavicle. Frankie regarded Ståle's coarse hands. The sight of the wedding ring gave him a sort of reinvigorated tenderness for Lena. There was something self-destructive about her eternal search for a partner.

They didn't say much to each other. There wasn't much point, inside ear defenders, which transformed the howl of jet engines into loud but muted background noise. A cool breeze blew across the Gardermoen runways. Behind the immense glass walls passengers were stocking up with spirits and tobacco for holidays in southern Europe. A plane came in to land, low at the back, like a goose on its way down to the water. They passed caravans of baggage trailers, catering vehicles and passenger buses. In the corridors: line after line of tourists on their way home; sunburned and overweight, wearing gaily coloured shorts and expensive sandals with ergonomic straps and soles, bold choices of cowboy hats which would soon be stowed away and forgotten. Queues of passengers in the jet bridges that led to the planes, cabin staff on their way, as they always were, striding quickly across the tarmac: elegant, long-legged and uniformed, with downcast eyes and a good hold on their practical cases, into the long, round fuselages that would soon be speeding down the runways and tilting their noses upwards, then climbing towards the clouds, same aerodynamic heads and dorsal fins as sharks.

Where was Andreas Langeland?

Ståle pointed a fat, quivering index finger.

Frølich barely recognised the cameraman from the film set. No pirate's kerchief or drop-crotch trousers. The figure seemed thin and small in blue work pants and a hi-vis vest. He made the same boring impression as a reflection of Frølich's face on a grey weekday.

Shortly afterwards the three of them marched in file past the zinc toilet where the drugs smugglers have to sit until their bodies return the pouches they have swallowed, past the dressing rooms and scanners, into a sparsely furnished interview room. Andreas Langeland – pale but composed. Frølich realised at once that he was going to play it hard and asked him whether he understood why he was being questioned by the police.

The answer was impertinent. The police had a duty to issue a warning, didn't they.

'This is about Rosalind M'Taya.'

'Who?'

Got you there, Frølich thought, and said: 'Don't you remember me talking to your brother Mattis about her when you were filming in St Hanshaugen?'

He didn't.

Frølich presented him with a selection of CCTV pictures.

'Oh, her!' It had been one evening last week. She had asked the way to the airport bus.

'She asked the way to the airport bus? Standing on the station platform?'

The question worked. Andreas Langeland's eyes became pensive. Station platform. The cops knew something. Ståle and Frankie exchanged glances. They could almost see the cogs working behind the young man's lowered eyelids. Andreas Langeland elected to play a careful back pass:

'I didn't know what was on her mind, did I.'

'OK. Did you show her where the airport bus was?'

Nod.

'Answer properly.'

'Yes, I showed her where the airport bus was.'

'What happened next?'

'She got on the bus.'

Frølich and Ståle exchanged glances again. Cops 2 : Robber 0. The first lie was in the bag. This young man had to be more stupid than even he feared.

'So how come she was in your car?

'She what?'

'You've got a parking spot, P11, first level, right? Europark's CCTV shows you and Rosalind M'Taya getting into your car, a yellow 2007 Mini Cooper. Do you want me to read the registration number as well?'

Langeland's eyes went walkabout.

'Twenty-seven minutes later the car's registered at the toll gates in Alnabru, and this is only some of the stuff we've got on you, Andreas. Come on, you gave Rosalind a lift from Oslo Airport to Blindern Hall of Residence. Isn't that right?'

Andreas Langeland shook his head.

Ståle spoke up. 'Are you calling us liars?'

Frølich regretted using Ståle.

'I'm not calling you anything,' Andreas Langeland said. 'But I refuse to answer your questions. I'd like to ring for a lawyer.'

'Why would you like to do that?'

'You want me to say all sorts of shit which is not true and use it against me later. I know what you're like.'

'Do you know where Rosalind M'Taya is?'

Langeland was silent. Watched them, mouth closed, moist at the corners. Eyes defiant.

'Do you think a lawyer would be able to deny she got into your car?'

Andreas Langeland was still quiet. His expression was furious. Frølich had seen hundreds of such expressions. No amount of common sense would mitigate their defiance.

'Let's jump forward two days,' Frølich said. 'To last Friday, Friday before the weekend. Where were you then?'

'At work.'

'And after work?'

Andreas Langeland shrugged. 'Went home, played a game, watched a film, went into town late, here and there.'

'With Mattis?'

This was a shot from the hip, but it hit the bullseye. He could actually see Andreas trying to avoid the bullet, sitting there tight-lipped.

'Were you with Rosalind M'Taya?'

Andreas Langeland shook his head with a grin.

'Mattis says he met Rosalind at the student pub on Friday,' Frølich said. 'You heard that with your own ears.'

The young man didn't answer.

'He said he was with you that Friday.'

Andreas smiled, and Frølich saw through him at once, but he still didn't have enough to go on. He needed to know more.

'Have you spoken to Mattis since?' Andreas asked. 'I didn't hear him say anything like that.'

'You're saying you didn't meet Rosalind on Friday?'

'Have you got any photos to prove I'm lying?' asked Andreas Langeland with the same self-assured smile on his face.

Frølich studied the hard-won composure on his rough features. 'Clear off,' Frølich said.

Ståle squirmed uneasily on his chair, but Frølich took no notice.

'Do you mean I can go now?'

'Of course.'

The young man in the yellow vest and blue trousers stood up hesitantly. The chair scraped in the silence. He slunk to the door and turned.

'You should have informed me about my right not to make a statement,' he said defiantly. 'Now I can report you.'

Frølich nodded.

'I think I will.'

Frølich nodded again.

Andreas turned to the door and opened it.

'Andreas,' Frølich said.

He glanced over his shoulder. 'You've brushed up on your law since we last met. You're a good student. I'm very impressed. Just one thing though: why have you been swotting?'

When Andreas didn't answer, Frølich pointed a theatrical finger at him and fired.

'PIAOUW,' he whistled as the door closed behind him.

'You're too soft, Frankie,' Ståle Sender said.

'He's lying,' Frølich said. 'We know he drove her to the hall of residence on Wednesday. But Rosalind M'Taya checked in alone. The problem is we have nothing to go on after she checked in. She was alive and well, participated in activities at the summer school and slept two nights at the hall before she disappeared. So there are two whole days after meeting Andreas to account for. I'll question the lad again, but first I need to know more.' Frølich rose to his feet.

'Say hi to Lena,' said his colleague.

'Have you told her you're married?' Frølich asked. The comment was meant to be caustic, but it came out flat.

Ståle Sender grinned. 'Appearances deceive, Frankie. I told Lena the first time. You never know what's under the bonnet of car, I said, even if the car looks a bit battered. It's only when you sit behind the wheel you can put your foot on the gas.'

Frølich was lost for an answer, as he always was when he met this man.

'She's still driving, Frankie. And this is what I tell the boys: it might be cheaper to drive a sensible little car, but driving isn't only about money in the bank. It's about comfort too. In a small car you bump along and are thrown around on the bends. By the time you arrive you're a lot more tired than if you'd been sitting comfortably in an American sedan with a decent engine and decent suspension.'

Now what's that supposed to mean? Frølich wondered, but he couldn't bring himself to ask. He just spun on his heel and left.

13

'Veronika Undset's last day,' Rindal said, and stuffed both hands in his trouser pockets. In brown slacks and a white shirt, open at the neck, he looked like Gene Hackman, as always. Waves of blond hair over his ears, suntanned pate, all that was missing was chewing gum, thought Frølich. As though he had telepathic powers, Rindal unwrapped an Extra and put it in his mouth. Hackman in *Enemy of the State*.

Frølich's eyes followed an electric cable from the socket on the wall to the junction box and on to the neon light. It resembled the rally stripe on Karl Anders's kayak. One summer they had paddled almost every day in the two-man kayak on Lake Bogstad. Actually it had been Frankie's idea. He'd had a crush on a Swiss girl he had been watching several days in a row by a pontoon. She had been working as an au pair for a family in west Oslo somewhere, and she took the children with her every day to Bogstad to swim. He had to smile at his own transparency now – the excuses he made, ringing Karl Anders, the kayak ...

'Hello!' Rindal roared.

Frankie gave a start. Lena Stigersand and Emil Yttergjerde both avoided looking at him. 'You met Veronika Undset at her workplace at five minutes past three on Monday, 6 July – the day she was killed. When did you leave her?'

'At about half-past three. The conversation wasn't very productive. She admitted Regine Haraldsen was one of her clients, but denied tipping off Zahid about her or any of the other clients whose names you gave me. We talked for about twenty minutes max.'

'Anything else?'

'I urged her to co-operate with the police, told her about all of her clients who'd been burgled and said she could perhaps save her skin if she helped with our investigation.'

'And?'

Frølich told him Veronika had immediately grabbed her phone after he left. Most probably she had rung Zahid. That at any rate was what he had assumed.

'Could she have threatened to grass?' Rindal asked.

'Wouldn't our undercover agents have seen something – if Zahid killed her? They stick to him like leeches.'

'Zahid could still be behind the murder because he would never do the dirty work himself,' Yttergjerde pointed out.

Lena Stigersand sent Emil a patronising look: 'Hit man?'

The discussion veered off and Frølich was back with the Swiss girl. Her name was Irene and when she went to the lake with the children she wore a white bikini. Her skin was tanned brown. Every morning she mixed sea salt in a large bottle of water. She rubbed this saltwater over her body when the sun was at its peak. She thought saltwater gave you the best tan. The bottle had been his passport to teasing and dialogue. He had been in love with her, but she was mostly interested in Karl Anders. In fact, the two of them got together until her boyfriend from Switzerland appeared. A tall, flabby guy, a good ten years older than them. He rode a Harley in leathers and wore a German helmet from the Second World War. Frankie grinned at the thought.

'What's so funny?' Rindal asked, playing with the chewing gum between his front teeth.

'A thought just struck me.'

'Keep your mind on the job,' Rindal said. 'What we know is that Veronika Undset used her bank card three times that Monday evening. She paid at a chemist in Byporten Mall at 20.08. She bought a packet of nail files and some skin cream. The assistant remembers her. She was wearing a flowery summer dress and sandals and carrying a shoulder bag. Shortly afterwards she paid for a latte and a brownie at Stockfleth's on the corner between Prinsens gate and Dronningens gate. The pathologist reports that she didn't eat anything afterwards. But an hour after going to the café, at 21.23, she took out eight hundred kroner from the Nordea ATM on Karl Johan. This is the last sign of life we have.

'What was she doing in town though? Meeting someone most likely. Probably her fiancé – but I don't see a single damned report of any interview with Karl Anders Fransgård!'

The echo of Rindal's angry crescendo resounded between the walls. Everyone stared at Frølich. He met their stares. And held his tongue.

Rindal chewed like a man possessed.

Frølich glared back, still silent.

'I want to read that report tomorrow,' Rindal demanded. He turned to the board with the photos of the body and the chart showing relationships.

'Veronika Undset was found just before three o'clock in the morning, rolled up in plastic in a refuse container on Kalbakken, rented to a housing co-op by the firm Ragn-Sells.'

'She was naked.' Rindal pointed to the photos of the body. 'One of the residents in the co-op rang Stovner Police Station to complain about outsiders throwing rubbish in their container. Strangely, the police investigated further. Police Assistant Bodil Sydengen discovered the body at 02.48. None of Undset's dress, underwear, sandals, bag, money or bank card have been found – the container's been gone over with a magnifying glass and a fine brush. The body was rolled up in transparent plastic, which was sealed with brown parcel tape. The plastic is the type that is sold in rolls at all builders' merchants, in the damp-proofing section, and is used to insulate and weatherproof properties. Builders and DIYers all over the country buy it every day. We know where and when it was produced, but finding out where and when it was sold is harder than looking for the proverbial needle in the haystack. Ditto the tape. It's the kind that's used in post offices and private houses and is sold in all Norwegian bookshops and most supermarket chains.

'Whoever wrapped her up left no fingerprints.

'The victim was subjected to extreme violence to the head and stabbed multiple times in the chest. Death occurred between 23.30 and 00.30. After she died her stomach and genitals were washed in boiling water. There are burns to the vagina. In the pathologist's opinion, the perpetrator washed the body in order to remove biological evidence after a rape and he succeeded. The scene of the crime is as yet unknown. Door-to-door enquiries have so far revealed nothing. No one knows Veronika by sight. No one heard screams or sounds suggesting an attack in any of the co-op flats, but several residents heard a vehicle outside – at a time that could tally with when she was put in the container. Therefore, we must assume she was transported from the crime scene to the container – in a vehicle. No confirmed sightings. Enquiries will continue. The only concrete object we have from the place of discovery is an earring. A small diamond.'

Rindal nodded to Gunnarstranda, who lifted up a small plastic bag and passed it to Lena Stigersand. She studied the contents and passed the bag on.

Frølich held the bag. The earring was an insignificant little stone forming a flower above a rosette with leaves of gold. He couldn't remember having noticed it before.

Rindal looked at his watch. 'I wish you luck. I know you'll nail this. You're a good team. So let me leave you with Gunnarstranda,' said Rindal, making for the door.

Gunnarstranda waited until the door closed behind Rindal. 'No diamond in her right ear,' he started. 'Veronika Undset had both ears pierced. I suppose there is another diamond. I think the perpetrator missed the earring. Why would a meticulous person, like our perpetrator, who scalds the body with hot water to remove clues, why would this person intentionally let Veronika keep a diamond in her ear? If this diamond was missed the other one may have been too. In other words, the other diamond may still be at the crime scene.'

Gunnarstranda paused for thought. 'The clothes and possessions were removed, the body was washed, wrapped in plastic, taped up like a parcel, carried into a vehicle and thrown onto the rubbish container. This person is thorough, takes his time and works slowly. The murder was committed in a place where he could work without disturbance, for example, at home. Veronika had a coffee in town, took out money and met someone at their home. She probably took a taxi there. Her photo's circulating among taxi drivers, but no one has come forward. On the other hand, Veronika was engaged. So the simplest explanation is that she met her fiancé. He picked her up, they drove home and had a row that got out of hand.' Gunnarstranda directed his gaze at Frølich. 'What's your friend like? Is he prone to violence?'

Frølich looked down at the table while absent-mindedly fidgeting with his phone. He cleared his throat. 'I wouldn't like to speculate.'

'You know the man,' Gunnarstranda persisted.

Frølich studied his phone. His hand was trembling. 'We haven't had any contact in twenty years,' he said, and had to clear his throat again. 'I think you're right that she met the perp in town, but it could have been anyone. I saw her myself visiting Zahid last Friday. How random was that? Veronika came out of his house and was fined for possession of cocaine. Afterwards she's accused of leaking information about her clients to a big-time criminal. I put it to her straight, I accused her of being party to theft and organised crime. I'm sure she contacted Kadir Zahid after I left.'

'Zahid's house was under surveillance on Monday night,' Gunnarstranda said grumpily. 'No one went to the house. No one left the house – according to Rindal.'

'Zahid himself says he was at home with two brothers,' Lena interjected.

'But no one knows for sure if he was there,' Frølich countered.

Gunnarstranda angled his head. 'You'll have to explain that comment.'

'The surveillance was scheduled for overnight, to catch Zahid if he made a move. If he stayed away *all* night, it's conceivable that our under-cover officers were watching an empty house or only the brothers. It's possible that Zahid may have met Veronika *and* killed her.'

Gunnarstranda held his chin in thought.

'The perpetrator is still a person in her circle anyway,' said Lena

Stigersand. 'Where did she come from that evening and where was she going?'

Gunnarstranda grinned. 'Where *do* we come from and where *are* we going? Isn't that what we all ask ourselves every day of our lives?'

He looked from one face to another. Coughed, then said: 'We have to find out what Karl Anders Fransgård was doing that night, OK?'

Frølich decided this was the moment. He squirmed on his chair.

'Yes?'

'I've spoken to him.'

There was a scrape of chairs as officers turned their heads. Silence. Everyone was looking at Frank Frølich, who sat up straight and eyed them all.

'Come on. What did he say?'

'He lied about where he was.'

'And you know that, do you?'

Frølich nodded. 'He claims he received a visit from his ex that evening. Janne Smith. I've spoken to her. She says she was at home – with her son, Kristoffer, who has confirmed what she said.'

'And you tell us this now?' This was Lena Stigersand. The bruising around her eye was barely visible.

'It was only when I spoke to her that I knew he was lying,' Frølich said calmly. 'I have, by the way, made it clear to Gunnarstranda many times that I consider myself compromised in this case and shouldn't be taking part.'

'Your request is turned down,' Gunnarstranda said, looking at his watch. 'From now on I'll take care of Fransgård and that's the end of the matter. Well, what are we waiting for?'

14

A fly had found its way into the car. It was crawling up the window. Gunnarstranda pressed the button for it to open. The fly flew off. He drove slowly past the entrance to Frogner Lido. Howls and squeals from children swimming wafted over the fences, along with the smell of chlorine in the water. He continued past the car enclosure near Frogner Park. Somewhere here there was supposed to be a pump sump – whatever that was. When he drew up beside the round Water Resources and Energy Directorate building he spotted a concrete wall with a door on the left. The sign on the wall said Oslo Council. He pulled in.

Actually now he was none the wiser. No one around. No cars parked. He picked up his phone and rang the number he had been given by the council switchboard again. There were three rings before the man answered.

'Fransgård?'

'Speaking.'

Gunnarstranda explained that he was in his car outside a large door in Middelthuns gate. Before he could say any more the door opened and revealed an entrance to a tunnel in the mountain.

Gunnarstranda put the car into gear and drove in. Bright paintings adorned the concrete walls on the inside. Graffiti too – homage to Pythagoras and Archimedes, a right-angled triangle with a corresponding mathematical formula and beside it a man in a bathtub shouting 'Eureka' as the water overflowed. Gunnarstranda stopped in front of a traffic light hanging from the ceiling which soon changed to green.

He let the car roll down in second gear. Passed the Munch graffiti. The cavern wound its way downwards, around bend after bend inside the mountain. Finally, the road culminated in a tarmacked car park. There was one other car, a dark Volvo.

Gunnarstranda got out of his car. There was a stench. Not exactly acrid, just unpleasant. The noise was noticeable. A drone from machines at work, and something louder over the top.

At the end of the car park a huge steel gate was bolted into place. Closer to the tunnel opening, a kind of construction site with cranes and staircases led into the mountain. Here, in a deep hollow, were six enormous blue machines mounted in a line. These were the source of the noise. All of them were bolted to the ground. Every attachment was reinforced with powerful steel stays. Gunnarstranda clambered up onto a metal bridge running above the hollow. There he spotted Fransgård behind a machine – a lean, sinewy man wearing a green hi-vis vest and blue helmet.

'Fransgård?'

The man swung around and climbed up the ladder. They shook hands.

Gunnarstranda shouted to be heard above the racket. 'So this is the pump sump?'

Fransgård nodded. 'Behind the wall there's a bloody huge basin. Most of the sewage and effluent from the town is collected here. These six pumps take the waste water up thirty metres to a big pipe that falls quite naturally into Slemmestad.'

They stood watching the pumps, without speaking.

'You spoke to Frølich before,' Gunnarstranda said at length.

Fransgård nodded.

'As you know each other from the past, I'm afraid you'll have to speak to me too – even if it's not what you'd like most. Shall we go somewhere a bit quieter?'

'Of course.'

'My car,' Gunnarstranda said, walking down and holding the door open for him.

'Are you responsible for maintenance?' he asked – after getting behind the wheel.

'I'm more of a libero,' Fransgård said. 'I'm the project leader, everywhere there's waste water.'

Gunnarstranda nodded, deciding that was enough small talk. 'What do you think happened that night?' he asked, remembering he had rung this man on his mobile. Coverage while sixty metres underground. Not bad. As an answer wasn't forthcoming he turned to Fransgård, who removed his helmet.

'It's unpleasant to talk about.' Fransgård took out a tin of snus and slipped a pouch under his top lip. Wiped his fingers, put the tin back in his pocket and sat thinking, his mouth shaped like a beak.

'People go into relationships with differing requirements and expectations,' he went on. 'You respect the other person, you think you know them. Emotions rule. You define that as love. Animals have it easier than we do, Gunnarstranda. They're on heat once a year and that's it. But in a way we humans follow two paths when we enter a relationship. One path is governed by emotion. The other is the rational one, governed by the everyday and work and routines. You find a tone in the relationship; you're quite open about some topics, others you don't mention. It's tied up with personality, I suppose. For some it's very natural to be open about everything. I have a cousin who can talk to complete strangers at a party about her haemorrhoids in detail. Some people find that revolting; others fall into conversation and think the topic is interesting and natural. Another case in point – one of my colleagues was almost neurotically open with his partner. They pooled their money, he insisted she should have access to his bank account, she should read letters addressed to him and of course expected the same in return. In the end, she couldn't stand it and moved out. It had become impossible to have any privacy. Why am I telling you this? My friend Frølich, whom you referred to, arrested Veronika one night last week. She told me about it, but only after she met Frølich at my party and realised he and I were friends. Then she told me – to get in before Frølich told me, to give *her side of the story*, you see? She had a little cocaine on her, but she didn't tell me *why* she had cocaine on her. Where or who she'd got it from. She clammed up and didn't want to talk about it.

'I had no idea she was taking drugs. What I'm trying to say is that when she decided to tell me these things, she was selective in what she told me. She didn't mention, for example, *what* caused the police to stop her or where she had been *before* she was arrested, where she was *when* she was arrested or *why* it happened. But – after this conversation a few things fell into place. I suddenly realised I didn't know Veronika. And that is quite a shock. You've been together with a girl for a long time, you're engaged to her, you've decided to spend the rest of your life with her and you discover you don't actually know her! Your mind starts working, you examine the relationship in depth and become even more paranoid. You think: she doesn't want to meet me on that and that day, why not? Why does everything in this damned relationship have to be so calculated? Is she living a double life? Are there friends and people and elements in this other life I know nothing about?'

Fransgård rested his hands on the helmet in his lap.

'You haven't answered the question,' Gunnarstranda said. 'What do you think happened the night she was killed?'

'There was a lot going on around Veronika. I have to say these things. It's important to me, and it says a lot about her. Once I had a strange experience. Well, I had it many times. But there was a guy who stuck close to us on the tram. We were going home from town and the tram was full, but he was particularly persistent, if I can put it like that. I thought it was a chance encounter with a loony, but after a while I saw him again. I saw him twice. One night I'd been to see her and was going home and there he was, on the pavement, watching me as I came out. I walked over to my car and was about to get in, then I noticed him still there, looking at me with weird eyes. I returned his stare and then he went away.

'I remember thinking: goodness me, how is that possible? It's the kind of thing that preys on your mind, but which eventually you repress. But then it damned well happens again. I come out and almost collide with this guy, who backs off and disappears as though I were carrying a contagion. I didn't think twice, I ran after the guy, but he got away. I walked back and took the matter up with Veronika, but she didn't seem to understand anything. A guy? On the tram? Outside here? What are you talking about? And I … well, I dropped the matter. But then I'd promised to look after my niece – she's ten. My sister and her husband were going on a weekend cruise to Kiel, to regain the spark in their relationship, so to speak. Veronika and I took the girls, my niece and her friend, to Tusenfryd Amusement Park. It was a lovely day. The girls had tickets and money and ran wild. Veronika and I took it easier, had a bite to eat, went on a rollercoaster and so on. Among other things we did what they call the water ride. You can buy photos of yourself afterwards. She bought one of us.

'Afterwards we went back to hers. In her bag was the photo of us and I went to have a look. Then I discovered there were two photos. One was of her and me. The other was of this pest. The photo was taken a few minutes after ours.' Karl Anders Fransgård shook his head and brandished a hand, as if to say what was all this. 'She insists she doesn't know what I'm talking about when I mention the guy, but then she sees a photo of him in the kiosk at Tusenfryd, buys it without saying a word to me and hides it in her bag.'

He fell quiet.

'Did you confront her?'

'No.'

'Why not?'

'It's a shock to be lied to your face. A slap is nothing by comparison. Anyway, I didn't want a scene with the two girls present. Later … I didn't dare. Or at least I let sleeping dogs lie. I don't know why. But I've wondered about it hundreds of times since.'

Fransgård sat with his eyes closed. A kind of self-reproach pose, Gunnarstranda reflected, and asked: 'Why are you telling me this?'

'I think this man killed her.'

'A man?'

Fransgård nodded.

'This man? And you don't know his name?'

Fransgård nodded again.

'What does he look like?'

Fransgård deliberated before answering: 'Pretty run-of-the-mill, between forty and fifty, thinning hair, few strands over his forehead, otherwise a very ordinary person.'

'Ethnic Norwegian?'

'Yes.'

'Is that all you know?'

Fransgård nodded. 'He can't live so far away from her as I saw him outside her door twice. I'd guess he lived there, close by.'

'And Veronika has a photo of this man, taken on a water ride at Tusenfryd?'

'Don't you believe me?'

Gunnarstranda didn't answer. Instead he asked: 'Do you know where she was or where she was going the night she was killed?'

'No.'

'She hadn't said anything?'

Fransgård shook his head.

'Not even a hint?'

'No.'

'There was nothing she used to do on Mondays that could give us a clue as to her plans for that day?'

'No idea.'

'You don't have any suspicions?'

Fransgård glanced across at him without saying anything.

The silence in the car persisted. The din outside was audible through the window. Fransgård looked at his watch. He cleared his throat and was about to say something, but Gunnarstranda got in first:

'You said you ran after this pest once. When was that?'

'It was a Wednesday. A few weeks ago.'

'You remember it was a Wednesday, but not how long ago?'

'We were together on Wednesdays. That was a fixed arrangement.'

'You said he got away?'

Fransgård nodded.

'Can you be a bit more specific?'

'What do you mean?'

'How did he get away?'

'I gave up, stopped running.'

'He was a good sprinter?'

'What are you driving at?'

Gunnarstranda inhaled and counted. He was going to fire a rocket and so a countdown was appropriate: 'Isn't it obvious what I'm driving at? You're talking bollocks and you know that yourself.'

Fransgård was taken aback. He pressed his shoulder against the door and glared at the policeman with wide-open eyes. 'What?'

'Blast off,' Gunnarstranda muttered under his breath. Aloud he said: 'According to Frølich, you claim you were with Janne Smith the night Veronika was killed. Is that true?'

Fransgård ran the back of his hand over his forehead. At length he said in a forced voice: 'It's true.'

'Janne Smith says it isn't. What do you say to that?'

Fransgård regarded Gunnarstranda with a distant stare. 'I have nothing to say.'

'Do you wish to change your statement?'

Fransgård twisted his head and stared vacantly into space, as though he hadn't heard the question.

'Do you wish to change your statement about what you were doing and where you were when Veronika was killed?' Gunnarstranda repeated.

Fransgård swallowed and shook his head. His eyes were evasive.

'May I interpret your answer as that you don't wish to change your statement? You still claim you were with Janne Smith on Monday night and not anywhere near Veronika?'

'Yes.'

Gunnarstranda turned the ignition key, put the car in gear and drove into the tunnel that led up to the open air.

'What are you doing?' Fransgård asked, dumbfounded.

'Fransgård,' Gunnarstranda patronised. 'Every player with any ball sense knows when the game's over. I'm arresting you in the name of the law, as they say in old films. Now we two are going to drive to the police station and take your statement properly.'

They passed through all the bends without saying a word.

Gunnarstranda stopped in front of the locked door.

It stayed locked.

He turned to Fransgård, who was staring into the air, perplexed. The Munch painting on the concrete wall behind Fransgård's head was 'The Scream'.

'My car,' Fransgård said. 'I can drive my own car.'

'You're not listening,' Gunnarstranda replied in a gentle voice. 'You're under arrest.'

Gunnarstranda eyed the locked door and recognised the irony in those words without a smile. 'Open sesame,' he mumbled.

As though the mountain had heard him, the door slowly slid open.

He drove out, stopped and saw the door closing again in his rear-view mirror.

15

Lena Stigersand always felt ridiculous when she fiddled with the police radio. There was something silly and crime-series-like about fiddling with a radio when you were in uniform, but she was sitting next to Rindal in the leading police car and was obliged to do her job. They had radio contact with undercover officers in Karihaugen and were being updated constantly. Abid Iqbal reported that the delivery van parked on the forecourt of Dekkmekk had now opened its doors.

Rindal grinned and winked at her.

Shortly afterwards there was a report about some activity. The van reversed towards the back of the building. Shutters that were padlocked were opened. There were three men around the van.

'Can you see Zahid?'

'No.'

Rindal glanced at Lena and grimaced, started up the car and drove off. Abid radioed in: 'The van's got a logo on the side – *Go-getters* AS.'

Rindal looked at her. 'Heard of them?'

She shook her head.

Rindal grinned and informed all the units to stay calm.

Abid radioed in: the three men were inside the building.

Rindal again asked for calm.

He chewed his lower lip.

Lena looked through the side window. They were passing Lindeberg. Rindal was keeping to the speed limit. There was a long tailback of vehicles; no one dared overtake the police car.

Another report by Abid: one of the three men had walked around the building and just opened the shutters of Dekkmekk.

'Yesss!' roared Rindal into the mike.

Another report: the man had taken a pallet truck from the Dekkmekk workshop.

Rindal switched on the blue light and sirens. Pressed the accelerator to the floor. The automatic gear gave a jerk and Lena was thrown back in her seat.

Rindal yelled. 'Now. Go, go, go!'

When they arrived the forecourt was crawling with cops. Lena jumped out. She wanted to see this. Three men were accompanied to a waiting Black Maria. She didn't know any of them. They were wearing jogging trousers and dated anoraks; one had ragged shoes on, the other two wore slip-ons without socks. From Poland or Lithuania, she thought, Eastern Europeans anyway, a provenance that made her see this raid with fresh eyes.

She walked around the delivery van. The shutters that had been closed last time were open now. Narrow room, like a long garage. Flatscreen TVs, gaming machines and computers were stacked on top of each other. Cardboard boxes full of digital cameras, mobile phones, big boxes full of silver cutlery. There was no doubt that this was stolen goods. Nevertheless, an uneasy feeling had grown stronger and stronger.

Rindal turned to her. 'Bingo, Lena. Nice work.'

She shook her head. 'Got a nasty feeling. Think we should have let them load up and drive off.'

Rindal eyed her for two brief seconds. He understood, but used his argument: 'The pallet truck. It belongs to Zahid.'

Lena surveyed the scene. Emil Yttergjerde was talking to one of the three men in anoraks. The latter was waving papers. It seemed to be a long discussion.

Rindal jumped onto the lift gate at the back of the van. He towered half a metre above everyone now.

'OK,' he shouted. 'Empty the place. Seize the stolen goods. Come on!'

Lena turned to take in the residential area a hundred metres away. He, Zahid, was probably training his binoculars on them now. She raised her arm in an act of defiance and gave the finger to the whole district.

16

The sun had retreated behind a veil of mist in the sky, which had a dampening effect on the intense heat. Afternoon was turning into evening. Frank Frølich was standing in front of the fireplace staring at the beer can Karl Anders had left behind. It had caused him to reflect. When he looked at the can and remembered the conversation the words jarred. He turned his back on the can and concentrated on the rack of DVDs instead. He skimmed the titles in case he felt like watching one of the films again: *Heat, Once Upon a Time in America, Departed, Casino.* None of them tempted him. He was restless and wouldn't have the patience to watch a film right through. Should he just sit down on the veranda with a cold beer and pretend he was sitting on the edge of a harbour? Should he eat something? No, he wasn't hungry. Listen to music? He couldn't even be bothered to switch on the stereo.

There was a ring at the door.

For some reason he stared at the bell. Why did he stare at the bell when there was a ring at the door? He strolled into the hall. Lifted the intercom receiver with a 'Yes?' while pressing the switch to open the door below. There was no response from whoever it was. He heard only the buzz of the lock and the bang of the door as the visitor came in.

He waited in the doorway while the lift rose between the floors. The lift stopped. The door opened.

Out of the lift came Janne Smith.

'I have to talk to you,' she said.

'Of course. Come in.'

He tried frantically to tidy the worst of the mess. No underwear or dirty towels out. Thank God! He bent over the coffee table and removed the old newspapers. 'Can I offer you anything?'

'No, thank you.'

The intonation made him straighten up. She was still in the doorway. Yellow top, shorts, sandals, red toenails. Small shoulder bag and hands in her pockets. Her eyes roamed around the walls.

The silence was palpable. She was the one who broke it.

'Why are you doing this?'

'Doing what?'

'Putting Karl Anders in prison.'

In his heart, he had known what this was all about. Nevertheless, his disappointment was hard to hide when she revealed the purpose of her visit. He heaved a heavy sigh and slumped down into a chair. 'You know this is hopeless, don't you?'

She was angry. Her lips quivered as she said: 'Karl Anders might have been lying when he said he was with me when Veronika was killed. But you're his friend. You have to know he can't have killed her. You must know him well enough! And then you end up putting him in prison.'

'I didn't.'

Her eyes were cold and hard. 'Really? Is he on holiday inside, then?'

'He's being questioned. Afterwards perhaps he'll be held in remand. If so, it's a court, in other words the judge, who will decide whether he'll be imprisoned or not.'

'But you must know he's innocent.'

'I had nothing to do with the arrest.'

'Didn't you? Who cast doubt on what he said about the night Veronika was killed, then?'

'I had to say that.'

'You didn't *have* to.'

'It was an ethical dilemma. But I concluded it wasn't right to withhold information in a case.'

She regarded him with eyes filled with contempt. 'My goodness, how pathetic you are,' she said in a low voice.

He was getting sick of this hassle, but decided to control himself: 'Karl Anders can change his statement at any point, but he hasn't done. Take a step back and try to see what this case is actually about…'

'I *know* what it's about,' she interrupted shrilly.

'There's only *one* victim,' he continued in an equally controlled manner. 'Veronika suffered a brutal death. It's the police's job to find the perpetrator and take him to court so that he gets the punishment he deserves. Whoever lies in such a serious matter *has* to take responsibility for his actions.'

'But you're his friend!'

'That has nothing to do with him telling the truth.'

'What's the point of friends if they don't support each other in situations like this?'

'I do support him. That goes without saying!'

'Oh, really?' Her eyes were still cold and hard, her lips thin and venomous. 'If what you're doing is friendship, what do you do to your enemies? He's not allowed any visitors. If this is the treatment handed out for his ridiculous white lie, then I can easily change my statement. Call me in. I can say I'd forgotten. Of course he and I were together. You haven't got much of a case then, have you. Eh?'

'I'm afraid that won't help much.'

'See, you admit it. This is not about lies and the truth. It's about your revenge on someone who regards you as a friend.'

'Revenge? What do you mean by that?'

Janne looked away and said: 'I know what happened.'

Frank Frølich stiffened. His chest felt like a block of ice. He wasn't sure he had heard correctly and chose his words with care: 'What do you mean?'

'I know what happened between you two, why you broke contact.'

'So you know, do you? Now I'm really interested. Come on, tell me!'

His attitude surprised her. Her eyes revealed uncertainty. 'You don't need to be like that,' she said quickly.

'I'm not being like anything. I find it hard to believe that Karl Anders would tell *anyone* what happened then.'

She gave him a worried glance, but he was tired of her now. He was angry. This was his home. He didn't want to be plagued with work or gossip here.

'What do you mean?' she retorted.

'Nothing. I have nothing to say. And now I'm tired of being shouted at in my own home!'

Janne Smith plumped down on the sofa. Hid her face in her hands.

'Go home,' he said sternly. 'As soon as Karl Anders gives an honest answer to a couple of questions he'll be out and you can celebrate with waffles and champagne. If you trust him, everything'll be fine. Go home to your son. I presume Karl Anders will be along in the course of the day.'

She stood up. Seemingly having sloughed off a skin from her delicate body. She ran a hand under her eyes. Looked at the make-up. 'I'm going, but I just have to use the bathroom.'

She went in and left the door open behind her. She washed her face and looked into the mirror. Fetched some mascara from her bag, put it on and spoke at the same time. 'I spoke to a neighbour who's a lawyer. He said that if Karl Anders isn't out already he'll be held on remand.'

'I know nothing about that. Nor do lawyers from the street.'

She studied her reflection.

'Janne,' he said.

He got up and followed her. Met her eyes in the mirror.

'Why *did* you break up with Karl Anders – *actually*?'

'Actually? I said we went through a bad patch. He and Kristoffer didn't get on well. I felt forced to choose. So I finished it … or … you know how it is. You ask for a break and so on.'

'Nothing happened?'

She turned and looked at him, uneasy. 'What do you mean?'

The silence hung in the air for a few seconds. His self-assurance grew in that moment. Whatever Karl Anders had told her about the past, it wasn't the truth anyway. He looked into her eyes and said coldly: 'I don't mean anything. I was only asking if there was a specific incident that lay behind the break-up, but now I know there wasn't. You moved away from each other, as in novels.'

He could see the answer made her uneasy, but he didn't dare follow up.

She said: 'We didn't meet for several months, maybe six. When we did it seemed hopeless. We dated once or twice, but it felt as if there was no point starting afresh. We still stayed in contact though, at parties and such like. That was how he met Veronika, at a party.'

She stared vacantly into space. All of a sudden an arm shot out and she leaned against the wall.

'Everything all right?' he asked.

'Now Kristoffer's grown up,' she said, regaining her composure, 'things are different.'

'What about Veronika?'

She closed her eyes.

He turned away and left her in peace.

When she came out of the bathroom she seemed more composed and assured. She stood with her arms crossed. 'I know this will sound cold and cynical,' she said. 'But Veronika's dead. She's gone. Neither I nor Karl Anders can stop living … because she's dead.'

She considered carefully before continuing: 'I might've had a different view if I hadn't known Karl Anders so well from before. When we got together again it felt so right. A profound sense of loss disappeared for us both. We would've got together again sooner or later anyway. I know that. He knows that. That's why it's so important for us that Veronika's fate isn't allowed to destroy everything for us as we start up again. I loved Veronika. Karl Anders loved her too. But they didn't love each other. I know it sounds odd for me to claim that, but it's true. I know it is. Deep inside, I know it is. And after she died I made one mistake. It was wrong of me to tell you the truth. If I'd known what Karl Anders had told you, I'd have happily lied. I'd have said Karl Anders and I were together the night she was killed. Then no one would've had any reason to suspect him, no one would've had any reason to arrest him. That's why I have no option but to blame you. You tricked me. When you tricked me you let down Karl Anders. By doing so you sullied the few remnants of love he and I have tried to cling to for a fresh start. I'll never forgive you … and nor will Karl Anders. You've played your part so neatly, you've even dragged Kristoffer into this and deprived me of the chance to lie, deprived me of the chance to save Karl Anders. But you know as well as I do that Karl Anders can't have killed Veronika. We don't believe that for a second – neither of us.'

He walked past her. Opened the front door and held it there.

She didn't move.

'Out,' he said.

She hesitated for a few seconds, but then walked past him and out.

Frølich closed the door without looking at her. Stood on the same spot when the lift stirred from somewhere higher up the building. Stood on the same spot when it stopped, the door opened, closed again and took Janne Smith down to the ground floor.

Then he went into the sitting room and collapsed on the sofa, leaned his head back and observed the can of beer on the mantelpiece above the fire. It was as though the can was the image of his old friend. It had seen and heard everything, on behalf of Karl Anders.

17

'And what are you doing?' Gunnarstranda asked from the doorway.

Frank Frølich peered up from the table guiltily. 'Rosalind M'Taya,' he explained. 'I'm trying to reconstruct her movements before she disappeared.'

'Isn't the Veronika case more important?'

'You made an arrest,' Frølich commented.

Gunnarstranda didn't answer at once. He closed the door behind him. 'CCTV,' he sighed, lifting a DVD and shaking his head. 'I hate CCTV cameras. All these hi-tech things are crap. Electronic trails, they say, trying to make me believe the world is different from what it was yesterday. It isn't. People are the same. Twenty years ago there weren't any base stations registering people's mobile phones, no toll gates or stationary radar devices recording where people drove, nor did we have any surveillance cameras on every street corner. But we nabbed the criminals who committed murders anyway. We did police work. We used our training and our experience. Now you have to sit at a desk with a magnifying glass like some bloody stamp collector, studying lists of who's logged on to the internet or texted someone at such and such a time. That's not how I want to spend the working day. That's not police work. Police work is talking to people, questioning them, interpreting their reactions, recognising psychological mechanisms ...'

'Or sitting on your arse in a car half the night while the main suspect's nicely tucked up in bed,' interrupted Frølich, piqued because Gunnarstranda was stopping him work. 'You don't need to be so frightened of progress,' he said. 'I'm sure veteran sleuths used to whinge like you when fingerprinting became police work. When they began to search for skin under the fingernails of rape victims there was the same outcry and even more when DNA was accepted as evidence and—'

'Are you calling me a veteran? Do you see me as old?'

Frølich closed his eyes, not wishing to be sidetracked. 'I don't think it's the office work you dislike. You're just allergic to progress. New technology means training, and training means changing your mindset.'

Gunnarstranda rolled his eyes heavenwards.

Frølich continued undaunted: 'With respect to Rosalind M'Taya, I'm not even sure a crime has been committed. But I can't rule out the possibility. If she's lying croaked somewhere I have to find out who had the motive and the opportunity. The same job they did a hundred years ago. The difference is only that I have a better chance of proving who could have carried out the crime. My intuition tells me Andreas Langeland knows what's happened to Rosalind. So, he's lying to me. Looks me in the eye and says he hasn't seen the woman. But the camera at Gardermoen *proves* he's lying. He works there, he loads and unloads suitcases. When he finishes work he sees her there in the arrivals hall. He follows her down to the train platform and persuades her to go with him. Two days later she's with his brother at a student pub in Blindern. How come it's his brother she talks to the night she disappears? The answer's logical enough. One brother has introduced her to the other. My gut instinct tells me Andreas Langeland met Rosalind at the pub. He knows she's new to the country and wants to meet people. He got to know her in the car. On Friday he contacts her: come to the pub. Meet Norwegians, my brother and all our friends. She goes there. There's a girl at the bar who's head over heels in love with Mattis Langeland. He's a charmer. He's got a scar by the side of his mouth and blah blah blah. The girl at the bar doesn't see Andreas, but he's there, one hundred per cent. It *has* to be like that. Mattis doesn't try to pick up Rosalind. She's his brother's girl that night. Mattis goes and the other two stay. I'm sure Andreas made a move on her. Yet *he's* the one who denies having seen her.

'Imagine: this girl takes part in the summer school for two days. Then she goes to the pub and disappears. Just like that!' He clicked his fingers. 'Not one of the other students knows what's happened. Not one of the teachers knows. So my question is: why does Andreas Langeland deny having seen her? What's the point? There are two days between the Gardermoen CCTV shots and her disappearance. He didn't need to deny that he'd seen her and driven her in his car. There's only one reason for his denial: he knows what's happened to her.

'I can't prove she's been murdered, but my instinct is that she has been. She leaves behind her money, her toiletries and clothes. Has she disappeared of her own volition? No. Has she been kidnapped for a ransom? A poor woman from a poor country in Africa who's given money by the Norwegian Foreign Office for her plane ticket? Hardly. After this evening could she have killed herself? A girl getting the opportunity of a lifetime, travelling to affluent Norway for a prestigious course – a girl about to spend forty-two inspiring days in an international setting, with highly qualified teachers, new friends, new networks abroad and at home, a wealth of opportunities. No, she couldn't. Rosalind M'Taya was new to Norway and met the wrong man at the wrong time. Andreas Langeland killed her. My sixth sense – if I have one – is screaming at me. I'm furious he's killed her. I'll catch the sack of shit and lock him up. I know everything stands and falls on one thing: I have to find the body. I don't know where it is, but I can work out what he was doing that night by examining his electronic trail. I'll get an idea of where his car went, which toll gates he passed. Then I'll find out where his phone was at any time afterwards, where he spent money and took out money on his card. In that way I'll be able to circle a geographical area. Once that's done I'll get the bloodhounds out if I have to. I'll find the body and get the bastard sentenced!'

'Amen,' said Gunnarstranda. 'If she's poor enough and attractive enough she might be in some hotel right now performing blowjobs. She wouldn't be the first African girl in this country to earn her kroner that way.'

'I'll treat that with the contempt it deserves,' Frølich said, irritated.

Gunnarstranda shrugged. 'I can't ignore new technology. My point is only that I don't like going through lists of data for hour after hour instead of talking to people of flesh and blood.' He paused, added, 'By the way,' and turned to go out.

'By the way what?'

'I wish you would show the same commitment as this in the Veronika case. Is your indifference perhaps because of your friendship with the main suspect?'

Frølich had to let the words sink in and the meaning materialise before he could bring himself to answer.

'Who says that?'

'Frølich. Get a grip,' Gunnarstranda said softly. 'The point is that Veronika Undset has been killed. The body has been found. Most probably an old pal of yours croaked her. But you're scrabbling around for a body no one knows anything about. That's a waste of energy!'

Frølich angled his head. 'Unusual for you to show such emotion,' he said casually. 'What's happened?'

'The fish is off the hook!'

Frølich stood up. He breathed out. The arrest of Karl Anders had tied his stomach in a knot. Janne Smith's visit had tightened it. Now it was loosening. He was breathing lighter. In fact, he felt better. He had to look away to conceal a smile.

'How did Karl Anders react?'

'How do you think he reacted? I've just come from the court session now. We were too hasty,' Gunnarstranda said. 'The judge got caught up in the relationship between Veronika and what she calls verifiable organised crime, with Regine Haraldsen as the burglary victim. All the other clients of Veronika who were also burgled. Mess and contradictory statements from the officers carrying out surveillance on Zahid. They were unsure whether they were spying on him or his brother. In the end, the icing on the cake: your arrest of Veronika. The seizure of the cocaine in her bag. The judge got it into her head that this murder's like the American muck she watches on TV. Well, anyway. Karl Anders Fransgård walked out of court a free man. He gave me the finger two hours ago – who wouldn't have done in his shoes? But we're back to square one. Right back.'

Gunnarstranda headed for the door. 'And so we'll need your help,' he said, acidly. 'Now Fransgård's free and you're no longer compromised. Just so that you know.'

The door slammed after him.

Frølich stared at the door with a smile on his face.

18

Gunnarstranda could feel his irritation chafing as he waited for the bus. Finally, he reached for his phone and rang Oslo Council. The woman in the personnel department was not very forthcoming. Rumours that Karl Anders Fransgård had been released had reached the ears of the council. She didn't want to say anything.

'But surely you can tell me when he started with you, can't you? Where did he work before?'

The woman reluctantly consulted her files. She took her time. Three minutes. The electronic display in the shelter warned that the bus was coming. A voice spoke in his ear. Karl Anders Fransgård came from a job in the Norwegian Water Resources and Energy Directorate. Gunnarstranda thanked her and switched off.

There was a problem with the electronic display, so he decided to do something useful while he was waiting. He rang the directorate.

*

Three-quarters of an hour later Gunnarstranda dropped into the armchair by the bookcase at home. He was only there for a few seconds before he stood up and opened a second window. He sat enjoying the draught. The trumpet solo on the stereo was satisfying and matched the heat and the mood. 'What are we listening to?' he asked.

'Paolo Conte.'

Tove was on the sofa, bent forward. Between her thumb and first finger she was holding a piece of thread. At the end of it swung a screw. 'Italian jazz,' she said, 'and *so* wonderful.'

Gunnarstranda focused on the lamp on the ceiling. She was right. Music harmonised the draught from the semi-open window and the clinking of the two latches. He closed his eyes and felt his stress slowly dissipate. The sound of metal on glass made him open his eyes again.

Tove was still playing with the screw on the thread.

'What are you doing?'

She passed him the thread.

'It's a pendulum,' she said. 'Hold it.'

He sat up and took it. Then held it.

'Ask it a question.'

He let out a sigh and put the thread and the screw on the table.

'Oh, no,' Tove said, shaking her head. 'You're not allowed to back out!'

Reluctantly he picked up the thread again. Held it between his thumb and middle finger and let it dangle. 'You want me to ask a screw a question?'

'We're talking a human energy field here, between your perception and what still is you, but about which you know nothing.'

'Then I prefer a whisky on the rocks. The best bridge between rationality and irrationality is built with a good drink.'

She got up.

'Stay where you are,' he said. 'We're modern adults and I'm more than happy to fulfil expectations of my role. I can pour us a drink.'

'You might be a modern man, but you're not quick enough,' she grinned and went to the American trunk, opened it and looked down at the collection of bottles. 'A Talisker?'

He shook his head. 'A blend.'

'Chivas?'

He nodded.

She went into the kitchen with the bottle. With his eyes closed, he followed the sounds. The fridge was opened, then she banged the ice-cube tray on the sink.

He opened his eyes and accepted the drink. They raised their glasses. Tove sipped and said:

'Why do you always reject as humbug anything you can't control with your senses? You know some animals can hear sounds that cannot be perceived by the human ear, don't you? There are sounds you can't hear, so why shouldn't there be things in the world your eyes can't see? What is it that makes you think you're so perfect you're able to perceive everything in this world? Don't you understand that when you reject the supra-sensible, you do that on supra-sensible terms? Your supposition that there is nothing in this world other than the physical phenomena you can see or sense in some other way – is simply a circular argument.'

He had to smile at her passion and waited for the conclusion:

'Whoever claims there are no truths, is using truth as an argument.'

'Amen,' he said, and took a sip.

Tove grabbed the tarot cards from the bookcase. She held them up to his face and said: 'The cards in themselves don't say anything.'

'I've told you a hundred times. I don't want to have my future told,' Gunnarstranda interrupted.

'The cards in themselves don't say anything,' she repeated undaunted. 'The cards are symbols that awaken possibilities. They can evoke options for you. They can be part of the awakening process.'

He had to smile again at her choice of words. Tove had two sides to her. She shared his scepticism in many areas, while also cultivating the irrational and fostering a deep fascination for anything in the field of parapsychology.

She said: 'It'll always be you who makes the decisions. I shuffle the cards, but you cut the pack. I spread the cards on the table. You pick out the cards that are read. What is it that determines your will? What is it that makes you choose precisely the cards you do? We don't know. Actually it doesn't matter which cards you choose until they're laid on the table and read. It's only when the cards are face up on the table that I can read them, but my reading only has meaning if there's an intention behind what you do. Accordingly, I'd like you to think about an unclarified problem when you choose a card. Ask yourself a question. Bring some dissonance into the situation.'

'Please,' he yawned. 'It's been a long day.'

Tove deliberated, then came to a decision: 'OK,' she said, 'I'll let you off if you try the pendulum. Ask it a question and it'll answer with a swing.'

He took the thread with the screw attached. 'You're telling me that this screw knows something about me and my life?'

She shook her head. 'If you ask the pendulum a question which is outside the field you control, it won't give you an answer. This is neither magic nor hocus pocus. The cards and the pendulum are only instruments of your own consciousness.'

Gunnarstranda could feel tiredness creeping in and nodded dreamily. He didn't quite know where to begin, but made an effort:

'You know, I brought a case to the remand court, a charge. We moved too quickly and the accused was set free. What do I do in this situation? Do you think the screw can help me?'

'I do not, and you know that very well.'

'But will it be able to answer?'

'Depends on whether you're really interested.'

'If I wasn't interested, I wouldn't have asked.'

'OK,' Tove smiled. 'First of all you have to have a framework. You have to know which way the pendulum swings for yes and no. Ask, for example, if it's daytime now. The answer you'll get is yes. Ask afterwards if night has fallen. Whichever way the pendulum swings is no. If the pendulum doesn't know it will rotate. Do that now,' she explained, and got up. 'That way it'll be over faster.'

She shuffled towards the kitchen, stopped at the doorway and smiled. 'I've bought some shrimps, fresh from the harbour.'

Gunnarstranda drained his whisky with the thread and the pendulum in his hand. This is idiotic, he thought, holding the pendulum in the air. For a joke he asked: am I an idiot? The pendulum started swinging. He let go of the thread. The screw fell to the table.

Gunnarstranda sat looking at the screw. Eventually he went to the kitchen to give a hand.

Tove was arranging the shrimps on a plate. He sliced a lemon, then a loaf of bread.

'White wine or beer?'

'Both,' he answered, and sat down. 'And I don't care what the bloody screw says.'

19

The Dandy Warhols were playing on the stereo. The same CD as the last time they were in the car together.

'Number twelve.' Gunnarstranda pointed to the rows of low-rise flats in front of them.

'I've been here before,' Frølich said, and stopped by a gap in the line of cars. He reversed into it. Even felt proud to pull it off at the first attempt.

From the bells outside the front door they could see her flat was on the second floor. Gunnarstranda fumbled with the keys, but eventually managed to open the door.

They entered a tiny hallway. Three brown doors led into rooms.

Gunnarstranda opened the sitting-room door. Frølich opened the adjacent door. It led to the bathroom. He saw himself. The opposite wall was covered by a mirror. An expensive steam shower in the corner, an integrated sink. Shelf upon shelf of cosmetics. He imagined Veronika's slim figure pushing the shower door to the side, walking naked onto the narrow floor and studying her body in the mirror.

He lifted the lid of the laundry basket. A pair of jeans above a jumble of underwear. He recognised the seams of the jeans. She had been wearing them when he last saw her. So she had been home to change after work. She had arrived at the office by taxi. How had she got home afterwards? Metro? Bus? Or … he didn't get any further.

'Come here!' Gunnarstranda shouted.

Frølich closed the door and went into the sitting-room-cum-bedroom.

The double bed was wedged into a tight alcove. Made, covered with a white, crocheted quilt. A shelf beneath the window was stacked with CDs. The stereo was good quality – NAD player and tall, slim Dali speakers.

Gunnarstranda was waving an enlarged photo. Frølich took it. It had been taken in an amusement park, probably Tusenfryd. Veronika and Karl Anders at full speed down the water ride in a canoe, both screaming and laughing.

Gunnarstranda went through the desk drawers with renewed energy, mumbling:

'He talked about photos when I banged him up, your friend.'

'Photos?'

'Yes, plural, photos.'

Frankie stood studying the photo. It was a bit blurred, but the movement and the emotions were there to see. She was sitting at the front, him at the back. Her hair was flying; her face shone with pleasure, while Karl Anders's was partly obscured by her hair.

He went back to the CD shelf and read the titles. There were Nice Price editions of early Stones, seventies' Dylan, Led Zeppelin and a few female vocalists – Nina Simone, Aretha Franklin, Etta James and the songbird of all songbirds: Eva Cassidy. The latter lay on top of the others, opened, so this disc must have been in the stereo. He switched it on.

His eyes found a framed photo on the wall. Her and Karl Anders in a classic embrace for the photographer. Seeing the photo made him feel sad.

Eva Cassidy's clear voice filled the little flat. 'Fields of Gold.'

Frølich took two paces back. The sound was exceptionally good and he shuddered at the words of the lyrics. *You remember me…*

Gunnarstranda was gesticulating. He wanted the volume turned down. Frølich obeyed.

'Who's this?'

Gunnarstranda had found another photo taken at Tusenfryd. The same scene, but the canoe on the way down contained just one man.

Not Karl Anders. A stranger, white, wearing light-coloured trousers and a red jacket with a zip, sporty type, around fifty, slim. The man holding on seemed focused. His facial features weren't very clear, but what hair he had was dark, with a strand over his forehead, a pointed nose. Frølich shook his head.

'Time and date,' Gunnarstranda said.

Frølich held a photo in each hand. At the bottom were the times and dates. The photos had been taken less than a month ago. On the same day, fewer than three minutes apart.

'This tallies with the statement your friend made,' Gunnarstranda said. 'He's telling the truth. Perhaps the judge was right.'

Frølich arched both eyebrows.

'These photos are shown on a TV screen by the exit,' Gunnarstranda said. 'People can see themselves, their strange, terror-stricken grimaces. I can understand her buying a photo of herself and her fiancé, but why buy a photo of the guy behind them?'

Frølich shrugged.

'Your friend reckons it was this man who did it,' Gunnarstranda said, tapping the photo with a bony finger. 'He thinks this man killed Veronika.'

Frølich scrutinised the photo with renewed interest.

'I thought he was talking rubbish, but he wasn't lying, Frølich. He maintained he had absolutely no idea who the man was. Veronika bought the photo in secret, without him seeing. She hid it and he saw it quite by chance afterwards.'

Frølich grinned.

'What is it?' Gunnarstranda asked.

'The perpetrator follows them, to the amusement park, onto the water ride.'

'He must have got a kick out of that.'

Frølich's grin was even broader.

Gunnarstranda eyed him with obvious annoyance.

'You don't seem to believe what Karl Anders says?'

Gunnarstranda waited quietly for a response.

'I suggest we drop Karl Anders,' Frølich said. 'You didn't win at the remand court. If you continue getting stressed about things he's said, about him in general, you'll get tunnel vision. You have to open your eyes, delve deeper into the case. It's futile getting obsessed by Karl Anders.'

'I bungled it,' Gunnarstranda confessed. 'He was apprehended too early and got off the hook. On the other hand, *we have to know more*. I'd like to know who the man in the photo is, for example. I want to talk to him and hear his version of events.'

'You're losing focus.'

Gunnarstranda frowned in astonishment.

'Karl Anders is an old friend,' Frølich said. 'I asked to be kept out of this case, but no. I had to be thrown in. You humiliated Karl Anders and hauled him in with everyone watching at his workplace – for one lapse, he had no alibi, but there was no motive—'

'What are you talking about?' Gunnarstranda broke in angrily. 'He was alone, sixty metres below Frogner Park. No one saw anything at all.'

Gunnarstranda took both photos. 'You should be interested in this. The photos are, as far as I can see, a new lead in the case. Veronika Undset was a woman who kept a lot of secrets – even from the man she was going to marry. I don't think we'll crack this case unless we find what these secrets were. Well, this is one of them: she bought a photo of this man *without* telling her fiancé. That's pretty unusual.'

'You've got tunnel vision,' Frølich stated.

'I have not.'

'No? Actually I feel partly responsible for Veronika's murder. Her hell started when I arrested her outside this door. Before that she was an independent businesswoman who was going to get married in Rome in the near future.'

Gunnarstranda observed him in silence.

Frølich stared back, his hands in his pockets.

On the floor between them lay a round crocheted mat. The scene reminded him of the ring for sumo wrestlers. All that was missing was an old man chanting and throwing rice onto the floor.

Gunnarstranda said: 'I don't want to talk about friendships here, neither mine nor yours, but I'd imagine it would be in your interest to find out the truth about Veronika's death. My thinking is: if it was me who knew Fransgård, I'd want to have the truth out in the open rather than pushing it away at the expense of old memories. The worst thing you can do is to close your eyes to the truth. If you do, sooner or later you'll start wondering what was true and what was lies. Then conspiracy thoughts start creeping in. Then the good memories will be slashed to ribbons. If it gets that far, you have nothing – neither the truth nor the memory of happy moments to fall back on.'

Frølich didn't wish to comment on the phrase 'memory of happy moments'.

Neither of them said anything for a long while. It was Gunnarstranda who broke the silence. 'This is Veronika's secret whether you like it or not.' He waved both photos.

'OK,' said Frølich. 'I have an idea with regard to this guy.' He took both photos and headed for the door.

'Where are you going?'

'To Tusenfryd,' Frølich answered. 'That's where the photos were taken, isn't it.'

20

Even though there was a nip in the air and ominous black clouds were forming above the mountains, the car park outside Tusenfryd was full of cars and buses. The man who met Frølich outside the administrative building was a tall, thin Vestlander in a short-sleeved shirt and a tie of the same colour and pattern as a stick of rock.

'You're in luck,' he said. The person who was selling photos of the water ride now sold them on the day in question as well.'

Frølich inclined his head in gratitude and followed the man, who was explaining the system they had with young helpers over the summer: the most important attributes were work rate, a willingness to provide a good service and a cheerful disposition. 'We try to drum into them that they're ambassadors, they're the face of the amusement park.' He explained that the youngsters got points according to their behaviour and the cheery humour and service they showed customers. A certain number of points qualified them for an award, there was a scale, and employees were given coloured badges, more tangible evidence of their success. These badges gave them increased confidence and they climbed the scale. Those who excelled over several seasons might be appointed group leaders. 'I believe in competition to develop leadership qualities,' the man said, with a Vestland roll of the 'r'. 'And I believe in women. Statistically speaking, the majority of our group leaders are women. Simple as that.'

Frank Frølich listened with half an ear as they trudged up the tarmac path and made way for children brandishing candyfloss with flustered parents at their heels. 'That's new this year,' the Vestlander said, pointing to a tower at the end of a long queue of people. From there you could hear a cacophony of screams as the new machine acrobatically turned visitors' stomachs inside out. The Vestlander picked up an ice-cream wrapper as he walked and threw the paper into a bin. He wiped his fingers on his handkerchief. Frølich trod on popcorn that had spilled from a paper cup the man had missed. Cooing pigeons with popcorn in their beaks ran from under their feet.

The Vestlander's phone rang and he answered it.

They stopped.

Frølich turned and surveyed the park. The wave-swinger rotated and customers clung on tight, screaming as they were swung around. A small distance away there was the rumble of a more traditional carousel. There was a collective groan from behind the trees as the new attraction performed another twist. Frølich was reminded of his own childhood, listening to the sound of running feet, the snorting of pneumatic installations, the rattle of the cars on the rails of the rollercoaster that slowed down more and more before hurtling down a loop and triggering whoops of glee. He breathed in the air of hot fat, burned sugar and wafts of perfume from young mothers out walking. *All these places have the same atmosphere*, he thought: Tivoli in Copenhagen, Liseberg in Gothenburg, Disneyland in Anaheim – he could draw connections all the way back to the wandering fairs of his childhood when long lines of lorries camped outside the museums in Tøyen and set up rinks for dodgems and stalls for raffles. Once, in their teenage years, he and Karl Anders had spent a whole evening shooting at small bears which climbed trees and ran between bushes in a square display case. They had won a lot of teddy bears, which they generously donated to the girl who loaded the airguns. He was still smiling at the thought when the Vestlander resumed walking, having finished his phone conversation.

Another chilly gust of wind made him shiver. The sky had darkened considerably in the ten minutes he had been here.

They moved into a new zone of noise, and here people's screams mixed with the sound of splashing water. Spray lashed the tarmac.

Where the paths divided they were joined by a uniformed teenage girl with a ponytail and a sun visor. She curtsied and said hello. In the stall at the exit of the water ride two teenage boys were selling photos that were displayed on TV screens.

The girl with the ponytail took over the photo sales from the two who would talk to the police officer. One boy was overweight and stank of deodorant. His head was as round as a bowling ball and there was a cascade of red freckles around his nose. The other was tall, thin and had bad posture. He had big teeth and wore a headband to keep his blond hair out of his eyes.

The Vestlander had brought up the two relevant photos on a laptop. The two youths shook their heads when they saw them.

'The woman in the first photo might have bought both of them,' Frølich ventured. 'Does that help?'

They shrugged their shoulders.

The Vestlander started serving up figures. Tusenfryd had so and so many visitors every season. So and so many thousand went on the water ride every day. Of these so and so many hundred photos were sold every day, each and every day,' he said. 'To try and remember one visitor from all of this is simply impossible,' he concluded.

Frølich fought to control himself. He was thinking, *What the hell am I doing here if it's impossible*?

He stared at the two youths and made one last attempt. 'This woman was very attractive and she bought two photos.'

The two youths looked at him just as blankly.

'Sometimes it helps if you try to associate the day with a particular event. In other words, distinguish this one day from all the others. Something or other that happened on this one day. You might have bought new clothes, played in a football match or seen a certain film. The point is that if you can differentiate this day from all the others, this incident might stand out in some way and you can remember what happened.'

They looked at each other. Then they shook their heads.

Overhead, an immense thunderclap caused the Vestlander to flinch.

The rain beat down. People ran for cover. No one was interested in the photos any more. An elderly woman with a newspaper over her head scurried past. Water ran in torrents down the hill. Soon there wasn't a single visitor to be seen. The girl with the ponytail reacted to the photos on the laptop. 'I know who he is,' she said, pointing to the lone man in the boat.

Frølich turned to her.

She nodded. 'He's the librarian at Deichman.'

The boy with the headband didn't like being outshone by a girl. 'Oh yeah? You don't even work here!'

'No,' she retorted. 'I'm a student and if you used your brain, perhaps you will be one day, too.'

The girl with the ponytail shut up when she saw everyone looking at her. Abashed, she looked at each of them in turn. Finally, she focused her gaze on Frølich. 'I often study in Deichman Library and the man in the photo is the spitting image of the librarian.'

21

'Sivert Almeli,' Frølich said.

'How did you find that out?' Gunnarstranda asked sceptically.

'It's the man in the photo. He's a librarian at Deichman and is off ill. He hasn't given a reason for his absence. He just said he would be away for three days and the doctor would decide if he needed any more time'

'Have you spoken to his boss?'

'Colleague. She says he's worked there longer than her, for decades apparently. He's a kind of institution at the library from what I can gather. Seems to be an easy-going, ordinary sort of person, but keeps himself to himself, rarely takes part in the Christmas celebrations or any others. No one at Deichman has heard of Veronika Undset or recognised her in the photo, but I think I know what the relationship is between them.'

'Oh, yes?' Gunnarstranda said, changing his grip on the phone. He was in Veronika Undset's flat, where he was searching through boxes of underwear in her wardrobe. On the bed there were piles of panties, nylons, tights, bras…

'Why haven't you spoken to the guy?'

'I have a good reason,' Frølich said. 'Where are you?'

'Where you left me,' Gunnarstranda said. 'Still in her flat.'

'That's what I thought. So you can speak to Almeli first,' Frølich said on his phone with a grin. 'He lives in the next block. Number eighteen.'

*

The entrance to Almeli's part of the building was locked.

Gunnarstranda found the bell and pressed. Waited with his hands in his pockets. Obviously no one at home. He rang again. The fingers of his left hand found something in his pocket. It turned out to be Tove's screw, still attached to the thread. The pendulum.

He pressed again, but the intercom by the bell was as silent as before. Then he pressed one of the others on the ground floor.

'Yes,' a small, hoarse woman's voice answered, her vocal cords quivering with a pensioner's anxiety.

'Police here.'

She was waiting on the landing and supporting herself on a Zimmer frame. Grey perm and wrinkled face, about eighty. Wearing a white blouse and dark trousers. 'What's this about?' she asked nervously.

'My apologies,' Gunnarstranda said sympathetically. 'I must have pressed the wrong bell. I was looking for Almeli on the third.'

She snorted with annoyance, turned around and stabbed her Zimmer frame back to her flat.

Gunnarstranda continued upwards, staircase by staircase. Blocks of more than three floors without a lift were an anachronism. He was beginning to pant. The doctor was right. His lungs weren't getting better, even though he had stopped smoking. He paused to regain his breath. Nevertheless, his lungs were going like bellows by the time he found the right door. The name plate was black, the letters white. *Sivert Almeli.*

The bell rang like a telephone from the Sixties. No one opened up. A draught in the corridor caused the door to move slightly. It banged against the frame. It was unlocked.

Should he? It was tempting. He glanced over his shoulder. No one would see him if he went in. He studied the neighbouring flat. No peephole in the door. Everything was quiet.

Gunnarstranda couldn't restrain himself. He pushed the door open. Stared at the hallway.

'Almeli?'

Not a sound to be heard.

'Police here. I have a few questions.'

Total silence. Or was that a sound?

He crossed the threshold warily. Closed the door after himself.

In the entrance there was a coat stand, but there was nothing hanging on it. No shoes on the floor, no pictures on the wall. Three closed doors shone uninvitingly. He raised his hand, but stopped as he heard a noise.

Where had it come from?

He knocked on the closest door.

'Hello?'

He knocked again.

No reaction. He concentrated.

That *was* a noise.

He knocked again.

Nothing.

He opened the door. It was the bathroom, which was empty. White bathtub, old-style, ditto the sink. A toothbrush in a glass on the shelf.

He turned around. Opened another door and found himself looking into the kitchen. Just as empty. Must have been the original from when it was built. Sliding doors in diagonal cupboards and an old-fashioned sink. Clean worktop, clean table, gleaming sink unit. Not so much as a salt cellar on the table.

The noise must have come from the room behind the third door.

He raised his hand. Turned the handle and slowly pushed the door open, and found himself looking into the sitting room. It seemed abandoned.

'Hello?'

No reaction.

Gunnarstranda went inside. Looked around. The flat was exactly the same as Veronika Undset's, a mirror image. A narrow bed in the alcove. Beside that was a bedside table with a small black battery-driven alarm clock.

By the facing wall there was a TV with a chair in front of it and a desk with a laptop. That was all.

'Hello?'

No answer this time, either. He was beginning to feel stupid. He walked over to the window. Saw Veronika's flat. He could see inside. He saw a bit of the floor and the TV screen. If he crouched down, he could glimpse the bed in the alcove.

A chill went down his spine. He had a strong sensation he wasn't alone. Someone was behind him.

The hairs on his neck were standing up as he turned – slowly.

The room was as empty as before.

He gasped for breath. He had never yearned for a cigarette so much. He was sweating. His vision blurred, the air quivered. He groped in his pocket for a nicotine chewing gum and pressed it under his lip.

He stood fingering Tove's screw. Held the thread between his forefinger and middle finger and swung the pendulum until it was coiled round and the screw hit his fingers. Then he let go of the screw and repeated the action.

This flat is empty, he thought to himself. As the front door was open, Almeli must have just gone out on a short errand.

He sat down in the chair without thinking. He was still flushed. Were his hands shaking? He held the pendulum to check, held it between thumb and index finger until the screw hung without moving. No shakes. Happy, he asked himself, mostly for fun, 'Is Almeli at home?'

To his surprise the pendulum started swinging. To and fro. Towards the north-facing window.

Gunnarstranda held the screw. OK, so the screw could talk. But what had it said?

'Am I in Almeli's flat?' he asked himself.

The pendulum began to swing, but the opposite way this time, east-west.

Sceptical, Gunnarstranda took a deep breath and placed the pendulum in his lap. It bothered him that it had swung in different directions. That could be interpreted as the pendulum giving two different answers – and therefore having an understanding of the situation. Almeli wasn't at home. He didn't need a screw to work that one out.

Nevertheless, he couldn't understand how it was possible for the screw to swing of its own accord and give two different answers by swinging in two different directions. Both of them correct. He was here, but Almeli wasn't. But, he thought, it must have been his own subconscious that provided the impetus. The swing had to be a kind of desired reaction, one he couldn't control. It had to be his subconscious that made his finger holding the thread start the movement – unbeknown to him.

On the other hand, he mused, it ought to be possible to control his subconscious in this case.

He waited patiently for the pendulum to be absolutely still. *A question of control.* In the end he couldn't restrain himself. He let the pendulum swing free and asked: 'Am I alone here?'

The pendulum swung, like the first time. If the screw was right, he *wasn't* alone.

The second the thought was articulated, the same sensation returned. The air in the room seemed to tremble. A chill went down his back and sent him into a cold sweat.

That's not right, he told himself. *I'm sitting here alone.*

He noticed he was staring at the wardrobe in the alcove where the bed was. Three closed doors.

Soundlessly, he rose to his feet. Put the screw back in his pocket. Stood collecting himself for a few long moments. Walked slowly towards the wardrobe. Stopped in front of the door in the middle.

He lifted his hand. Hesitated.

Slowly pulled the handle. The door opened. The hinges screamed.

He stood face to face with a line of jackets hanging from a rail.

Jesus, he thought. *This is ridiculous.*

He closed the door.

He spun on his heel.

Pressure had built up in the air. It was like sitting for too long in the sauna. He had to get out, away. He ran out of the flat.

On the landing he bent over panting.

What had happened? He had no idea. He checked the door. It was unlocked, as Almeli had left it. Almeli would expect to find it unlocked when he returned.

Gunnarstranda sauntered down the stairs. Stopped outside the door of the woman with the Zimmer frame. Rang her bell. It sounded like dull clangs from a remote church.

Her name plate was of the same kind as those on the third: black and rectangular with white letters. *Solfrid Reine*.

He heard her fumbling with the Zimmer frame behind the door. The peephole was dark. The door was opened a fraction.

'Almeli? He's the strange fellow on the third, isn't he? No … I really don't know.'

She articulated every word with special emphasis and a familiar tune in the upper-pitch range. 'You're from Trondheim, madam, aren't you?' said Gunnarstranda, careful to observe decorum.

The wrinkled face broke into a nice smile. Her eyes narrowed with delight. 'How did you guess?'

'My wife grew up in Rosenborg.'

'Well I never. What's her name?'

'She's dead,' Gunnarstranda said, not mincing his words. He regretted his charm offensive and wanted to get back to the case in hand. 'Are you sure you haven't seen Almeli today?'

Fru Reine was friendliness itself. 'You know, it might be his laundry day. Erm, that is a possibility as his door isn't locked. If so,' she reasoned with a finger in the air, he must be downstairs in the cellar. Wait and I'll check the list.' She turned and pushed the Zimmer frame in front of her. The door shut behind her. When she returned she was holding a piece of white paper in her hand. And, yes indeed, it was Almeli's laundry day.

'Might I borrow your key, Fru Reine?'

'Of course.' She smiled again. 'I'm really sorry. I'm so direct. I've done it so many times. I didn't mean to pry into your private matters.'

'No harm done.' Gunnarstranda was almost starting to like her.

'Don't mess the place up now,' she joked, passing him the key with a wink.

He waited until she had closed the door, then he hurried down the cellar steps. Unlocked the door and looked along a long, dark corridor that culminated in an illuminated, bombproof room.

His fingers searched for the light switch on the wall as he stared into the darkness. The feeling from Almeli's flat returned – a kind of quiver. Something that made him reluctant to stay down here.

His fingers found the switch and he told himself, *You're in a block of flats in Oslo. Children play here every day of the week, now pull yourself together*.

He turned on the switch. The neon tubes on the ceiling lit up one by one.

On both sides of the corridor ran a long row of padlocked cages. He listened for the noise coming from the washing machines.

Nothing, apart from the dry clicks of one neon tube that wouldn't light up.

Watchful, he moved down the corridor. Passed cage after cage and approached an opening. He got it into his head that someone was waiting for him around the corner. He stopped. Glanced over his shoulder. No one behind him.

He looked ahead again. The standard steel doors of the bombproof room were wide open at the end of the corridor. That had to be the residents' laundry room. He took a deep breath and collected himself. Took two steps. His legs came to a halt. Slowly he turned his head and looked into the pitch darkness of the side corridor. He started to imagine that this *wasn't* a dark room he was looking at, it was black smoke billowing up, it enveloped and hid the creature that had followed him from the moment he entered the block. He stood with his back against the timber-lined wall and waited. His face was soaked with sweat as he pressed himself backward and stared into the blackness until his eyes got used to the sparse light and he could make out the outline of the corridor – which was completely empty. The feeling didn't disappear however. He glanced back again. No one. He forced himself to delve further. His shirt was sticking to him. He had to stop and look back again. No one there.

At last. He staggered into the illuminated bombproof room with white concrete walls and a green floor.

Two washing machines and tumble dryers stood against each wall.

Water was running from a tap set in the wall beside a washing machine. It ran in a broad stream down to the drain in the middle of the floor.

He walked across the concrete and turned off the tap. Total silence.

The glass door of one tumble dryer was open. He felt the clothes in the drum. They were damp. Someone had put them in there not so long ago and hadn't closed the door.

Then he caught a scent; a very familiar smell.

He turned quickly, took one step and slipped in the water on the floor, almost fell, but managed to regain his balance. He hadn't been wrong. The floor around the second washing machine was red and the red was slowly, slowly spreading.

Gunnarstranda took his phone from his pocket. His fingers were trembling so much he almost dropped it. His eyes glazed over as he went to key in the number. He had to lean back against the wall to hold the phone still.

Then he saw the figure lying on the floor behind the washing machine. The man lay with his legs tucked beneath him, face and chest to the floor. The slash across his throat tilted his head at an unnatural angle. The amount of blood and the whiteness of his skin told its own story.

The phone rang in his ear. Twice.

'Frølich? I need back-up. Almeli's been killed and I think the killer is still in the vicinity.'

Gunnarstranda slowly backed away from the body. For two long seconds he stood quite still watching. The outline of the bombproof doors blurred.

The next moment he ran out of the room. The sight of the long corridor brought him to a halt. Where could the perpetrator be hiding?

Nevertheless, he had to get out. He took the same route as when he came in. His spine tingled. But there was no one behind him. The dark side corridor approached. He slowed down. His breathing was laboured and he stopped. Told himself: *there's no one here.*

He gritted his teeth and carried on, past the black hole and along. Unable to stop himself. He cast a last glance over his shoulder.

He tore open the door to the stairwell. Took the first staircase two steps at a time. Passed the Trondheimer's flat. She opened the door and shouted after him:

'My dear, what about the key?'

He couldn't waste any energy on her now. He pressed on.

He dragged himself up by the banister. Three sets of stairs left. What had happened to the cavalry?

On the landing he stood fighting for air by the window. Scanned the street.

The first patrol car rolled up, and he forced himself onward. With ID in one hand he banged on the brown door. Pulled at the handle. The door wouldn't budge. It was locked.

But he had left it unlocked. There was a flood of pent-up anger in the torrent of curses Gunnarstranda unleashed on the door. He wasn't so much angry because of his poor physical shape, but because the bloody screw had been right. He hadn't been alone. Someone *had* been in there; someone who had shut the door on their way out.

22

There was a throng of vehicles outside and the front entrance was cordoned off with police tape. A scene-of-crime officer in blue overalls with her title written in white letters on her back was taking items from the boot of a car. Frølich exchanged a few words with her, went back and was lost from sight under the entrance roof.

Gunnarstranda turned away from the window. Sat down on the chair. He observed the officer kneeling on the floor to look under the bed. 'Nothing,' Gunnarstranda said, and added: 'I can see from here.'

The SOC officer got up and examined the rest of the room.

At last they heard the heavy footsteps of Frølich on the stairs. He was out of breath. 'I spoke to a couple of neighbours,' he explained.

'Who?'

'The woman whose key you borrowed and a younger woman who lives on the floor above her. Biology student doing an intensive course in Spanish who stays at home all day studying. She heard Almeli talking to someone on the staircase, on his way down. It could fit the time scale.'

'Man or woman?'

'She doesn't know. She recognised Almeli's voice and assumed he was speaking to someone. The sound of the footsteps suggested two people. Fru Reine thinks she saw a car roaring off,' Frølich said. 'Her neighbour, Elise Andersen, confirms she saw a car driving off at great speed, and that may tally with the time when you were in the cellar.'

'So the car drove off *while* I was in the cellar?'

Frank Frølich nodded.

'We're talking seconds here,' Gunnarstranda sighed. 'Any description of the driver?'

'No.'

'The student?'

Frølich shook his head. 'Elise Andersen heard a squeal of tyres, looked up from her textbook and caught a glimpse of a dark car.'

Gunnarstranda sat looking at the desk by the wall. 'Someone must have seen the driver. We just have to keep making enquiries.'

'Bård,' Gunnarstranda shouted.

The SOC officer in the alcove turned around.

'Have you moved anything here?'

The man in the white overalls shook his head.

'There was a laptop on the desk, a white Mac. It's gone.'

The SOC officer and Frølich exchanged glances. Both stared at Gunnarstranda, who said: 'The door was open when I got here, so I left it like that. When I returned it was locked. Someone …'

The SOC officer, who had opened one of the wardrobe doors in the alcove while Gunnarstranda was talking, motioned them over. 'Look here,' he said with a smile.

He pointed at the inside of the wardrobe. Someone had been in there, that much was obvious. Behind the right-hand door the clothes had been pushed aside and several pairs of shoes had been trodden on.

Gunnarstranda eyeballed the scene. 'The door on the right,' he whispered.

Frølich gasped. 'That can't be possible! He was hiding while you were in here.'

Again, both officers turned to Gunnarstranda, who didn't appear to be registering anything.

'That's just not possible,' Frølich repeated.

Gunnarstranda sat stiffly staring into the air.

'Everything OK?' Frølich enquired.

Gunnarstranda raised a finger and asked: 'Bård, what's that?'

The man in the white overalls turned, stretched up on tiptoes and took a flat object with an attached cable from the hat shelf. He held it out. 'An extra hard drive.'

They looked at each other. Gunnarstranda took a deep breath.

'The person who hid in the wardrobe grabbed the laptop, but didn't take everything. We ought to ID the body in the laundry room. Are we completely sure the murder victim is Almeli?'

Frølich shrugged.

'If the body is someone who didn't live in these flats, Almeli could be the perp we're looking for, couldn't he?'

The other two officers looked at each other again. Neither made any objection.

23

It was approaching seven o'clock in the evening. Frølich was eating crispbread and listening to the weather girl on TV2 forecasting a continuation of the hot days, and possibly nights, at more than twenty degrees. He was sweaty after a long day at work and went for a shower. Despite the heat, he stood next to the jet of water waiting for it to become hot. Shampooed his hair and rinsed it. Then there was a ring at the door. He wrapped a towel around himself, went into the hall and lifted the intercom phone.

A woman's voice answered. 'Are you the Frølich who works for the police?'

'Yes.'

'I'd like to have a word concerning Andreas Langeland.'

He pressed the buzzer, jogged back to the bathroom and pulled on jeans and a T-shirt. Managed to towel down his hair, but not comb it by the time the bell rang for a second time.

The woman outside was wearing black linen trousers and a matching jacket. She was in her late forties, had thick blonde hair and narrow, loud-red glasses.

He angled his head in an enquiring manner.

'I should have phoned you first, of course,' she said. 'My name's Iselin Grav.'

He held the door open for her. 'Sorry about my appearance, but I was in the shower.'

She came inside. Her shoes were the same style as her glasses. They were also a strident red. Her blonde hair was collected in a bun with a large slide.

'I don't want anything,' she said as he began to clear the coffee table. 'This is a short, very informal visit.'

He abandoned his efforts at clearing the table.

'I got your name from Andreas,' she said. 'He phoned me last night.'

Frølich slid onto the sofa. Pointed to the armchair. 'And what is your relation—?'

'With Andreas?' She sat down. 'I'm a social worker at what's known as the Pedagogical-Psychological School Service – the PPSS. We work with pupils at school who for some reason need support because they have either specific learning or psycho-social problems. Andreas is over eighteen and finished anything to do with school a year ago, but before that he had been with the PPSS for several years, right from when he started at school until he left upper secondary. I don't wish to go into why, but it was all tied up with his family situation.' Iselin Grav spoke with her eyes downcast and the red glasses on her nose, as though she were reciting from a manuscript for a reading test. At the first intake of breath, Frølich grabbed his chance.

'They're two brothers, Mattis and Andreas, aren't they?'

'Yes, but they have different fathers. Mattis probably had a better childhood than Andreas, but he's had an unfortunate influence on his brother. As I said, I don't wish to go into detail – I'm bound by an oath of confidentiality anyway – but as I worked with Andreas for some years I'm someone he knows and trusts. There are not *many* adults Andreas trusts. Well…'

She gazed at the ceiling for the right words. 'Yesterday he phoned me, as I mentioned, and he seemed pretty manic. And that – just him ringing me – is an alarm signal in itself. It suggests, well, we can come back to that. He says the police – that is, you – think he's killed a woman.'

She paused and looked him in the eye.

Frølich stared back.

Iselin Grav looked down.

He asked: 'Why have you come here?'

'You have to understand,' she said, getting up restlessly. She walked over to the window. Stood with her back to Frølich. 'The relationship between Andreas and me is built on trust established over many years. I have nothing to do with him any longer, and I try as best as I can not to get involved with my patients – privately. But when he calls me and is so desperate it wouldn't really be ethical to reject him.'

She turned, put her hands in her pockets and fixed her eyes on him again – awaiting a response.

Frølich had his own ideas about that. She could have given the young man some good advice on the way, but she didn't need to call on the police officer who was investigating a case where the boy was a witness. Had she come to fish for information? He chose his words with care:

'No one has actually mentioned murder,' he said. 'Andreas has been asked some simple questions with regard to a specific case, and it's clear he's lying. He's been confronted with the fact that he's lying.'

She didn't move. Her eyes flickered behind the glasses.

'Well?' he said, very aware of how dismissive and brusque his attitude was.

'We spent a lot of time and invested a lot of resources in Andreas,' she said. 'He has an extremely tragic background. You're wondering why I've come and what I want. I understand that. Well – call it a registration of concern. On the phone yesterday I thought he gave certain signals which were worrying. I've never known him to be so agitated, if I may say so. I think Andreas feels under a lot of pressure now.'

'Pressure?'

'Yes, pressure. Any talk of murder makes me feel quite anxious, and what you've said doesn't exactly diminish my concerns.'

She removed her glasses and looked at him. Without the red lines across her nose her face became more human, in fact quite interesting. Her top lip was full, which gave her mouth a knowing, sensual character. A long, blonde lock of hair had fallen from her slide. She flicked it behind her ear. Narrow hands, long fingers, short nails. No wedding ring.

'Andreas is easily led. He wants to fulfil others' expectations, to be accepted by those he admires. And that's the nub of the problem. His idols have always been bad choices. There's still the odd bit of trouble, which Andreas has never instigated, but you can be sure he's left in the mire. I've never known Andreas to be so distraught as yesterday. I'm very nervous, Frølich, very nervous. Did anything happen? Did the police do anything to him?'

Frølich shook his head. 'Not yesterday, not as far as I'm aware.'

She stood looking at him without adding anything further.

'Iselin,' Frølich said gently. 'If you can exert any positive influence on Andreas—'

'You misunderstand,' she interrupted.

'Your registration of concern has been heard,' he continued undaunted. '*My* concern, however, is for a poor African girl who's alone in this country. She seems to have vanished into thin air. I think Andreas has had something to do with this case, and what you've told me only strengthens my suspicions. The best thing you can do, if you talk to him on the phone or in any other way, is to advise him to tell the truth. If he has a clear conscience, to use a worn cliché, he has nothing to fear, nor any reason to lie. The truth must come out. He must tell us what he knows about this missing girl.'

She leaned against the wall, silent. 'Sorry,' she said as the silence became awkward. 'I'm thinking.'

'I'll have to talk to him again,' Frølich said. 'What you've said tells me it's important to do that.'

She nodded pensively. 'His call last night made me think something had happened – yesterday.'

She took a deep breath and checked her watch.

He accompanied her to the door. Iselin Grav waited for the lift with her back to him. It was only now he noticed her figure. The curves.

The lift came.

She opened the door and turned towards him.

'I don't think she's dead,' she said.

The door closed behind her.

Frølich wondered what she had actually hoped to achieve with this visit.

He walked back to the window and looked down. After a while Iselin Grav came out. Blonde hair, black clothes and red shoes. She got into a Saab cabriolet. She had style anyway – a blonde in an open-top car.

As she pulled away from the pavement he turned back to the room. That was when he saw the red glasses.

He put them on the mantelpiece beside the beer can.

With his hands in his pockets, he stared at the two objects, rapt in thought.

The sun coming through the window made it difficult to see the writing on the screen. Gunnarstranda drew the curtain. Then his mobile beeped. It was a text from Tove. She wanted to know which version of 'Come Rain or Come Shine' he liked best. What sort of question was that? There were loads of versions, each one better than the last: Sarah Vaughan, Art Blakey, Ella, Chet, Bobby Hatfield, Ray Charles, Judy Garland – even the lyricist, Johnny Mercer himself. While he was thinking he remembered the words. Then he cottoned on to what the real message was and closed his eyes with a shy smile.

Texts like these were Tove's way of prodding him. They made him look forward to the time after work. It had taken him years to get there. Not so long ago leisure had been synonymous with sitting at home and not understanding how people could bear having nothing to do. He could no longer remember when this stopped. But he knew why. Clumsily and laboriously, he typed with his thumb: *Your version*. She would have to work out the meaning for herself.

'Gunnarstranda?'

The inspector dropped the phone as if he had been caught red-handed stealing it.

Lena Stigersand stood in the doorway.

'Yes?'

'These cases are beginning to revolve largely around photos,' she said, entering the office. In her arms she was holding an open laptop which she placed on the desk in front of him. The screen showed a blurred picture of Veronika Undset, seen through a window, taken from above.

He peered up at Lena with a strained smile.

She clicked on the screen.

Another photo. A zoom shot of the subject. The sash bar of the window was a dark shadow. Veronika Undset sitting on the side of the bed unhooking her bra. Next photo: Veronika Undset pulling a nightie over her head.

'We've uploaded the hard disk we found in Sivert Almeli's flat,' Lena said. 'It contains more than seven hundred photos. Half of them are nature photos, flowers in Nordmarka, shots of boats from the islands in Oslo Fjord, the sunset over Akershus Fortress and so on. The other half is paparazzi-style photos of Veronika Undset, mostly in similar scenes to this one, but also when she's eating, reading a book, coming out of the front door, walking along the pavement.'

Gunnarstranda reached out his hand and fiddled with the keyboard.

'There,' Lena Stigersand pointed politely.

He clicked the mouse. Another photo: Undset on her way down the pavement. Then: Undset lost in thought waiting for a tram. Next: a close-up. A study of a woman's profile. Eyes downcast. Blurred at the edges.

'Arty-farty photo,' Gunnarstranda mumbled. 'Do you think she knows she's being photographed?'

Lena shook her head. 'This is psycho stuff. Peeping Tom hardly covers what he does. Stalker is better. He's taken photos of her in all sorts of places: in front of the fountain at Eidsvolls plass, even hiking in Nordmarka.'

'And she never knew?'

'All the – what we might call *intimate* shots – were taken through the window. That suggests he was spying. But he's followed her as well. I think it's pretty unlikely she *didn't* know he was tailing her. My guess is he was a stalker she knew about.'

'She had a photo of him – taken on the water ride in Tusenfryd.'

'Ergo,' Lena smiled wryly, 'she must have known what he was doing.'

Gunnarstranda leaned back in his chair with a furrowed brow: 'She could have reported him for this.'

'The report would've been shelved before she was out of the door,' Lena said. 'Provided that he wasn't violent and didn't issue threats.'

'But we should be able to find the report.'

Lena gave a sceptical grimace. 'The officer who spoke to her would've asked about any specific threats and so on. It's very unlikely she could've come up with anything. She would've had to turn on her heel without leaving a report, like a good citizen. Probably muttering to herself that at the next elections she was going to vote for the right-wing populists.'

Gunnarstranda grinned. 'Good, Lena, that's your old self. Carry on like that and you'll soon be the boss.'

'I'll check anyway,' she said, clicking through the photos.

He watched the screen. 'Have we got the camera?'

She shook her head. 'No camera and no laptop found. Nor any memory cards for the camera. Everything indicates the perp was after the photos.'

'Almeli could've accidentally photographed Veronika's murderer when he was taking photos of her,' Gunnarstranda said.

Lena smirked. 'Looks like you and I think on similar lines.'

Gunnarstranda stroked his chin. 'The perpetrator could be someone who knew both Veronika and Almeli.'

Lena shrugged. 'These photos are from the extra hard disk the intruder didn't find or didn't take with him. The photo he was searching for could just as well be in this selection as in the camera or on the laptop. Thought I should show you a series of photos that is a bit special.'

She took the laptop and looked for another series. 'Here,' she said. The subject this time was a man crossing a road. He was around forty with short hair and a trimmed, unattractive beard. His hair was greying. He was wearing a short jacket and dark jeans. The next photo was of the man sitting in a dark green Mercedes. The third was the car driving off.

'Three photos are quite unlike all the rest,' Lena Stigersand said. 'The rest are either studies of Veronika Undset or shots of nature. But these three were obviously taken in secret. And there's one thing that's particularly interesting.'

'What's that?'

'The photos of the man were saved onto the disk the day after Veronika's body was found. The same day Almeli rang in sick to the library.'

'So he wasn't ill. He was out taking photos,' Gunnarstranda said, leaning back in his chair. 'Let me see the first one of the man again.'

The subject was walking fast – unaware that he was being photographed. By the back foot there was a black shadow.

'Why's the background so out of focus?' Gunnarstranda asked.

'Almeli was zooming in with a type of telephoto lens, three hundred mill or more. He was snapping shots from quite a distance. This is spying, this is.'

Gunnarstranda pointed to the shadow by the man's foot. 'That,' he said, 'is a central reservation.'

Lena Stigersand nodded.

'We're probably talking here about a road into town divided by a central reservation. '

'Kirkeveien?'

'Possible, but not definite.'

'Gyldenløves gate?'

Gunnarstranda shrugged and clicked again through the three photos. The man crossing the road. The man getting into a car. The car driving off.

'This rings a bell,' he mumbled, and added, 'no registration number. Why didn't Almeli get the number of the car?'

Lena Stigersand shrugged. 'Perhaps he was too nervous. I would've been if I was taking secret photos of a murderer.'

Gunnarstranda leaned back again. 'It *can't* be Kirkeveien,' he said. 'The car's heading towards a crossroads without traffic lights. In Kirkeveien there are traffic lights the whole way.' He inhaled sharply. 'Show these photos around. I want to know where they were taken. I want to get hold of this man.'

25

It was a dream that wouldn't let go. Stark colours and a closeness to water and skin. Iselin Grav's skin. One image especially from the dream had etched itself firmly in his brain. It was when her body sank into the water. Frølich couldn't remember whether she had slipped in accidentally or jumped in; he only remembered that the water was green and deep and that the figure plunged down with both legs together. Her blonde hair billowed in slow motion above her body, like a curtain. He couldn't recall whether she was wearing clothes or not, but he had jumped in after her. Dived down, grabbed hold and lifted her onto land with consummate ease. Afterwards he had laid her across a huge log so that the water would run out of her mouth. So that she could breathe.

Absolutely crazy dream. But thoughts about Iselin Grav continued during the day. Her cryptic words. *I don't think she's dead.*

He was sure she was holding something back.

After lunch he could stand it no longer. He left Police Headquarters for Urtegata. Strode to the block of flats where Andreas Langeland lived. Rang the bell. No reply.

He took out his phone and tried to reach the boy on his mobile. Got his voicemail. He thought, *If Andreas is at work it would be normal for his phone to be switched off.*

Back in his office, he sat down with the papers describing the movements of Langeland's phone. Went through them again. The problem was the proximity between the base stations. In Oslo there were so many of them. The strange thing was that the phone wasn't in Oslo every day. Could Andreas be leaving it at work?

Gardermoen Airport, he wondered, and studied the movements. The phone was *not* in the north of Oslo, it had moved west and south.

Frølich started sweating. *How thick-headed can you be?*

He rang Langeland's phone once again. It was still dead.

Could it be outside the coverage area?

He took the base-station map. The furthest bearing outside Oslo was a station in Buskerud. It lay between Filtvet and Tofte, about a hundred kilometres from Oslo. The stations followed the arterial road south. Frølich examined the map more closely. Inland, west of Filtvet and Tofte, there was forest, roadways through it and small lakes. Lake Røskestad. No base station for kilometres.

He rang Oslo Airport. Was passed from pillar to post. Andreas Langeland wasn't there. Well, where was he?

Andreas Langeland was on holiday.

Frølich sat scrutinising the papers in front of him. He checked the times of day. Checked his watch.

Rosalind's first meeting with a Norwegian: Andreas Langeland. Two days later: Rosalind has contact with Mattis Langeland. She goes missing. Andreas Langeland is grilled by him and Ståle Sender. No reaction. Andreas Langeland goes on holiday. Shortly afterwards, he rings a social worker at PPSS who describes his behaviour as worrying, ominous signs…

He followed the succession of movements on Langeland's phone. It had to be possible to trace a pattern.

He studied the sheets as if they contained a cleverly contrived puzzle in an IQ test. The writing blurred. He rubbed his eyes, stared at the sheets again. Searching for links without seeing anything at all.

He called Telenor and asked for the last movement on Langeland's phone. Rang off. Waited. Went out to buy a can of Coke in sheer frustration. Back: no paper in the fax machine. Went back out, paced up and down. Greeted people in a distracted fashion.

At last the fax started up. He grabbed the sheets. The latest movements. Langeland was now in a coverage area. In other words, he was moving along the forest roadways. His phone had passed Filtvet a short while earlier, so he was on the R281, along Oslo Fjord towards Drammen or Oslo.

Again, Frølich remembered the moment when Iselin Grav turned by the lift. *I don't think she's dead.*

Not yet?

26

Gunnarstranda fumbled with the CD as he put it in the player. It is illegal for people to talk on the phone when they are driving, he mused, but this was surely worse. He almost drove into the ditch because he couldn't find the slot it was supposed to go in.

He decided to take Ring 3 west, turn off by Tåsen to go via Sagene, down Uelandsgate and Maridalsveien and get to Deichman Library from the rear – across Fredensborgveien. He might even find a parking spot there.

The opening track on the CD was a duet between Jimmy Buffett and Frank Sinatra – a pretty good version of 'Mack the Knife'. Two quite distinct voices. Buffett, soft, almost sensual; Sinatra, seasoned, a touch rough. Alternating between verses and then every line. Gunnarstranda drove down Tåsenveien towards Nordre Gravlund, snapping his fingers. An uneasy feeling took hold of him. He pulled into the side of the road and stopped. Turned down the volume.

He couldn't explain his unease. Got out of the car and scanned the road. Not much traffic. The noise level was so low he could hear the shouts of the people training on the Voldsløkka sports pitches. He was reminded of the allotments hidden behind the estate in Stavangergata. One summer he had hung out with Evelyn, who had an allotment cabin in Oslo. He had even slept there sometimes, many years ago.

Was it memories of Evelyn that had made him stop?

No, he concluded. The thought of her didn't strike him until *after* he got out of the car. *Something else* had made him stop the car and get out? But what?

He lived not far away. East of Tåsenveien was Voldsløkka and the allotments while the post-war town planners had squeezed in high-rises around Gråbeinsletta further south. A ridge of green treetops towered over Nordre Gravlund.

Gunnarstranda turned and glanced up the road. To the north and west of Tåsenveien there were detached and terraced houses, on the outskirts of that gem in the old version of Norwegian Monopoly – Ullevål Hageby. Between the functionalist blocks and the cemetery lay the upper reaches of—

Uelandsgate.

Once Uelandsgate had been a modern avenue. A four-lane road with a central reservation in the middle.

The realisation hit him at that very moment: *this is where Sivert Almeli photographed the as yet unidentified man.*

But he was standing in the wrong place.

He was in the middle of the photo. Almeli had stood with the camera further down the road, pointing it in this direction – to the north. Gunnarstranda couldn't restrain a grin. This was *his* stamping ground. Half his life he had lived in a flat barely seven to eight hundred metres away as the crow flies. He had walked around Voldsløkka on innumerable occasions in the evenings to clear his head.

Sivert Almeli must have been by the roundabout where Uelandsgate meets Kierschows gate. He had stood there taking photos of a man getting into a car that was parked ...

Gunnarstranda walked slowly down the road. A chill ran down his spine. The car was still there.

It was a dark green Mercedes Benz. Gunnarstranda carried on past the car, down to where Sivert Almeli had most probably stood when he took the photos. A bus shelter. Inside the shelter was a narrow bench.

Almeli had either sat waiting for the bus or pretended to. From here he had taken the photos of the man getting in the car and driving off.

Gunnarstranda called Lena Stigersand and asked her to check the registration number. Three minutes later she was back on the line.

'The car belongs to a man by the name of Erik Valeur,' she said, and spelled his name. 'I checked the *Yellow Pages*. The man's a psychologist. He's got a practice in Hortengata, but he lives in Bærum. What shall we do?'

He considered her question. 'Give me his phone number.'

The phone rang five times before the answering machine cut in.

'This is the answerphone of Erik Valeur. At the moment I'm busy with a client, but I have a contact hour between twelve and one every day. If you need immediate help, I'd advise you to ring…'

Gunnarstranda pressed *Off* and strolled back to his car.

27

The lift doors were closing when a running shoe kicked them open. In strode Mustafa Rindal wearing shorts and a Red Bull singlet. He was on his way to a training session. His clothes smelled of sweat and he was chewing gum. Strangely enough, he seemed to be in a good mood.

Gunnarstranda couldn't for the life of him understand why some people had to change into training gear in their offices instead of the dressing rooms. He was working on a caustic remark, but Rindal beat him to it.

'My commiserations, G, old boy.'

Gunnarstranda didn't answer.

Rindal grinned. 'We have to treasure moments like these. Imagine seeing you with a long face!' He whinnied.

'What do you mean?'

'Veronika Undset's fiancé. I thought I read in the papers something about a defeat in court.'

'Oh, did you?' Gunnarstranda answered acidly. 'Did you read that in the papers? Perhaps as someone in a responsible position you ought to pay more attention to internal communications?'

'There are two kinds of losers, Gunnarstranda: those who mope and those who grit their teeth ready to fight back. What are you waiting for? Chin up, young man, as our poet Bjørnstjerne Bjørnson wrote.'

The lift stopped on the second floor and the doors opened. A distinguished lawyer stepped in. They nodded in silence.

There was a ping for the first floor. The lawyer stepped out.

'Being a leader brings two challenges with it,' Rindal announced out of the blue. 'One is to guide others. The second is to motivate.'

'You're confused,' Gunnarstranda responded. 'What you just said is the intro to your talk at the next seminar. At the moment you're in a lift with me.'

'Exactly. And I've decided to motivate. Regarding the psychologist you tracked down.'

'What about him?'

Another ping. They were on the ground floor. The doors opened and they walked out.

'Lena's good,' Rindal said. 'The girl's got potential. She checked the name of Valeur on the database and do you know what she found? Erik Valeur worked at the Child and Adolescent Mental Health Services in Troms.'

'So?'

Rindal grinned. 'The psychologist is registered. You know what that means, don't you?'

'If you could get to the point instead of giving yourself airs.'

'Think about Finnsnes 2006.'

'And what's that when it's at home? A new team in the basketball league?'

'Oh, very droll,' Rindal parried in the same tone. 'You're forgetting something, Gunnarstranda – ultimately your sarcasm will go nowhere, it drives intellect down a cul-de-sac. In coronary terms it's like eating sausages and pizza – unhealthy in the long term.'

'Sarcasm? I made the assumption based on your outfit. I have no idea what you're talking about.'

'Use your head, Gunnarstranda, your head! Finnsnes, on the island of Senja. May 2006.'

'Murder?'

'You're getting warm, Gunnarstranda, you're getting warm!' Rindal jogged on the spot and punched him on the shoulder.

Two of Rindal's training pals ran past, and he called after them: 'Coming, lads!' He almost spat out his chewing gum in the process, but caught it with a flick of his head and a very quick tongue. *Like a fly-catcher*, Gunnarstranda thought, impressed.

'Teenage girl killed by a drunk, that's as much as I can remember,' he said.

'Signe Strand,' Rindal said. 'Nineteen years old.' He lowered his voice and whispered: 'Psychologist – Valeur's name is in the interview reports!' Rindal's face was one big smile. 'Signe Strand was one of the psychologist's patients – she had an eating disorder. And Uncle Mustafa has given you a helping hand: I asked Kripos to fax over the case documents, and what do I find? The murder on Senja is nearly a carbon copy of Veronika's. The girl was raped, stabbed to death and afterwards dumped on a refuse heap. Holy moly, G, play your cards right and this'll be a media coup. Serial killing, old chum, eh? Cool or what?'

For the first time in many years Gunnarstranda was speechless.

'See what a good boss you've got,' Rindal beamed. 'A friend in your hour of need, who gives you hot tips. Cheer up. Chin up!'

'Are you serious?'

'Of course.'

'I've just found Veronika Undset's neighbour has been murdered. And then you drag up this old north Norwegian case. Which end do you want us to start at?'

Rindal grinned. 'Well, don't ask me, as the man said when they found his wife's body in the freezer.'

Rindal sprinted out of the door. Gunnarstranda caught a glimpse of the soles of his shoes and an erect back on his way down the path. It had been a long day. Now he was going home.

28

It was six o'clock in the morning as Frølich parked his car outside the block of flats in Urtegata. It was relatively quiet. A newspaper boy appeared pulling a cart half-full of papers. He stopped. Ran into the entrance. The sound of running feet on the steps carried into the street.

Frølich poured himself a cup of green tea from the Thermos he had in his very full rucksack (coffee would be killing for the stomach after two hours). The rucksack also contained a packed lunch consisting of four slices of bread and two apples, two smaller flasks with cold water and ice cubes, two empty flasks closed with screw tops, binoculars, a camera with a zoom lens, a Maglite, suncream, swimming trunks, towel, sandals, iPod and earplugs, as well as a spare pair of shorts.

The sun rose and the buildings slowly came to life. People were on their way to work. Young men in helmets and cycling gear that Norwegians call condoms unlocked ferocious bikes in the stairwells of apartment blocks, then sped off. Mothers of small children with the wind in their hair and time against them pushed sporty buggies. Cars wriggled their way out of tight parking spots and drove off. Two builders started a compactor plate and began banging sand into a hole in the pavement. A clap of thunder as a lorry unloaded a consignment of paving cobbles.

The din of the compactor rose and fell.

Some small boys started taking turns to kick a ball against a wall. Frølich had done the same when he was their age. They had called it wallie: you had to hit the ball on the rebound and if you missed you were out.

At long last the compactor stopped. It was like regaining peace on earth. He almost expected to hear birdsong. But didn't.

Frølich was getting stiff and hot. He looked at his watch. It was ten o'clock. The sun was baking down and would soon have nibbled away at the morning shadow afforded by the high-rises. Before long it was going to be unbearable in the car.

At half-past ten he pushed his door ajar to get some air, got out his iPod and started on the John Mayall recordings he had compiled. Was almost through *Blues from Laurel Canyon* when Andreas Langeland came out. Wearing black pirate trousers and a scarf again with a white singlet revealing suntanned skin and a colourful tattoo on his shoulder.

Andreas got into a yellow Mini Cooper parked further down the street and set off. Frølich turned the ignition key.

The Mini Cooper headed towards Grønlandsleiret, Tøyenbekken and Schweigaards gate. Frølich set the tripmeter to zero.

They were taking the right road – to the west, onto Drammensveien, past Sandvika and on past Asker.

Up towards Lierskogen the Mini Cooper was keeping a steady 120. It was difficult to tail him with several vehicles in between. Frølich hung back. The yellow car took the turn-off to Tranby and went down the Lier hills. This tallied with Langeland's phone movements. The guy would probably drive south along Drammen Fjord. Frølich hung back even further. He was almost down on the plain when he spotted a flash of yellow moving south-west between the cabbage fields. Andreas Langeland had turned off for Røyken.

He passed the car without wanting to. The yellow bubble was parked outside a Kiwi supermarket and Frankie caught it in the corner of his eye as he drove past. He did a U-turn and drove back. The problem now was finding a suitable place to wait. He did another U-turn and reversed into the forecourt of a private property; from here he could see the shop entrance. But now there was activity in the house behind him. Shadows in the window. The occupants were wondering what he was doing.

Frølich glanced from the shop to his mirror and back again. The front door of the house opened. A spindly old boy tottered down the steps and moved carefully towards the car. Frølich buzzed down his window.

'Good morning,' the man said, sticking his head nearly halfway into the car. Grey hair, grey bristles on his chin, the remains of egg on his lower lip.

'Good morning,' Frølich said.

The man was about to say something else, but the supermarket door opened and Andreas came out carrying shopping in both hands.

Frølich started the engine with a roar. He showed the old boy his police ID and put a finger to his lips. The Mini Cooper was off. Frølich waved to the old man, who clicked his heels together and saluted like a grenadier guard.

The road was the type that tamed motorists with the use of speed cameras. The car in front kept to fifty, sneaked up to seventy and braked back down before it reached the next grey box. Langeland knew the route.

Despite the hours he had waited undercover, at this moment the job felt like building Lego: the pieces slotted into each other. Frølich had John Mayall and the Bluesbreakers on his iPod – *A Hard Road*. He hung back again and was content with the day's progress so far.

Then the Mini Cooper was gone. He drove over the crest of a hill with a view of the road ahead. No yellow car. He pulled in to the verge and stopped.

The Mini Cooper had left the main road, but where? He switched off the music, turned around and drove back to where he had last seen it. He turned again and drove slowly back, too slowly; a lorry with a flatbed and trailer full of blasted rock braked behind him and blared its horn. Frølich wasn't ruffled. Bend after bend followed. He could positively feel the annoyance of the lorry driver searing the rear window. Keep the nastiness at a distance, that was his motto. He put the music back on and kept a sharp lookout for a turn-off. Finally, a straight. The lorry driver angrily hooted as he overtook.

The turn-off was almost impossible to see. He found it only because he was driving so slowly. He entered the gravel roadway that gently ascended to the ridge of a mountain. The state of the road was poor, with sudden inclines and narrow stretches. If Andreas came back down, he couldn't fail to see him.

Ah, there he was. A flash of yellow between the trunks of spruce trees. Parked behind a little crag.

Frølich drove past, to where the road culminated in a gravel circle. Grey logs piled in a heap. No shade anywhere for the car. It would have to do. He got out, played alpine tourist and headed for a promontory a few hundred metres higher up. That should give him a good view.

When he arrived he was dripping with sweat. He leaned against a crag. The place was perfect. He glimpsed some yellow behind a clump of trees. Oslo Fjord was a gleam of blue far below. On the mountainside, a few hundred metres north, hovered three felt-covered cabin roofs, like enormous birds with outstretched wings. Very far apart. Frølich took the binoculars from his rucksack and examined the terrain.

It was unbearably hot. He lowered his binoculars and smeared suncream over exposed parts. Raised the binoculars again. A fly had developed an interest in his right eyebrow. He swatted it away for the nth time. Some jackdaws were conversing in the trees, their noise halfway between screeched laughter and the hoarse cries of a crow. A large bumble bee flitted from flower to flower among the wild roses that stretched out thorny branches from tiny cracks in the rock. The sun was remorseless. His back and neck burned. Some small black ants crawled over one foot. He must have been blocking their path. One of them climbed up his calf and bit him. He lowered the binoculars and flicked it off. The mixture of suncream and sweat was making his skin wet and sticky. His brain was boiling over. He took the Thermos of iced water and quenched his thirst before pouring the rest of the water over his head and neck. Wonderful.

Frølich lifted the binoculars to his eyes again. A movement led them to the place. The cabin lay deep in a hollow, well hidden. Through the foliage of the treetops he could vaguely make out the wooden frame of a terrace. Here, perhaps invisible to the naked eye, a sunbather was turning over onto their stomach.

29

People take against certain words. Gunnarstranda had once observed a professor of Norwegian going completely berserk over the misuse of a preposition. The man predicted the downfall of Norwegian culture and language and appeared ready to commit murder in the cause.

Upon reflection, Gunnarstranda found there were words he took against, too. Such as 'serial killer'.

This morning he dropped by to see Schwenke at the Forensic Institute and met the pathologist in the corridor. Schwenke was easily recognisable, a man notable for his gaunt figure and an unusually large head adorned by a mass of hair and a thick beard.

'Couldn't we have done this over the phone?' Schwenke grunted, but opened the door to his office anyway. Gunnarstranda ensconced himself in the worn leather chair by the window while the pathologist opened and closed the drawers of his desk searching for some papers. His desk overflowed with reference books and documents. Atop a gently sloping volcano of typed sheets sat a black laptop.

'If I'd rung, you wouldn't have answered the phone and I would've forgotten to ring back.'

'There it is,' Schwenke said, lifting a sheaf of papers from the drawer and placing it on top of an already teetering pile.

'What's bothering you?'

'There's something wrong with the way we're approaching the case of Veronika Undset. We're assuming the perpetrator is smart.'

'Aren't murderers smart?'

'Never,' Gunnarstranda replied.

Schwenke raised his leonine head suspiciously. 'How stupid is a murderer, actually?'

Gunnarstranda deliberated. 'Let me give you an example. There was a man who needed money. When the daughter's student loan was in the bank, their mother was supposed to pick up the money on her behalf. Outside the bank the husband would fake a robbery and hit his wife over the head with a spade. Unfortunately, he hit her so hard she died. He didn't even earn any money either because the bank only pays one month's loan at a time.'

'So?'

'My point is that this is the mental level of murderers.'

'In practical terms, why are we assuming Veronika's murderer is so smart?'

'Scalding the body with hot water. Why does he do that?'

Schwenke chewed on that one. He sat pensively staring at a point on the ceiling.

'He beats her up and rapes her and he ends up stabbing her to death,' Gunnarstranda said. 'Afterwards he thinks: DNA, have to get rid of any traces of semen, so he washes her with water so hot he scalds her. Wouldn't he have scalded himself?'

'He must have done it in two stages. First he washed her and then he poured scalding hot water over her to be sure.'

'OK, but for a plan like that to work, aren't the odds a bit like winning the lottery?'

Schwenke regarded him with watery eyes beneath his bushy brows. 'Where are you going with this?' he asked suspiciously.

'I just want some help. If the perpetrator left biological traces, would he be able to remove them all?'

Schwenke was still crabby. 'The man won't be any worse at looking for clues than us.'

'But he didn't operate on her. You did.'

'What do you want me to say?'

'Is it possible that she wasn't raped?'

'You mean the burns caused by the water might have a purpose other than concealing traces of a rape? What would that purpose be?'

Gunnarstranda smiled wanly. 'In other words, you're not sure—'

Schwenke interrupted: 'You're not listening.'

'But what do you think?'

Schwenke shook his head and banged both palms on the table. 'You're going too far, coming here and babbling on about stupid murderers to make me say something you'd like to hear. No way. I don't want to put my name to things I don't know. I stopped having any faith when I took on this job. I leave that to people like you and priests.'

Gunnarstranda was not going to be browbeaten: 'When you came to the conclusion a rape had taken place, what did you base your decision on?'

'Why are you nagging away at this?'

'Purely professional interest.'

'You're bluffing. Out you go, come on.'

'OK.' Gunnarstranda raised his hands in defence. 'Rindal's discovered that one of our witnesses, a psychologist, had a patient in Troms a few years ago. This girl was murdered. Very similar case.'

'Which case?'

'Signe Strand, on the island of Senja, 2006.'

'Hm.'

'Your analysis of the MO in Veronika's case is really important,' Gunnarstranda emphasised. 'It will have an effect on resources, the press and the way we approach this case.'

'Let me say what I'll say when I'm in the witness box,' Schwenke said, getting to the point. 'As well as stab wounds, Veronika also received a blow to the head. She had head injuries. It's not clear which caused her death.'

After a moment's thought, Gunnarstranda asked: 'She was hit, stabbed and murdered, yes, but was she raped?'

'Let me ask you a question: Do you want to solve this case or battle it out with Rindal?'

'I asked first.'

Schwenke sighed. 'Try to accept the following: Veronika Undset met the wrong man in the wrong place at the wrong time. There are hundreds of similar cases all over the world. Victims and abusers fight. He lies on top of her and bangs her head on the ground until she loses consciousness and is unable to resist. Then he carries out the rape. Afterwards he stabs her a few times to silence her. A man who does such things *must* be pretty disturbed, *unstable, crazy, psychotic*. Psychiatrists have written shelves of books about such nutcases. But the man you have to find is even more unusual – he scalds the body with boiling water to remove any DNA. He wraps the body in plastic and drives around until he finds a suitable place to dump her. I can't and I don't want to speculate. I have to make a global assessment. I haven't found any traces of semen or other biological evidence on Veronika Undset's body. The most likely explanation for the state of the body is that she was subjected to grievous assault, raped and then killed. And if we go further and for one tiny moment *assume* it was the same perpetrator who killed the girl on Senja and Veronika, I would imagine he learned from the first murder. It was well known generally that he left biological traces. Every single newspaper in the country wrote columns and columns about the rape of Signe Strand. After killing Veronika he took care to remove any traces.'

'So we're confronted here with two cases that have several similarities and two specific differences,' Gunnarstranda summed up. 'Veronika was beaten up—'

Schwenke shook his head and interrupted him: 'You can be damned sure that Signe Strand was beaten up, too.'

'But Veronika's body was washed in scalding hot water. Signe's wasn't.'

Gunnarstranda rose to his feet and went to the door.

'Gunnarstranda,' the pathologist called after him.

'Yes?'

'You've got a mouth and a half on you. A bloody big mouth.'

'I'll take that as a compliment.'

'Read the Strand files. You need to know about the man's psyche. There could be useful material in that case.'

Gunnarstranda left without answering.

30

Frank Frølich blinked the sweat out of his eyes, lowered the binoculars and adjusted the distance between the lenses. Raised the binoculars again and focused.

The cabin was a greyish-blue; the terrace woodwork black. The figure was lying on a blanket, without a stitch on. Apart from a pirate's scarf. It was Andreas.

Was this an anti-climax – had Andreas driven to the cabin to sunbathe?

No. Frølich could feel a fire burning in his stomach. Thoughts piled on top of each other. Suspicions, impatience.

The second hand crawled round. The minute hand hit like a hammer when it did finally move. He was sweating profusely. His clothes were sticking to his body. Close on an hour passed. It was a long hour. His head was whirring.

Then something happened. Someone came out onto the terrace.

Frølich gripped the binoculars harder. This guy was stark naked as well – suntanned and muscular, even his bottom was brown. But who was it?

Frølich pressed the binoculars to his eyes. The figure moved behind the foliage, and reappeared. Crouched down. Two naked men on the terrace. Andreas kept nodding. Frølich could see only the back of the second man. *Turn around, for Christ's sake. Turn!*

The suntanned man stood up, lit a cigarette, blew out smoke and took something off his lower lip. At last he turned.

Yes!

It was Andreas's brother, Mattis.

Frølich could positively hear the pieces in the jigsaw puzzle falling into place.

He couldn't contain himself any longer and ran back to the car. Grabbed the disposable restraints and handcuffs, breathless.

His heart was beating hard. Throbbing in his ears. He paused. *No. This is different. You know nothing.*

But all he could hear was his heart. His heart and the insects. He wiped the sweat from his brow. Hyperventilated. Collected himself. Straightened up. Looked around. *There are no insects of that kind in this country.* But the sound was there. The song of the cicada and the hammering of his heart. He covered his ears. *I'm here, on a mountain in Vestfold!*

He caught sight of a bumble bee crawling over the car bonnet. Concentrated on listening to it move.

At last the chirping stopped.

Only then did he tear himself loose. Ran back to where he had left his rucksack and binoculars. He raised them to his eyes. Mattis was alone now. He was lying on his back on a lilo and sunbathing. Reading a comic. He held it in the air, keeping the sun out of his eyes.

Frølich was still hyperventilating. Trying to think. Mattis alone. First of all, Andreas had been alone.

His worst nightmares *didn't have* to be right. But they *could* be.

He grabbed the Maglite, the handcuffs and the plastic restraints and set off. Jumping soundlessly from rock to rock in light trainers.

As long as he stayed on the mountain his progress would be soundless.

The mountain ended in a deep crevice and now the cabin wasn't far away. He crouched and edged his way down with his eyes fixed on the terrace railing further ahead.

In the end he had to jump. Landed with both feet on leaves and dry twigs.

There was a crunch. He stood still, bent over. Held his breath to listen. Heard nothing. Had he been rumbled?

He breathed out, his mouth open.

Without moving a muscle, sweat pouring down his face, he waited until he was sure that all normal sounds were back. Leaves rustling, the wave-like rumbling of a plane in the distance…

Setting off again, he concentrated on placing his feet on rocks.

The cabin appeared between the trees. A narrow wooden construction, on two levels, small base, deep in a hollow. In front of the cabin someone had tried to lay a lawn. On the edge grew straggly scrub. Frølich sat on his haunches between the thin trunks, hidden by the bushes.

The last ten metres had no cover. The leaves of the asp rustled as a gust of wind blew across the mountainside. He heard Mattis turn a page.

Two black plastic pipes on the ground revealed the source of summer water.

Two entrances. One through a broad door straight ahead. The second on the floor above, via the terrace where Mattis was.

Which way should he go?

How?

Then he heard voices. He listened. They came from inside. No. There was only one voice. It rose, but then it broke off.

He looked at the cabin. Hostile windows and greyish-blue walls. The countryside, the trees and the sky were reflected in the glass.

He stood up without making a sound. Placed a foot on the grass, then one more. If anyone looked through the window now, the game would be up. Six more metres. Four metres. Three. Then he realised the blinds were drawn. He sidled along the wall. Pressed his ear to the wood. Listened. Heard crying. In a flash he was back in the past. Had the same taste of blood in his mouth as twenty years ago. The same panic. He couldn't bear it.

His body moved on autopilot. He ran across the grass, found the staircase up to the terrace and covered it in three strides.

Mattis Langeland heard the footsteps and sat up in astonishment.

The next second Frølich was above him. The policeman grabbed his arm. Rolled him onto his stomach. Forced a knee into his back. Wrapped an arm around his neck. Tipped him backward. Mattis screamed. Frølich tied his hands with the plastic cuffs and finally understood what Mattis was screaming:

'Andreas! Andreas!'

Frølich turned to the glass door in the cabin. No one around. He turned back to Mattis, who was making a dash for the staircase, with his hands behind his back. Frølich put out a foot and the naked body crashed down on the wooden planks.

He grabbed hold of one ankle and dragged the howling figure back. Handcuffed the ankle to the terrace railing. The wood wasn't very strong, but it would hold.

Eventually Mattis shut up. They exchanged glances. Mattis was panting and got to his knees. Frølich turned his back on him and walked slowly towards the glass door.

He opened it. Inside there was silence. He stood listening. Still silence.

There seemed to have been a party in the room. Empty cigarette packets and beer bottles on the table.

A staircase led to the ground floor.

Iselin Grav's voice in his brain: *I don't think she's dead.*

Frølich glanced through the window: green treetops.

Peered over his shoulder. Mattis Langeland had stopped yanking at the railing. Their eyes met.

Frølich moved into the room. Tiptoed down the stairs. No one to be seen. Not a sound to be heard.

The staircase ended in a corner. All he had to defend himself with was a torch.

On the landing halfway down he stopped. His heart. He could hear it pounding. His eyes misted up. The chirping of the cicadas returned. He blinked to see better, wobbled and said to himself: 'There are no cicadas here. Keep going.'

Frølich tore himself away from the wall. Breathed through an open mouth until his lungs were functioning normally.

He took a step and had to grab the banister to stop himself falling down the stairs. Carried on down to the bottom. No one there; no one waiting. He became aware of a pungent smell. Vomit. Sweat. Stale air. He continued. There was a smell of bedrooms here.

Frølich kept walking. The air quivered. There were two open doors. One to the left and one to the right. One was a room. The other…

A window smashed. The tinkling of glass was followed by the sound of running feet over rock. Andreas was trying to escape, but he wouldn't succeed. Frølich moved to leave, but as he turned to go, he caught sight of something. He froze on the spot. On the bedroom wall was a large mirror, which revealed details of the room. The spotlights on the ceiling. Two cameras on stands. The body on the bed.

Frølich let Andreas run. He walked slowly towards the open door and went inside.

31

As he approached the entrance to the block, the front door was opened by a large, fat woman in a long red dress. Gunnarstranda slipped in smartly before the door closed, turned and stared after her. She seemed to be gliding on an undercarriage; she reminded him of a robot moving on invisible wheels.

Valeur lived on the second floor. Gunnarstranda had to ring three times before the door was opened by the man in the Peeping-Tom photos – wearing jeans and a loose yellow shirt which suggested a paunch behind the line of buttons. His short beard was grey with coarse bristles, which made him look unkempt. Valeur observed the policeman with his head held back to spare his eyes from a thin line of smoke coming from the cigarette in his mouth. The sight impressed the former nicotine slave so much that Gunnarstranda felt he had to comment on it.

'Nowadays smokers are usually found shivering on street corners or a balcony. I thought indoor smokers were an extinct species. To have such freedom I don't suppose you can be married,' Gunnarstranda concluded.

Valeur removed the cigarette from his mouth. 'And who are you?' he asked tartly.

'Gunnarstranda, Oslo Police, Violent Crime and Sexual Offences.'

The psychologist looked him in the eye for a few long seconds before moving aside to let him in.

The hi-fi sound in the sitting room reminded Gunnarstranda of the

Sixties. A low coffee table was covered with catalogues and files. 'Excuse the mess.' Valeur grabbed the remote and turned down the volume. 'I'm a collector, you see.'

The flat was one long run through with a balcony at each end. The panoramic windows with push-doors created a light, pleasant atmosphere. Gunnarstranda walked over to the windows and confirmed that the neighbours had a clear view inside.

'Hits,' Valeur said, tidying the files and catalogues spread across the table. 'Top-Twenty hits in Britain, the US and – naturally – Norway.' He lifted a dog-eared booklet. 'This is the Top-Ten lists from 1960 up to the end of the radio programme.'

'And what are we listening to now?'

'"Pretty Flamingo" by Manfred Mann. Made its entry at number eighteen in the UK Top Twenty in April 1966. Within a fortnight – mid-May – it was top and stayed there for three weeks before slipping down the charts and disappearing after nine weeks. In Norway the record went straight into the number-three slot on 3 June, held its place on the radio, but then dropped down to seventh and out. Summer holidays, of course. I've always loved Manfred Mann and I'm sure it would've done better if it'd been released earlier.'

The room was equipped for vinyl. The two free walls were full of tightly packed shelves of old 45s, black, with and without sleeves, some green, others red.

'It's my obsession,' Valeur explained. 'Get hold of the records, cross them off the list. We're herd animals. You know that, as a policeman. There are cultural differences, however; some years there's a very distinct difference in musical taste between the US and the UK, and it's interesting to see where they diverge. What's unique in Norway is the position of the Top-Ten radio programme because it was based on a customer feedback button. People decided on the basis of their taste, so it was a momentary experience that determined a song's place on the list, not the sales figures. That is unique. What was your name again?'

'Gunnarstranda.'

'What can I do for you?'

'A few years ago you had a patient called Signe Strand.'

There was a sharp intake of breath and Valeur sighed. 'Don't tell me *Oslo* Police are working on the case!'

'Your name did come up.'

'*Come up*? My name?'

'She was your patient, wasn't she?'

Valeur sat scrutinising Gunnarstranda. At length he made a decision.

'She had eating issues. Signs of anorexia. Her gym teacher had flagged it up. The weight loss was significant, but not alarming. I worked for the Child and Adolescent Mental Health Services at that time. A couple of weeks after she was killed I spoke on the phone to someone working at Kripos. I don't even remember whether it was a man or a woman. They wanted to know if I had any inside info, if I knew about any secret boyfriends or if she'd had fears regarding any specific men. I can barely remember what I answered. The conversation lasted less than two minutes.' He hissed in annoyance. 'And so you say my name came up?'

'Do you know someone by the name of Sivert Almeli?'

Valeur shook his head. 'Should I?'

Gunnarstranda put his hand in his pocket for the photographs. He laid the three of them on the table.

'Goodness gracious,' the psychologist said. With his eyes firmly fixed on the photos he stubbed out the cigarette in a well-filled, round aluminium ashtray. 'That's me,' he confirmed and eyed the police officer for an explanation.

When this was not forthcoming, he took a packet of Teddy from his chest pocket and tapped out a cigarette.

He offered one to Gunnarstranda, who shook his head.

Valeur held the cigarette up to the light for a few seconds, then lit it with a red disposable lighter and talked out of the corner of his mouth. 'I'm into nostalgia, Gunnarstranda. That's part of my personality. I'm looking for some happiness from the old days – even though I know that this state is actually an illusion. But what can you do when you have an obsession? I wish I could go back to the times of Radio

Luxembourg, the old songs, the chord riffs. When I was a teenager and started smoking, you could go into a shop and buy decent cigarettes. The selection was immense: Camel, Rothmans, Benson & Hedges, Pall Mall, South State, Kent, Merit, Blue Master, Red Virginia, Gitanes, Gauloises, Lucky Strike. In those days the brand you smoked was part of your personality. I like nostalgia, Gunnarstranda. I'm continually looking for a form of bygone harmony.'

'Mummy, I want to go back,' Gunnarstranda said. 'Back to the warm, secure womb before reality hit with all its problems and complicated decisions.'

'I wasn't thinking of *that* far back,' Valeur countered forcefully. 'What has my mother got to do with this?'

Gunnarstranda pointed to the photos. 'Aren't you wondering why I've shown you the photos?'

Valeur tapped one of them. 'Naturally. I'm assuming you're the same as my patients. Eventually you will get to the point.'

Gunnarstranda glanced up. His glance was expected. A different Valeur was looking out from behind the man's eyelids. A devil inside him flashed and glinted until the policeman saw and tried to lock onto him. Then he slid back inside and was gone.

Gunnarstranda focused on the photos again.

'These photos were taken by Sivert Almeli a few days ago. He was a librarian at Deichman Library.'

'Was?'

'He was murdered.'

Valeur raised both eyebrows. 'Why did he take photos of me?'

'That's what we're wondering.'

Valeur shook his head. 'You must have heard this so many times, but I don't understand anything.'

Gunnarstranda laid the photo taken at Tusenfryd on the table. Almeli on the water ride. 'Have you ever had this man as your patient or met him in some other way?'

Valeur took the photo. He studied the picture from various angles. At length he shook his head. 'Sorry. I'm afraid I can't be of any help.'

'What's your connection with Deichman Library?'

'Thirty years ago they had a branch in Valkyrie plass. I grew up in Majorstua, in Bogstadveien. I often used to borrow books about the Hardy Boys or the Bobbsey Twins. Of course, the branch is closed now. It must have been too expensive to hire rooms and pay the librarian. But in those days books were so important for people that they wanted a branch close by, as you know. Do you understand what I mean when I say I want to go back to another time? Well, now I mostly read non-fiction and order whatever I need off the net.'

Valeur took small puffs of the cigarette.

Gunnarstranda was intrigued by what he had just seen and wanted to evoke the same reaction again. He took a strip of chewing gum from his pocket, undid the silver paper and put it in his mouth. 'I used to smoke more than you once,' he said. 'I'm developing COPD and will die in agony – according to the doctors.'

'They print the same message on the packets.'

'But you still won't stop?' Gunnarstranda said.

'Of course not,' Valeur said, placing the cigarette on the edge of the ashtray.

Neither of them said anything. Eventually Valeur stood up, a sign the visit was over.

'I'd like to ask you one more question,' Gunnarstranda said.

'Be my guest,' he answered in English.

The policeman passed him another photo. 'Do you know her?'

Valeur didn't need to answer; his expression said everything. 'Why do you ask?'

'Her name's Veronika Undset. She was also murdered. Again by unknown hand. It's been in the papers, by the way.'

Valeur slumped back onto the sofa.

'Something tells me you knew her.'

'Not very well.'

Gunnarstranda sat quietly. Absent-mindedly, Valeur took another cigarette from the packet and held it between his fingers without lighting it.

'You've already got one on the go,' Gunnarstranda smiled, pointing to the smoking cigarette in the ashtray. 'I'm sure you know I love reactions like that – you being a psychologist.'

Not even this caustic remark could elicit the response he wanted. Valeur smiled wearily. He took the cigarette he had lit and put it in his mouth.

'She had one session, last week. We hadn't even got to know each other.'

'What impression did you have?'

'She seemed frustrated. Of course, that's true of everyone who comes to see me. But I didn't have the impression she was suffering from angst or neuroses; she just seemed frustrated. She said she needed someone to talk to, to sort herself out, to sort out her life. She told me she was engaged, so I imagined she might want to discuss things because she'd become unsure about her relationship. I don't know – we didn't have time to delve into her problems.'

'She didn't mention the name of this man, Sivert Almeli?'

'No.'

'Did she talk about her fears?'

Valeur shook his head.

'Did she mention anything about strange men harassing her, stalking her?'

'No. The conversation was very banal, about general matters, the situation with her fiancé and so on. Naturally I assumed the *real* problem lay much deeper and it would come out in the course of therapy.'

'What about the fiancé?'

'She wasn't sure about him, whether he loved her as he claimed. Anyway, she had her doubts and that made her doubt herself.'

'Were you able to help her?'

'In fact, I'd been thinking of suggesting they should both come for therapy, together.'

'But you didn't. Why not?'

'I wanted to get to know her better first. I thought perhaps there might have been other things depressing her – as she chose to come for therapy alone. When people come to a psychologist the reason given can be based on some form or other of rationalisation.'

'You mean there could be other causes behind it?'

'Precisely. But I never managed to get that far.'

Gunnarstranda leaned forward.

'This man – Sivert Almeli – was her neighbour. He was killed shortly after she was. We have reason to believe there was a, shall we say, unusual relationship between them, psychologically. Almeli spied on Veronika Undset. He secretly photographed her. *He* was a case for a psychologist. But she didn't mention any of this to you?'

'If anything we talked about had been in any way relevant to your case I would've told you.'

'Why did she choose you in particular?'

Valeur shrugged. 'I would've asked her, at some point during the therapy, but I didn't have the opportunity.'

'So she wasn't referred to you by a doctor?'

'No. Those patients have to put up with long waiting lists. Veronika Undset belonged to the group of patients who come on their own initiative and cover their own expenses, without any support from the public purse.'

'Are there many patients like that?'

'Quite a few. Norway's a rich country, and many people are willing to pay the full price to avoid having to wait.'

'The strange thing is,' Gunnarstranda said ruminatively, 'that this Almeli has taken shots of you without you realising. He took them the same day Veronika's body was found. He's off sick from work, but he doesn't stay at home. He takes three photos – only three – and you're in all of them. Why would Almeli do that?'

Valeur doesn't answer at once. His stereo has gone quiet. There is silence in the flat. 'I think I have an explanation, even if it might seem a bit odd.'

Gunnarstranda inclined his head, interested.

'After the session – she was the last client I had that day – after the session I gave her a lift home. I suspect—'

'That was very generous of you,' Gunnarstranda interjected.

Valeur gave a smile of embarrassment. 'Pure courtesy, nothing else. I suspect this man was spying on her and saw me drop her off. Perhaps he wondered who I was, did a bit of sleuthing and found out.'

'Do you usually drive your patients home?'

Valeur shook his head. 'This was a gesture. She was the last of the day and didn't have a car. When I got in to drive off I saw her waiting in the bus queue. It was nothing more than a gesture of politeness.'

'So what did you say to her?'

'What do you mean?'

'What did you say to her when you saw her waiting for the bus?'

'I don't remember my exact words … I offered her a lift.'

'But you live here, in Bærums Verk, and she lived in Simensbråten. You were going the opposite way, several kilometres off your route, and yet you offered this patient a lift home, someone you barely knew.'

Valeur fell silent. He took a leisurely final puff of the cigarette and gently stubbed it out in the ashtray. He said; 'The way you're twisting this conversation it seems as if you, the police, think I have something to do with the case.'

'Signe Strand was raped and stabbed. Veronika Undset was—'

Valeur raised his arms and interrupted him: 'Now just take it easy, will you.'

There. The same glint was back in his eyes.

But as though Valeur had sensed what was in the policeman's mind, the steel blade in his eyes slid back out of sight. *As though he were playing hide-and-seek*, Gunnarstranda thought, and said: '*I'm* very much at my ease.' He rose to his feet. 'So that *you* can be a little more at your ease, *I* need to know where you were when these two people were killed. And I'd like you to write down the names of anyone who can confirm your whereabouts…'

Erik Valeur grabbed a pen from between the two catalogues. 'Of course. What dates and what times are we talking about?'

32

In the doorway to Police HQ Gunnarstranda narrowly avoided collid-
ing with a woman. It was Leyla Rindal on her way out. She had warm,
dark eyes and the world's biggest and whitest smile. Gunnarstranda
paid tribute to this divinely endowed woman by holding open the
door and taking a deep bow, like an ice dancer. She waved to him and
pointed to her watch to tell him she was in a hurry.

Gunnarstranda stood watching Leyla as she scuttled towards Grønlandsleiret. She was dressed in jeans and a white blouse, but hid her hair
in a blue and white hijab.

At the meeting Rindal appeared, surprisingly, in uniform. He introduced Stephan Borge, who was the spitting image of Buddy Holly – the
thick black glasses, the shape of his head, the hair and, not least, the
narrow mouth led to thoughts of the uncrowned king of rockabilly.

Borge, Rindal explained, was an acclaimed profiler from Sweden
who had examined two case files – those of Veronika Undset and Signe
Strand.

Borge spoke in Swedish. He didn't want to prejudge their investigation, but nor could he refute the evidence suggesting that the Oslo
Police were dealing with a serial killer. He began to underpin this thesis
by stating how similar the victims were in appearance. Both had red
hair and strikingly similar hairstyles. They were approximately the same
height: Strand was 1.61; Undset 1.64. There was a disparity in age. Strand
was nineteen years old; Undset thirty-five. Both were remarkably
attractive women who, according to reports, exhibited their sexuality in

the way they dressed. Strand had been stabbed thirty-four times in the breast region. Undset twenty-two times, also around her breasts. Both had been subjected to violent behaviour. Signe had probably been more co-operative than Veronika and didn't have such widespread injuries from punches and kicks to the body. Veronika had been hit so hard her skull was broken. The murders were committed in a state of emotional frenzy at some place other than where they were found. Neither crime scene was identified. Both victims were transported to the place where they were found after their death, a refuse site on Senja and a skip for building rubble in Kalbakken in Oslo respectively. Signe Strand was found au naturel. Veronika Undset's body had been wrapped in plastic.

On Signe's body investigators had discovered biological traces of rape.

Veronika Undset's body bore signs of scalding and burning in the genital area. There was no DNA on her from the unknown perpetrator and therefore no opportunity to compare DNA to establish whether it was the same man. But if the two women had been killed by one and the same person, Borge presumed the man had learned from experience with Strand and accordingly washed away any tell-tale signs on Veronika.

Other differences between the murders included the geographical area. Signe Strand was a student at Finnbotn School in the county of Troms, which is 1,500 kilometres from the capital of Norway. And as regards the murder weapon there were differences too. Signe was killed with a long, pointed weapon. Based on the depth of the wounds, the hypothesis was that the attacker had used a long Sami knife. The blade of the weapon that killed Veronika Undset couldn't have been longer than seven centimetres and the profile of the cuts suggested it was very probably the type of knife used for wallpapering and DIY – a Stanley knife with replaceable blades.

'Yes?' said Stephan Borge, nodding to Gunnarstranda, who had raised his hand.

'The geographical distance and the time difference – to what extent do they weaken the theory that we're dealing with a serial killer?'

'In my opinion,' the Swede started, taking off his horn-rimmed glasses, cleaning them and putting them back on his nose – he wanted to appeal to the experience of the murder investigators present – 'killers who have got away with remaining undetected once are very likely to murder again.'

The police around the table nodded in approval.

As regards geographical distance, that didn't necessarily militate against the hypothesis, if, for example, you were dealing with a perpetrator who had lived in two places or had a peripatetic job – such as a lorry driver or salesman – or the murderer had a job that meant working in two different places. The combination of the time difference and geographical distance could, in fact, reinforce the theory of serial killings.

Rindal spoke up: 'The reason we connected these two cases was that a witness in the Veronika case – Erik Valeur, who now lives in Bærum – was in contact with Signe Strand when he worked at the Child and Adolescent Mental Health Services in Troms. It's highly likely we're about to crack that case.'

Gunnarstranda raised his hand again.

Borge nodded to him.

'One of our witnesses worked in 2006 for the Norwegian Water Resources and Energy Directorate, inspecting streams and waterfalls re: licences for power plants on farms and suchlike. He travelled a lot in the spring of 2006. Including to the Harstad region. That's a fair way from Senja, but...'

'That's interesting, very interesting...' Borge said.

'Who was it?' Rindal butted in.

Gunnarstranda smiled.

Rindal eyed him sternly.

Gunnarstranda whispered something to Yttergjerde and there was an awkward silence, which Borge ended by continuing his talk.

'So to my profile,' the Swede said and explained that the perpetrator was a man with a very patronising view of women. He was a victim of his own drives, but hated himself for them and projected this self-hatred onto women in the form of a fury that manifested itself in two ways:

first, he dominated them by abusing them sexually. Borge compared the perpetrator's actions with conquering soldiers' behaviour towards women. Soldiers are rewarded by being allowed to rape women; penetrating becomes a physical symbol of conquest, and so every soldier becomes his own tsar as he injects women with his seed – in other words, fertilising the conquered ground.

Unseen by Borge, some officers exchanged glances.

Borge continued: the perpetrator's contempt for his victims was further manifest in the murders themselves, then the treatment of them as refuse. Borge suggested the person concerned had a narcissistic personality disorder. Someone with a very high opinion of himself. Subject to a strong emotional conflict, despising and yet desiring his victims – a conflict resulting in a violent clash between two personalities. Two hurricanes meet head-on and the consequence is murder. What muddies the picture is that the murderer, after killing Veronika Undset, was so cold-blooded and calm that he took the time to remove any biological traces, which was a very demanding clean-up job, and – one must conclude – thoroughly unpleasant as well.

Gunnarstranda raised his hand again.

The Swede nodded to him.

'We have another murder and a proven relationship with Undset. The victim is a man aged forty-three. A neighbour of hers, most likely a stalker—'

Rindal interrupted and waved a dismissive hand.

Gunnarstranda ignored him and continued: modus operandi – cut throat, so no panic or emotion, no suppressed guilty sexuality, no symbolic need to conquer or self-hatred involved. Does this murder weaken or strengthen the contention that the murder of Veronika Undset is one in a series of killings?'

'I can't answer that,' the Swede said. 'My analysis is based on two quite specific cases.'

*

'What the hell are you playing at?' asked Mustafa Rindal when the meeting was over. He followed Gunnarstranda down the corridor and was so annoyed that he couldn't open his pack of chewing gum.

'Do you think he looks like Buddy Holly as well?' Gunnarstranda asked, stopping by the Coke machine and inserting money. A bottle rumbled down.

'Do you know how much it cost to bring Stephan Borge from Stockholm to Oslo? And you have to argue with the man and pin him down. Who the hell do you think you are? Columbo?'

Gunnarstranda gulped down the Coke and patted his chest to expel air.

'Who was it who reported on power plants in northern Norway? Was that the fiancé, Fransgård?'

Gunnarstranda nodded.

Rindal held his forefinger in the air and wagged it. 'Now you listen to me. You screwed up with Fransgård. You didn't even have the composure to do a DNA test.'

'A DNA test wasn't relevant.'

'I told you to listen,' Rindal repeated. 'You screwed up, Gunnarstranda. Take that on board. No one will be able to make Karl Anders Fransgård do a test voluntarily now. Cause you *forgot* to do it while you had the chance. So listen to me. Neither Fransgård nor Almeli should have been mentioned at the meeting. We brought in *real* expertise. And you've done enough damage!'

'The Almeli issue was extremely relevant. He was sitting on seven hundred photos of the murder victim!'

'So what? He might have had seven hundred thousand photos of seven hundred other divas! What do you know? His computer was gone. Almeli could have been killed by any cuckold. But the cases of Signe Strand and Veronika Undset have similarities and you have to take that into consideration.'

Rindal strode on. After ten steps he turned, still fidgeting with his chewing-gum packet. 'If not, there'll be trouble. Shit!' The packet split and all the sticks flew out. He knelt down and picked them up.

At that very moment Yttergjerde emerged from the R&R room. 'God is great,' he said, with an innocent wink. 'What next? Praying mats and a hijab as part of the uniform?'

Rindal jumped up and went to grab him, but Yttergjerde was already racing down the corridor.

Gunnarstranda went back to his office.

He sat down and opened the top drawer. Took out some darts and threw them at the pictures of Valeur, but missed.

Yttergjerde came in. He was playing air guitar and imitating Buddy Holly: 'P-p-p-pe-eggy Sue.'

'Must be the glasses,' Gunnarstranda winked. 'Didn't think it was possible to get hold of a pair nowadays. Perhaps he's a pal of Elton John. Could you bring me the darts?'

Yttergjerde loosened the darts. 'Just to be sure, I checked Erik Valeur out on the national register,' he said. 'He's been married, but his ex-wife is alive and well. She's a nurse in Tromsø. Do you need someone to travel north? If so, it's my turn.'

'What would you do in Tromsø?'

'Do? Have you heard about the Beer Hall?'

Gunnarstranda threw a dart at Valeur and hit him. 'No budget for it,' he said. 'Tromsø's full of cops already. They can talk to his ex-wife.' He lifted the receiver.

33

It was approaching midnight by the time Frølich had looked through the film material that Andreas Langeland hadn't managed to take with him as he fled. He stood up, stiff-legged and scarred by what he had seen. He had no idea how long it was since he had slept.

There were officers all over HQ. Someone was always on duty, some were waiting to be called out, drinking coffee to stay awake, reading, watching TV, playing Minesweeper or Patience on the computer to kill time, but he didn't have the energy to meet any of them now.

He didn't want to go home either. Couldn't bear the thought of staring at the walls, reflecting on the sight of the beer can, closing his eyes and being haunted by the poor woman's sufferings.

He sank his first beer at Teddy's and then headed west, Justisen, Stopp Pressen, Herr Nilsen, another pub, another attempt to drown sorrows. In the end he found an unoccupied table outside Steamen. The Pilsner went down nicely, and he began to take stock.

A party of youngsters at the next table was short of chairs. One of the girls asked him if the chair at his table was free. 'No,' he replied. 'It isn't free.' Miffed, she and her gallant looked. He wanted to protest, but she restrained him. 'We'll find a chair somewhere else.'

Frølich thought to himself: *she can see. She knows I'm on the edge.*

He got up, left a fifty-krone note as a tip and stumbled away. He knew he was drunk, but it didn't feel like that.

His legs found the way without involving his head.

There was a tractor wheel on its side in Sofies gate. He sat down on the tyre and peered up at the dark windows in the block opposite. Wondering which window could be hers. Wondering if there was any point ringing the bell. As she had approached him unbidden surely he could do the same.

Time passed. Thoughts crowded in, stopped and went off on separate paths, as though they weren't thoughts but long, unconnected ropes tangled up in an unruly backlash.

A car stopped and parked a few metres down the street. Saab cabriolet with the top up. The engine died, the lights went out. Two doors slammed. He didn't move.

He recognised her blonde hair. Iselin Grav together with a man wearing shorts and a short-sleeved shirt. They walked towards the block of flats on the other side of the street. As she fumbled in her bag for keys she sent a glance in his direction, presumably because he moved. She reacted. Said something to the man in shorts. Hurried across the street.

'What's up?' she asked.

'I have to talk to you,' Frølich said, looking up. No glasses today. Perhaps she has contact lenses, he thought, as though that were important.

She glanced from him to the man in shorts and back again. 'What is it?' said the man, coming towards them.

'Rune,' she said firmly. 'It's a bit inconvenient now. I'll call you.'

The two of them eyed each other. The guy seemed reluctant to go. They walked away whispering. Frølich looked up at the sky. Far above him flashed a green light slowly gliding east.

The whispering increased in volume. At length the guy swore and headed up the street at a furious pace. The white calves and black sandals slowly became one with the darkness.

Iselin Grav waited at the entrance. He got up. Neither of them said anything as they went up the stairs.

'You were right,' Frølich said as she was unlocking the door.

She stiffened. Held the key in a firm grip, thinking. Eventually she pushed the door in.

She didn't switch on the light. Hung her shoulder bag on a hook on the wall and turned to him. The darkness softened her contours. The silence persisted. At last she said: 'How is she?'

'Fine, in the circumstances,' he answered. 'She'll survive. Physically, anyway.'

There was a bean bag by a low white table brightened with a bunch of roses in a vase. He slumped down into the bean bag.

She smiled at the sight.

'Did you know?' he asked. 'Did he tell you?'

The smile died. 'No, but I knew there was something very wrong. That was probably what I was actually trying to tell you.'

'They recorded everything on video.'

'They?'

'He and his brother, Mattis.'

'And now they're in prison?'

'Mattis is.'

She spun on her heel.

A little later she returned from the kitchen with two tall glasses full of ice cubes. On the shelf was a bottle of Glenlivet. She poured. A hefty dram. He thought: *she's generous – I like that.* She passed him a glass.

He finished the whisky in one go and passed back the glass.

She refilled it and asked warily: 'And Andreas?'

'He ran off.'

She went into the hall and rummaged in her bag for her phone. Came back. Flipped it open. 'He hasn't called me.'

The clock on the opposite wall showed eleven minutes to three. Frølich closed his eyes. 'You forgot your glasses,' he said.

When he opened his eyes she was crouching down in front of him wearing only her underwear. She undid his jacket.

The clock showed it was five minutes to five.

'You can't sleep like that,' she whispered.

'We'd been drinking for four or five days non-stop,' he said.

'Did you have a dream?' She was still whispering.

'We hadn't slept for almost a week. We'd finished school. We were plastered all the time and lit fires on the beach at night. There were hardly any other Norwegians there, only four girls from Ålesund who were giving the local men the once-over. They didn't want anything to do with us and spoke English so that we wouldn't realise they were Norwegian. The locals regarded us as crazy loons. We fell in love with a girl serving at the café.'

Frankie suddenly realised that Iselin had no idea who Karl Anders was and would have understood hardly a word of what he was saying. Yet she was on her haunches listening. 'I don't remember the girl's name,' he whispered. 'Fourteen years old, only, long eyelashes and thick black hair way down her back, so attractive that it hurt to look at her. We were dumbstruck, both of us, and behaved like it. We sat in the café all the time. Her father got the picture and incited a local mob to sort us out. I've never had such a beating, before or since. Two policemen drove up in a 2CV, but by that time my friend had legged it. It was me against the rest. I was arrested. I think the cops took me in to make sure I didn't get seriously injured. I didn't have a passport or anything on me. I was taken to an office, which was ridiculous; it was like a sheriff's office in a Western. A small, fat policeman pointed to the cell and me and kept talking and talking and wagging his forefinger. I understood nothing of what he said, but I was pretty stressed, thinking only of my pal who was alone with the mob pursuing him. I was released after an hour. I went back. Then all the men in the village wanted to be my friend, they praised the way I'd fought and a big guy I'd given a black eye wanted to buy me a beer. My friend was nowhere to be seen. I ran back to the bonfire on the beach.'

Frølich got to his feet.

He swayed. 'Where's the bathroom?'

'In the hall.'

He staggered out. The toilet smelled of perfume. He bent over the bowl, stuck a finger down his throat and thought: *that was more than twenty years ago*.

Afterwards he rinsed his mouth, washed his face and stared at his watery eyes.

Stood there oblivious of time passing until Iselin knocked on the door. 'How are you doing?'

He went out. She was wearing a white bathrobe.

He looked at the clock. 'I'm a nuisance,' he said. 'Sorry. You're working tomorrow and must be very tired. I'll go.'

'I'll make us some coffee,' she said, and went to the kitchen.

He sat down. Barely noticed her putting a hot mug of coffee in his hands.

'I was shocked by what I saw in the film Andreas and his brother made. It was as though images were put to a soundtrack in my head.'

'What do you mean?'

'I ran out of the village, to the beach. Since then I've wondered why I ran. I didn't know anything, of course. But I ran. There were those cicadas in all the trees and they were making a racket. You know the kind of sound I'm talking about. I've hated that sound ever since. Then there were two noises. The chirping insects and her screams.' He patted his chest. 'My heart. Bang, bang, bang, and the taste of blood in my mouth and the screams that at first rose louder and louder and then fell to nothing. It felt like I was holding onto someone's hand, someone hanging over a precipice, and I couldn't pull them up, their fingers slipped out of my hand.'

He met Iselin's gaze and leaned back in the chair. 'By the time I arrived he'd finished. Then he went for a night swim.'

'Who did?'

'A man who works for Oslo Council.'

He lifted his head. It was light outside.

34

The wall was a collage of press cuttings, photos, arrows and notes in felt tip. In the centre: a portrait of Veronika Undset and some information. Arrows from the picture pointed to photos of Karl Anders Fransgård, Kadir Zahid, Sivert Almeli, dates, times, descriptions of where bodies were found, photos of the psychologist Erik Valeur, crossing the road and in a car driving away. Above this a school photo of a girl with a strained smile. Her head at an angle, doing her best for the photographer. A life, a collected history of private moments, laughter, tears, celebrations, joy, achievements, ambitions, goals and, not least, lost illusions – of which Gunnarstranda knew not a thing. Apart from one, an assumption based on his own personal predispositions: sitting for the portrait Signe probably had only one thought on her mind, if not the climax of her youth, then definitely of her years at school – to get drunk day after day and boogie through the post-exam period. The way she had done at the party in Finnsnes before leaving for some fresh air, never to return. *First you dream, then you die* – who had those words on their conscience?

At the time Kripos had considered charging Signe Strand's boyfriend. He was six years older than her and had often been violent towards her. Once she had even ended up in hospital. But the DNA they found in the sperm on her body was not her boyfriend's.

Gunnarstranda looked back at the photos of the psychologist – Erik Valeur. Driving a patient home after the first session. Perhaps it wouldn't be so suspicious, if Veronika hadn't been so attractive, if she weren't dead now.

Gunnarstranda recalled the meeting with Valeur and his unusual demeanour, totally laid back when the police come calling, talking about the Top Twenty and the herd mentality. Did that necessarily mean anything? The guy had been cultivating his mania for collecting and, after all, Gunnarstranda had interrupted a ritual. There is something deeply human about collecting, he thought. Most people he knew were collectors of one kind or another. Before the Lillehammer Winter Olympics collecting commemorative pins had been a national epidemic. Fairs were held nationwide and some pins changed hands for phenomenal sums. Who collected them now? Gunnarstranda didn't know anyone who did. But he knew of people who collected wrist watches, wine, cars, bottles of cognac, stamps, coins, banknotes, biros, disposable lighters, even matchboxes. Collecting has been handed down from our evolutionary past; you have to survive a long winter, storing wood, food, fodder for the animals.

But there had been something.

The caustic remark about his visit – accompanied by the look of cold, hard steel in his eyes that vanished as soon as Gunnarstranda sensed it. The same hard steel that had risen to the surface when the psychologist was put under ever such slight pressure.

The coldness. What else had it been but his own damned intuition? So nothing. None the less: Gunnarstranda couldn't get Valeur out of his mind.

The telephone rang. He grabbed the receiver and asked the caller to be brief.

It was Emil Yttergjerde.

'There's something creepy about that psychologist. It's taken him over two hours to wash his car.'

Talk of the devil, Gunnarstranda thought. Or as his mother would say: *Life's strange. Every time I think hard about a friend, she rings me.*

Yttergjerde continued his report: 'First he put it in the car wash at Statoil, but he wasn't happy with that, then he rented a space to wash it himself. He went over it with a vac and ammonium chloride, took out all the mats and any detachable parts inside, crawled in and scrubbed it.

He's changed the water in the bucket several times and is still doing it. If he's trying to remove clues, I think he might be successful.'

'We haven't got enough on him yet to do anything,' Gunnarstranda said.

'That was what I thought, but it's worth taking note, don't you think?'

After hanging up, Gunnarstranda sat staring at the photo of the girl from Finnsnes. It was time to hear what Erik Valeur's ex-wife had to say. He lifted the receiver and rang the police in Tromsø.

35

Even eating out became a round of the differences between them. Ståle wanted to go to one of the flashy places in Aker Brygge and order a dry hamburger at the price of a fillet steak. He wanted to see the chicks (it embarrassed her every time he used the word). She had asked him three times what he saw in her if what *actually* turned him on was twenty-somethings with silicon tits as a confirmation present and he was unable to imagine anything cooler than having sex on a TV reality show.

She won anyway. Lena never went out and ate west of the river Akerselva. She was as finished with cafés as she was with puberty. On her way down from Brugata to Grønlandsleiret there were restaurants with international menus at affordable prices cheek by jowl with Narvesen kiosks selling bottles of Farris mineral water and steamy novels about Norwegian milkmaids. People queued in front of telephone exchanges to talk as cheaply as possible with family and friends on the other side of the globe. Lena liked being in the crowd thronging between colourful apartment buildings interspersed with elements of foreign architecture, such as the minaret in Åkebergveien, where all that was missing to complete the exoticism was the mosque's call to prayer above the low rooftops.

They arranged to meet at the Alibaba restaurant in Grønlandsleiret. She was early and killed time by wandering back and forth. She knew he was careful to arrive a quarter of an hour late. At a quarter past there he was, scanning the tables on the pavement.

He was always nervous about colleagues seeing them together and would pretend they were two workmates who had bumped into each other in town. Out of pure defiance she sat down at one of the tables outside. He wanted to go inside. She acted as if she hadn't heard or understood and started flicking through the menu. Soon some of the customers began staring at him. Only then did he sit down.

Losing in a situation like that went against all his instincts. When he started to criticise, she didn't beat about the bush. She looked into his eyes and gave it to him straight. 'If you don't want to eat here, now, with me, please leave.'

That annoyed him even more, but she didn't give a damn. Ignored him. Instead she explained what the various dishes were. 'Lahmacun is a kind of pizza, really tasty, especially with lamb.'

Ståle stressed that he wanted to have steak and made an unpleasant reference to her holidays in Turkey – wasn't it actually Turkish men she liked?

She ignored his vulgar insinuations and explained that there was no problem ordering beef. He could have a shish kebab, for example.

The waiter came. Ståle immediately ordered a beer. She ordered half a bottle of red wine for herself. Santa Rita. She noticed he didn't approve of that either. She had driven him hard and defied him several times. How would he exact his revenge? The thought of it was repugnant. At last she realised what was about to happen. This was their farewell dinner.

Two women, one in a black burka, the other in blue, pushed their prams past them. A young, more Western-looking couple strolled by, carrying shopping bags. Two men tried in vain to sell hash to passersby. She hoped they would move towards the river before Ståle saw what was going on.

'Why did we come here?' Ståle asked. 'We could've been enjoying the sun at Beach Club instead.'

The two drug barons disappeared as the waiter came with the drinks. Wine for her and a glass of water. The beer for Ståle took longer. She had to smile; this was not Ståle's day.

A tall, athletic man wearing a white gown and white turban walked past. She followed him with her eyes.

His eyes widened. Not a good sign. 'Don't think so much, Ståle,' she said.

'Shut up,' he snapped. 'I'm sick to death of hearing you say that.'

She distracted him by waving for the waiter. 'He's waiting for a beer,' she said.

'Of course.'

They exchanged glances. He couldn't bear that either – her taking the initiative and bringing order to chaos.

The waiter appeared with the beer. Poured more wine into her glass. The bottle was empty. 'Another?'

She looked up at him. A handsome young man from Iraq or Iran. Brown eyes and golden skin. 'I'll wait.'

'They turn you on, don't they?'

She didn't answer, just looked away. Somewhere deep inside her she was glad the final act was drawing closer and closer: *vaya con Dios.*

'There's something we have to discuss,' she said. 'You and me.'

He smirked. 'I'm going on holiday.'

She cast a sidelong glance to gather strength.

He gripped her hand.

She freed it and felt strong. 'You're travelling alone, of course?'

He shook his head.

The waiter appeared again. Were they ready to order?

'We'll wait a bit,' she said.

The waiter left.

'Shit, Lena, I'm hungry.'

'Where are you going?'

'Crete. In the south, where we usually go.'

She was almost impressed by how casually he talked about it. A pain shot through her stomach. This confused her. She was the one who should be able to talk casually about it. 'Didn't we talk about travelling together – one day?' she asked, took a sip of wine and felt her strength return. She repeated the question.

Ståle looked down at the table and smiled shyly. 'That won't work, you know that. But I'll be back on the first. Then we two can go away for a weekend.' He called the waiter, who stood at the ready with pad and pencil. 'I'll have one of those,' Ståle said. 'Number four.'

The waiter made a note and looked at her.

'I don't want anything,' she said.

The waiter took the trouble to refill her glass of water before going.

'Am I going to eat alone?' Ståle asked, annoyed.

Lena took her handbag. 'Just going to the toilet.' She squeezed her way inside and through the tables to the toilet. She gazed at herself in the mirror. A hair above her right eyebrow stood up like a horn. She pulled it out. Studied a wrinkle above the bridge of her nose. Tried to smooth it out. But couldn't.

At home in Lønnåsjordet where she grew up, on the floor above them lived an attractive, dark-haired woman who was visited twice a week by an older man. They never talked about this at home. You never talked about the neighbours. This woman had an English setter she walked every morning. At lunch on Sundays, come rain or shine, the family watched the woman and the dog. One Sunday morning thunder rumbled and the poor dog trudged reluctantly behind its owner, wanting to go back indoors. Her father lifted his coffee cup to his mouth and remarked: 'A majestic poetry lingers over a lover's loneliness.'

Lena had reacted: 'It's pathetic you mean, don't you?'

Her father had smiled and left the conversation there. He had only meant to be witty. She felt sorry for the woman who seemed so abandoned and couldn't understand how she could bear the eternal self-sacrifice.

And now she was in the same position herself. *No.* She met her own eyes in the mirror and shook her head. She wasn't. Not at all. She unlocked the door. But instead of going back to Ståle she turned right between the shops and over to the opposite side.

Sitting on the bus home, she sent Ståle a text message.

Owe you for the wine. I'll put the money into your account. Holiday money. Have a good trip, Lena.

She leaned back thinking life wasn't so bad.

36

Rindal stopped Frølich leaving.

'Good work, Frølich. Re the student from Kampala and all that. Any news on the kidnapper who ran away?'

Frølich shook his head. He knew Rindal, and Rindal had never been interested in the African woman.

'We're looking for him. Usual channels.'

Rindal nodded.

'They made films,' Frølich said. 'There's enough evidence.'

Rindal gave a non-committal nod and said:

'What do you reckon about Undset and Zahid? Has Kadir Zahid got anything to do with the murder?'

'It's possible Veronika and Zahid had an old-pals' act going, I don't know. That was my first impression when I arrested her. But then it turned out she was getting married to Karl Anders Fransgård. So, it's more likely she and Zahid were telling the truth. Their statements matched. Both said they grew up together, were in the same class, both said they were good friends. Both said they liked each other blah blah blah. So I can't imagine Zahid killed Veronika.'

'OK,' Rindal said reflectively. 'How do you think the case is going?'

Frølich shrugged. 'There's one matter that should be followed up more closely,' he said. 'The cocaine trail.'

Rindal furrowed his brow, confused.

'We arrested Veronika Undset for possession of five grams hidden in a Zippo. She denied—'

'Exactly,' Rindal interrupted, nodding, distant. 'Exactly, we have to take a wider view,' he said. 'A broader view. Don't you agree?'

Frølich realised Rindal hadn't asked for his opinion because he was interested, but because he wanted him to do something else.

'Look at this,' Rindal said, passing Frølich a pile of papers. 'An inventory of objects seized on Zahid's premises.'

'Why do you ask my opinion about a case when you don't give a shit what my answer is?'

Rindal reacted defensively, both hands raised. 'I don't care what you say. But there are two types of detective, Frølich: those who have to be briefed first and those who are already au fait with the material. This lead has to be followed up and you're a man who knows both the Veronika and the Zahid cases. There could be things among the confiscated goods which link them.'

Frank Frølich was unable to hide his irritation. 'This is office work.'

Rindal was already on his way. 'Just have a look,' he mumbled. 'A little peep can't harm.'

Frølich continued into Gunnarstranda's office. 'There's something I have to talk to you about,' he started, but fell silent when Gunnarstranda gesticulated with the telephone receiver.

'Eugen? It's me. Have you spoken to the psychologist's ex-wife?'

Gunnarstranda glanced at his watch. 'OK, talk later.' He hung up. Turned to Frølich. 'Suddenly Eugen Bendixen's very busy. It's ten to ten in the morning and he asked me to ring back in two hours. How can I help you, Frølich?'

'Look at this.' Frølich passed him the papers.

Gunnarstranda put on his glasses and scanned the papers. 'What about them?'

'Rindal's drawn up an inventory of the seized items at Zahid's.'

'Good. Kadir Zahid hasn't got an alibi and he could have a motive. For example, he might have felt threatened by Veronika Undset if she knew about the burglaries.'

'But then we have to prove that there's a link between the murder and the burglaries!'

'Exactly. The inventory is a good starting point. Start there.' Gunnarstranda pointed to something on the list.

Frølich lifted the sheet and read: 'Atmos? What's that?'

'The closest man has come to perpetuum mobile, Frølich. A clock that's like a standard mantle clock, but which is quite different. An Atmos is driven by atmospheric pressure changes. Fantastic mechanism. A clock made by the Swiss manufacturer Jaeger-LeCoultre. Atmos is a collector's item. Kadir Zahid, who believes that finesse is about shaving your balls and buying expensive cars, knows absolutely nothing about the certificates attached to the Atmos. If the owner of the clock is on Undset's list of clients, their name will still be on the certificates. Zahid will never be able to explain away this mismatch. So Rindal will have a case that is as reliable as the clock.'

Gunnarstranda had taken off his jacket while he was talking. He went out. The door slammed. 'Roger,' replied Frølich in a broad American accent. He wondered if there was anyone he could con into taking this crap job. Anyone who might be motivated.

37

Frank Frølich had treated himself to lunch at a sushi bar and was late. When he entered the office, Gunnarstranda was already briefing the others on the report by Eugen Bendixen of the Tromsø Police.

'Eugen spoke to Valeur's ex. She's a nurse and said that she and Valeur had what's known as an *acrimonious* divorce. She had to go to a Crisis Centre before the separation. She was on the point of reporting Valeur for threatening behaviour and violence, but never did.'

'How is it possible for a man like that to practise as a psychologist?' Yttergjerde said.

'I presume because she kept her mouth closed and struggled through. She didn't want to carry the blame for him losing his livelihood. She says she discovered his negative sides early on. They met on a Hurtigruta boat after making contact in a chatroom for the unmarried.'

'For singletons,' Lena Stigersand responded, setting the record straight.

'What's the difference?'

'If you say *unmarried* there are only negative associations. A large part of the Norwegian population is single. It's a lifestyle – a decision you make.'

Gunnarstranda regarded her in silent astonishment, which caused the others to turn their heads in his direction.

'OK,' she burst out angrily. 'I'm a singleton. Now you know!'

'What about ... ?' Frølich asked.

Lena was about to answer, but Gunnarstranda banged the table. 'Pay attention, will you,' he thundered. 'Valeur's ex-wife moved here from the US, where she'd lived with an oil man from Houston. She and the American met in Stavanger. He worked for Statoil, she worked at the hospital. That was apparently also a turbulent relationship, which they hoped would improve if they moved to his homeland. But in the US things got worse. He became more and more violent and she moved back to Tromsø ten years ago. After chatting on the net she met Valeur on the Hurtigruta. Fell for him and related her sad story. He was very considerate, a psychologist and so on and so forth. They got married after six months. She was then thirty-seven and wanted a child. According to her, however, Valeur's attitude changed after they were married. He turned out to be a notorious womaniser. After six months she discovered he was doing online chatting, on sites with live sexual activity, whatever that is.'

'Webcam,' Yttergjerde said.

The others looked at him.

He coughed. 'Striptease, masturbation and so on ...'

'The things you people know,' Gunnarstranda said in a distant voice. 'Anyway. He would boast to his wife about prostitutes he entertained on his journeys. According to her, he's a sort of Jekyll-and-Hyde character, pleasant and sympathetic at work, but privately a very disagreeable man with a strong need to dominate. She also thinks she has an explanation, namely that he hates his mother. There's some conflict stuff he can't resolve because at the same time he falls in love with women who are like her. And this Ragnhild – that's the name of his ex-wife – belongs in this category.'

'What does the mother look like?' It was Lena who asked.

Gunanarstranda looked up in surprise. 'No idea, but I'll ring Eugen and tell him to fax over a photo of the ex-wife. Don't keep interrupting me. I'll be brief: Ragnhild wanted to get out of the marriage. Valeur sent people to spy on her. Sort of provocateurs to chat her up in the street and suchlike. He obviously had some pretty sick ideas. At home he began to grill her about these incidents and especially her violent ex-husband. The latter turned him on and made him extra violent. On one occasion she was taken to hospital and there she was encouraged to move to the Crisis Centre. Where she was advised to report Valeur. She didn't. However, she did move out and now she's divorced.'

'When was this?' Frølich asked. 'When did she move out?'

'In May, 2006,' Gunnarstranda said, and added: 'Yes, you're on the right lines. That was when Signe Strand was murdered.'

'A psychologist?' Lena Stigersand looked at the others in turn. 'A person who works intimately with people for year after year?'

'What do you mean?'

'Every coin has two sides. We don't have to believe her, do we? She might be out to exact some kind of revenge. After all, Valeur's still working. There are *no* complaints from patients.'

When none of the others said anything, she carried on: 'Some women are attracted by dangerous men.'

Frølich and Yttergjerde exchanged glances.

Lena noticed: 'Don't you start that!'

Gunnarstranda peered at her over his glasses.

'Sorry,' she said. 'Those two get on my nerves sometimes.'

Gunnarstranda went over to the window and looked out.

Frølich spoke up:

'We don't believe Valeur's ex-wife any more than anyone else. What we do know is that when Valeur was working at the Child and Adolescent Mental Health Services in Troms he had sessions with Signe Strand because of her eating disorder. Kripos rang him and asked about this relationship. They never checked his alibi or his DNA – no one considered putting the psychologist under the microscope. As for Veronika Undset, he drove her home a few days before the murder. That's all we know about him. We also know that Sivert Almeli photographed Valeur the day after Veronika was killed. Erik Valeur is the one person who has a link with all three victims: Signe, Veronika and Almeli. That's quite significant, if you ask me. It's also very significant that the man beats up women he likes.'

'This is beginning to remind me of the Orderud case now,' Lena Stigersand said. 'We seem to be searching for clues to justify this one lead. Isn't it a bit early to point a finger at the psychologist? We know Veronika was his patient, but that's where it ends.'

'He also spent a lot of time washing his car,' Yttergjerde said, and added: 'It seemed clean to me at the start.'

Gunnarstranda shook his head.

'Valeur was at the opera when Veronika was killed.'

'Alone?'

'Alone.'

'So he hasn't got an alibi,' Frølich said.

'He might have,' Gunnarstranda said. 'He says he talked to people in the interval and has emailed us several telephone numbers.'

'His motive?' Yttergjerde enquired.

Gunnarstranda shrugged. He looked at Lena Stigersand, who said: 'His ex-wife claims he's violent and has an Oedipus complex, that's all.'

The others got up.

Lena banged her hands on the table. 'This is Orderud revisited. We *think* Almeli observed Valeur up to his tricks with Veronika and we *think* that's why he photographed Valeur and we *think* the photos gave Valeur a motive for killing Almeli. We can clear up all this doubt in one fell swoop.'

'How?' demanded Gunnarstranda.

'By, for example, letting me book a session with Valeur,' Lena Stigersand answered.

Frølich and Yttergjerde, who were heading for the door, stopped and turned to her.

A total silence descended.

Lena crossed her arms defiantly and looked at them, one after the other.

'Our job is to find out what actually happened,' Gunnarstranda said slowly. 'We don't do honeytraps, Lena. We don't want to incite crime.'

'I'm not talking about provocation; I'm talking about undercover work. A session with Valeur will give me an impression of what sort of person he is.'

No one said a word.

'I'll sit in the same chair, be in the same situation as Veronika Undset,' Lena enthused.

Still silence.

'If he killed Veronika, something must have happened between them.'

'Lena *is* a similar type,' Emil broke in with a smile.

Gunnarstranda eyed him sternly.

'Like Veronika and the girl on Senja,' Yttergjerde continued. 'Red hair…' He winked at Lena. 'Big boobies—'

Gunnarstranda interrupted: 'The answer's no.'

*

When Lena closed the door behind her she was annoyed. On the one hand, she reasoned, Gunnarstranda could take responsibility for what she did at work. On the other, he couldn't decide what she did privately.

She paced to and fro in the corridor. Nodded abstractedly to people passing. She cast a glance into the R&R room. Nobody there. She went in and sat down, pensive. Fiddled with her mobile phone. Placed it on the table. Beside the phone was the directory. She picked it up and thumbed through to the right page. Found the number. Looked up. And around. No one there. Now or never. She tapped in the number.

Valeur answered at once. She recoiled.

But his voice was pleasant. She hesitated for some seconds, nervously rose to her feet and cast a guilty glance around before saying she was ringing to book an appointment.

'There's a waiting list,' the pleasant voice explained.

'I haven't been referred, but I'm willing to pay the full price,' she answered.

Silence.

'Are you there?'

Valeur cleared his throat. 'Could you say specifically what the trouble is?'

'There's so much,' Lena said. 'Once I've started I'm afraid I won't be able to stop.' She paced back and forth, met her reflection in the window as she considered what to say. The man at the other end waited, didn't jump in. 'I'm worried about myself, my decisions, especially with regard to relationships – men. I need to sort out my thoughts. Sometimes I do things I don't understand, sometimes I despise myself...'

'Have you called me first?'

'Yes.'

'What's your name?'

She broke into a sweat. Lowered her hand and stared at her phone. *What am I doing?* She cast around panic-stricken. She was alone. No one was listening.

She cleared her throat. 'Lena. My name's Lena Stigersand.'

'It's summer now, Lena, and soon I'll be going on holiday. My schedule is absolutely full for the next few weeks before I go, but I can give you the name of several competent—'

'No,' she interjected. 'Please don't turn me away...' She paused, confused by her own outburst. 'I mean ... it cost me so much effort to make this call, and I'm sure...'

'If you start a course of therapy with me before the holiday, it might be wasted, Lena, because you'll have to wait at least four weeks for the next session.'

'That doesn't matter,' she said. 'I mean, the main thing is to get started, to cross this threshold. I couldn't bear the thought of a rejection now.'

The phone went quiet. Lena sat down again. Beams of sunshine angled through the windows. Specks of dust danced in the air. Doors opened in the corridor. She jumped up, headed for the door with the phone pressed to her ear.

'Let's see then, shall we. I'm looking for a window, but I'm afraid it doesn't look good.'

She gripped the phone tighter. Footsteps were approaching from the corridor. 'Ah, there you are,' said Frølich as he entered.

Lena gripped her phone even tighter. And wriggled past him without answering him.

'Lena?' Frølich said.

She glanced at him briefly. With her free hand she pointed to the phone to indicate how busy she was, then set off down the corridor. Now there were people everywhere. *Shit!*

'I have several good colleagues I can recommend—' Valeur started to say. She broke in:

'Please.' She strode along without seeing any of the faces.

'It would have to be after normal working hours, then.'

'When?' she asked. Opened the door to the staircase. People were standing by the lifts. Should she ring off? Pretend the call had been cut? She turned 180 degrees. Frank Frølich was waving and coming towards her.

'Today, at seven thirty,' Valeur said. 'My consultation room's in Hortengata. That's—'

'I've got your address here in the directory,' Lena answered. 'See you at half-past seven,' she said, and pressed *Off*.

'I need to ask you a favour,' Frølich burbled cheerfully.

She stared at him blankly. With the phone in her trembling hand. She had done it. The die was cast.

'As you were involved in the raid on Dekkmekk,' Frølich continued.

'What are you talking about?' she said.

'A favour, Lena. Could you do me a favour?'

She nodded, took the papers he passed her and left. She had to go to the toilet. Surely she would be on her own there.

38

Emil Yttergjerde and Frank Frølich were floppy in the heat – and in silly mode. Discussing what tortures would be suitable for Gunnarstranda. Yttergjerde suggested putting the old boy in a room with a code lock. The only way out would be to find the combination on a computer. The keyboard would be fiendish – missing three numbers, the ones he needed to restart the machine when he screwed up and the screen froze.

Frølich thought that was too complicated. He suggested a *Clockwork Orange* scenario, tying him to a chair with matchsticks between his eyelids forcing him to watch Saturday-night TV – all the programmes in the popular Norwegian series *The Great Class Reunion*. After that, Gunnarstranda would return to work in the same lobotomised state as Jack Nicholson in *One Flew Over the Cuckoo's Nest* – before Chief, the Native American, kills him out of sheer pity.

Emil Yttergjerde was in on this at once. They were picking the most unbearable celebrities in all of Norway for this torture when they were interrupted by Lena Stigersand.

'What are you doing?'

Yttergjerde, who liked to hear the punchline of a joke many times, gave her the highlights.

Lena thought of a much simpler solution. All you had to do was buy a carton of cigarettes and throw it down the refuse chute, the type you have in older Oslo housing-association flats. The torture would be to restrain Gunnarstranda and stop him jumping in after it.

She waved a piece of paper to get the men's attention. 'Regine Haraldsen,' she said to Frølich. 'You talked about perpetuum mobile – a kind of clock?'

'An Atmos.'

Lena beamed with pleasure. 'I've just spoken to Regine Haraldsen. The clock that was seized on Kadir Zahid's premises is hers. She has a certificate for it.'

Yttergjerde looked from one to the other.

'Which should prove,' Frank Frølich said, rubbing the tears of laughter from his eyes, 'that Zahid's behind the break-in at fru Haraldsen's, who was Veronika Undset's client. Seven hours before she was killed I accused her of leaking information about the lady's valuables to Zahid. The moment I left she got on the phone. And who did she ring?'

'Kadir Zahid,' said Emil Yttergjerde – who never understood rhetorical questions.

'That seems a bit too simple,' Frølich said.

Lena nodded. 'But it'll become complicated anyway. You see, Zahid denies any knowledge of the items we confiscated – including the clock. He says he rented the garage beside Dekkmekk to some Eastern Europeans. Illegal rental agreement, of course. No invoice and no name. What's up?'

Both Lena and Emil watched Frølich, who had risen to his feet and was staring into the air. 'The phone,' he said.

'What about it?'

'Veronika's phone. I turned and saw through the window that she had a phone to her ear. All the time thinking it was a mobile, but of course it was a landline.'

Frank Frølich was already out of the door.

The other two watched him leave, then looked at each other. They both shrugged.

*

Before she called it a day, Lena went through the statements of the three Estonians who were picked up at the raid on Kadir Zahid's garage. All three said they normally worked picking strawberries for a farmer in Minnesund. They hadn't understood a thing when the police appeared. Their version was that they had been in the fields when a guy in a car stopped and asked if they could do a transport job – filling a van with empty strawberry punnets and driving it to Nes in Hedmarken. When they saw what was actually in the garage they were in a state of shock.

Lena rang the officer who had interviewed them at Manglerud Police Station.

'Do you believe their statements?'

'Not for one second. But all three of them said the same.'

'What about the van?'

'*Go-getters* is a rental company. The vehicle was rented to one of the men two hours before our raid.'

'What about the trolley jack they borrowed from Kadir's garage?'

'They had no reasonable explanation for that. One of them claimed they'd been told there was the lifting gear they needed in the garage, so he went looking for it *until* he realised they must have come to the wrong address, as he put it – in other words a place crammed full with electronics and not a single empty strawberry punnet.'

'The padlock,' Lena said. 'How did they open it?'

'They maintained the place was unlocked, and we can't prove the opposite because we never found the padlock key on them.'

Exactly, Lena thought, she thanked them for their help and hung up. Everyone knew the three of them were lying, but there is no legal penalty for fabrication. The three Estonians were released after a night in custody. There was nothing they could charge them with. Now none of them answered their phones. Most probably they were back in Estonia.

She made neat holes in the papers, archived them in ring files and put them on the shelf. The working day was over.

Lena went home.

She had to prepare herself mentally and physically for her session with the psychologist.

*

The locksmith was sitting on the steps waiting when Frølich drove in and parked in front of the old display windows. Short-haired with a curl over his brow; angular head and a goatee around his chin. He looked like Abraham Lincoln.

Frølich signed the invoice and watched the man go before entering.

At first sight Veronika Undset's messy office looked the same as it had done the previous time: the low desk was still covered with papers and old newspapers. The mops in the corner, the piles of plastic buckets, cardboard boxes full of detergents…

He scanned the office. Something was missing.

There was no telephone.

He walked over to the desk, opened drawers and looked underneath to see if it had fallen on the floor.

It wasn't there either. He went over what had happened on the Monday afternoon. He had found the door locked and waited for some minutes. Then a taxi had pulled up by the pavement. Veronika got out of the car. They said hello, she unlocked the door, they went in…

He had been nervous to speak. Nervous because she was engaged to Karl Anders, because…

He remembered it as though it had happened a few minutes ago. Veronika went to the telephone and fiddled with it, and he had wondered if she was checking the display to see if anyone had phoned while she had been out.

Now the telephone was gone. There was no doubt. There was even a clear square in the layer of dust on the desk.

Whoever had taken the telephone must have had a key. There was surely only one place the keys could have come from – Veronika's bag.

Frank Frølich's eyes wandered across the walls. Kim's Game, he thought, walking around the confined office, careful not to touch anything. If any other objects apart from the telephone had been removed, he had no idea what they could be.

He used his mobile to ring Gunnarstranda.

There were three rings before he answered.

'It's seven o'clock, Frølich and I'm on my way home.'

'We need some assistance from Telenor,' Frølich said.

'Why?'

'Veronika Undset's work phone has been taken. Telenor can see who she phoned before she was killed.'

'Taken? As in stolen? Taken intentionally?'

'Yep. As I wrote in my report. She rang someone after I left her. All the time I've thought she used her mobile.'

'Me too.'

'Anyway, I'm here now. I came to check. The telephone's gone.'

'Telenor … have them run a trace … that could take time,' Gunnar-stranda said. 'I'll see to it tomorrow.'

39

It was eight o'clock in the morning and Gunnarstranda was pouring himself his second cup of coffee when there was a knock at the door. In came Lena Stigersand.

'Hi,' she said.

'What are you doing?' She eyed him and the coffee cup with despair. 'The coffee in the machine costs just one krone.'

Gunnarstranda screwed the top on his worn steel Thermos. 'Without this energy drink I'd have applied for a job elsewhere long ago. What's the matter?'

'Nothing.' Lena couldn't suppress a smile and was shifting from one foot to the other like a girl on the way to her first day at school.

Gunnarstranda allowed himself to be infected by her good mood and smiled. 'I can see there is something.'

'Voilà,' she said, holding up a little plastic bag. 'Thought you might poss–i–bly be interested in this!'

She placed the bag on the edge of the desk.

He observed it, still with the Thermos in his hand, eyebrows arched.

'Hair,' she said. 'Erik Valeur's. It can be analysed. You can see if it matches DNA from the sample you took in Almeli's wardrobe.'

Gunnarstranda was no longer smiling. He pushed the Thermos away. She involuntarily straightened up.

Gunnarstranda rose to his full height, walked past her and closed the door. Locked onto her eyes. 'Sit down,' he said coldly.

She sat.

He lifted the plastic bag from the desk and weighed it in his hand. 'How did you get hold of this?'

'Therapy,' she said. 'Private,' she added.

'You heard what I told you yesterday, didn't you?'

'It's private,' Lena said. 'I go to therapy, that's all. I took the hairs from his jacket hanging over the chair. He didn't see me doing it. I've also formed an impression of the man – interested?'

Gunnarstranda walked back to the desk and sat down. The silence was long and heavy.

At length he stretched out his hand and flicked the plastic bag with the few hairs inside. The bag sailed in an arc into the wastepaper basket.

Lena sat looking at the basket. Then she raised her gaze. Their eyes met.

'*That* was not necessary,' she said.

Gunnarstranda didn't answer, just stared at her. She was one of the few people in the building he liked. He remembered her from right back when he had held a couple of short lectures at the Police College. Lena had the bluest eyes he'd ever seen. Almond-shaped, resting harmoniously above a gently sloping nose and protected by long, naturally curled eyelashes. She had also the reddest hair he could ever remember seeing. And beneath the unruly mane was a quick brain which equipped this woman with intelligence, humour, self-irony, a chameleon's ability to adapt and a special skill for gaining perspective and drawing quick conclusions.

But now and then even the best go off the rails. He cleared his throat. 'Lena.'

'Yes?' She blinked. Probably knowing what was coming.

'I hope this investigation won't end up in a legal case.'

She sighed like a teenager before the teacher's reprimand comes.

He raised a hand to quell her reaction and continued:

'If DNA is produced as evidence in a court case I, or another officer, have to explain where the sample came from and why it was taken. I have to take responsibility for the progress of an investigation which should be both professional and ethical. Private psychology sessions do not come under accepted conditions for this type of evidence, and I think you know that in your heart of hearts. Why do you want to drop out of this investigation?'

Her eyes opened wide. 'I don't and you know that.'

'You've initiated a private relationship with a witness whose status might become that of a suspect.'

Her cheeks reddened and he could literally see the anger boiling behind her ice-blue eyes.

'Frølich's still working with us on the case,' she countered.

Gunnarstranda took a deep breath and leaned back in his chair, waiting for more to come.

'Frølich knew Veronika Undset,' Lena went on. 'He not only knew her, he—'

'That's absolutely correct,' Gunnarstranda broke in. 'But there's an essential difference, Lena. Frølich doesn't start a *new* relationship. He knows he's compromised with regard to some of the witnesses involved. He's told us which ones he knows and he's talked about the resulting problems. Can you do the same? Can you tell me why you booked a session with this psychologist?'

'I wanted to kill two birds with one stone. By using Valeur I wanted to get an impression of him. I had planned to write a report, but I can see you're not interested. Relax, I won't do it.'

'Why the psychologist, Lena?'

She stared into the air.

He waited.

'It's private,' she said.

'You have one more chance,' he said, noting the fury continuing to build up in her ice-blue eyes. It wasn't difficult to understand. He would have been livid himself. 'Both you and I know about Frølich and his childhood friend, and we know why he finds parts of his job problematic. We had to know that to decide whether he's compromised or not. You have to go through the same mill. What is it about you that makes—?'

She cut in: 'It's private!' The last word was pronounced with such force and volume that it resounded against the wall behind them.

He met her angry glare and regretted what he had to say, but said it anyway:

'I'll take this up with Rindal. I'll ask for you to be transferred.'

She rose to her feet, her back ramrod straight.

Seeing her like this sent a pain through his stomach. Her eyes were shiny and she was clearly fighting with herself, but said nothing. She went to the door.

'Lena,' Gunnarstranda said.

She turned and looked him in the eye. She had regained her self-control.

'Was that why you started the therapy with the weirdo? To hear what I just said?'

'Of course not!'

Then she was gone. Behind her, the door closed with a bang.

*

Gunnarstranda stared at the door. He swivelled to and fro in his chair. He glanced down at the wastepaper basket. Glanced at the door. The wastepaper basket. The door.

For ten long minutes he stared meditatively at the ceiling as he swung from side to side.

In the end he couldn't restrain himself. He pulled the basket over, bent down and fished out the plastic bag. He dangled it pensively between thumb and forefinger for a few seconds.

He picked up the receiver and pressed Schwenke's number. 'It's me,' he said. 'I've got some hair. Can you or one of your minions prioritise an analysis?'

While he was talking he took a form from a drawer to accompany the sample.

40

She was furious and packed her things. While she was waiting at the bus stop her phone beeped.

Text from Ståle. There were six messages from him in her in-box. All unread.

She breathed in and paced to and fro, hands in pockets, impatient. Telling herself: Ståle's on Crete. Walking hand in hand with his fragile wife on the beach. They'll find a restaurant with muzak playing, Whitney Houston or REM, and then eat moussaka, drink retsina and ouzo and gaze deep into each other's eyes before walking back and having sex, curtains fluttering in the wind.

Wasn't that the life she longed for?

It was irrelevant. She had been treated like shit by Ståle and now she was being treated like shit at work. She snatched up her phone and deleted all his messages unread.

The bus came. She got on. Found a seat and leaned her head against the window. Idly gazing at the cars and houses along Trondheimsveien. Fell into a sun-soaked bus-induced trance.

Aker Hospital. Changed buses. She stood at the head of the queue for a seat. The bus was packed, hot and soporific. She fell asleep. Dreaming about Ståle's sweaty chest and imagining she had the taste of saltwater and semen in her mouth.

She woke with a start thinking that life was like a swing rocking back and forth and never stopping.

At home she logged onto the net, finished writing reports that should have been done ages ago and sent them. As she got up to make tea she looked outside.

There was a dark green car in the parking bay for guests.

She had seen the car before. On a hard disk belonging to Sivert Almeli.

The sight froze her, and slowly she turned away from the window. Stood still, looking at the noisy kettle. When the water had boiled she switched it off, fetched a cup, filled it and added a tea bag.

Her hands weren't shaking. She spooned some honey from the jar and put it in her tea. Went back to the window and looked down at the roof of the green car, slowly stirring in the honey.

Lena worked through the session she'd had with Valeur the day before. What she had said; what he had said. His eyes. Still she couldn't fathom what had triggered this. Most probably it was something he did to many patients. He spied on them. Presumably this is what he did with Veronika. It must have been what Sivert Almeli had observed. An unfamiliar car outside. A stranger in the car. Something had happened. Something which caused Almeli to make a note of the registration plate, find the owner and photograph him.

What had happened?

There was only one way to find out; she had to go down. Lena was the patient being spied on.

She was Veronika Undset.

She moved away from the window and over to the mirror. But she *wasn't* Veronika. She was prepared; she was trained to master men like him – both mentally and physically.

She looked herself in the eye and felt herself go cold and determined. She went into the bathroom and changed into a tracksuit and trainers. Stopped and looked at herself in the mirror once again. Some back-up might be necessary, but not yet.

Anyway she would need a way out – if anything were to happen. *If.*

She went into the bedroom, opened the wardrobe and searched for her bumbag. Strapped it around her waist and tightened it. Her mobile phone was in the kitchen. She checked the display – the battery was fully charged. She put the phone on silent mode, placed it in the bumbag and zipped it up. She was ready.

She jogged down the stairs. Continued along the pathway ignoring the car park, followed the bend around it and set off down the hills towards the main road. Running sprightly with purpose and focus.

She heard the car after running only a few hundred metres. It followed her at a snail's pace.

Now was the time. She stopped.

The car stopped.

She turned. It was Valeur's Mercedes. The window slid down.

She walked over.

'Hi, Lena.' Erik Valeur looked at her from the driver's seat. His sunglasses made him resemble the baddie in a B-movie.

'Hi,' she said. And as much as she didn't want to be the one who covers over the strangeness of a situation with idiotic chit-chat, she heard herself wittering away like an adolescent: 'Oh, my God, is that *you*? That's a bit of a surprise.'

He didn't respond to her twaddle. The baddie black sunglasses were impenetrable. Eventually he nodded: 'Jump in.'

'I'm going for a little run and I'm quite sweaty,' she answered, wondering to herself: *why am I smiling stupidly like a schoolgirl*? 'Don't think it would be right in your car.'

'You've only been running for about a minute,' he said. 'I saw you.' His lips were dry. He licked around his mouth. Something nasty was going on in that head right now.

He leaned further forward and pointed through the open window. 'You live there, in the block on the right, second floor, third balcony from the right. The one with the spiraea in the window box.'

A car came down the hill. Braked and passed them. Lena waved.

'Who was that?'

'A neighbour,' she lied. She didn't know the driver from Adam.

'Jump in,' he repeated.

She waited, not moving.

He moistened his lips with his tongue again. Pulled a smile that wasn't a smile but a grimace. 'I only want to talk to you.'

The silence lingered for more long seconds.

'Why?' she asked.

The skin on his thin lips was cracked and flaked. 'Lena, do what I tell you.'

She looked at the black sunglasses, searching for his eyes without success. Then he leaned over the passenger seat and opened the door. She got in.

41

It was getting on for six in the evening. Gunnarstranda sat with his feet on the table opening another packet of Nicotinell chewing gum when the telephone rang. It was Schwenke.

'Congratulations, Gunnarstranda.'

The policeman popped some gum in his mouth. He placed it under his lip like a snus pouch. He did this instinctively, deliberating what these words actually meant. The investigation was going into a new and intensive phase.

'The sample,' Schwenke elucidated,' the sample of hair you sent has a match.'

'Almeli?'

'No. Almeli's killer is still unknown. The hair sample has a match in the Senja case. The man whose hair this is pumped his seed between Signe Strand's white thighs before killing her. What sort of person is he?'

'He's a psychologist,' Gunnarstranda said. 'The girl was his patient. Something about the treatment must have turned him on.'

'What about Veronika Undset?'

'She was also one of his patients,' Gunnarstranda answered stiffly.

Schwenke whistled.

Gunnarstranda was thinking about who had delivered the hair sample and quickly brought the conversation to a close.

'I'd have a look at Signe Strand's treatment history if I were you,' Schwenke said. 'At the interview you should go into the man's past. There must have been a trigger for how he acted.'

Struggling to retain his composure, Gunnarstranda answered: 'Thank you, thank you so much, especially because you prioritised it and were so quick.'

'Now you owe me a favour,' Schwenke replied with a laugh.

'Add it to the list,' Gunnarstranda said, and put down the receiver.

He immediately lifted it again. Rang Lena at home.

No answer.

He took out his phone where he had saved her mobile number. It rang. But she didn't answer.

He got up and hurried down the corridor to the R&R room where Emil Yttergjerde was engrossed in a car magazine.

'Lena?'

'Working at home today, I think. At least that was what she said when she left.'

'Seen Frølich?'

Yttergjerde shook his head. 'How come?'

'An arrest.'

Yttergjerde jumped up from his chair. 'Who?'

'The psychologist,' Gunnarstranda said.

42

They sat through three hours of authentic recordings of rape and abuse carried out by the accused. Frølich also had a statement from the victim. As soon as Mattis Langeland was confronted with the evidence he confessed to kidnapping, but not abuse and rape. His solicitor wanted to bargain. A dark-haired lady in her mid-forties, she played hardball and suggested two outcomes: either they would claim Rosalind agreed to have sex with Mattis and fight it out through the legal system or there would be a full confession and the full package. She wanted a reduced sentence and hinted at some irregularities in the arrest – presumably to put the skids under Frølich. He ignored the hints and left Rindal and the lawyers to get their hands dirty.

Rosalind M'Taya was discharged from Ullevål University Hospital. The students at the summer school had formed a support group which appointed a representative to take care of the information flow – Monica Johansson, a Swedish Ph.D. student who messaged the police about what Rosalind did and didn't want.

A photo of Andreas Langeland was sent to all police districts. He could hardly be labelled dangerous, so that was enough. He was a wanted man, suspected of kidnapping, rape and aggravated GBH.

Frølich himself knew little about Andreas. Iselin Grav wouldn't divulge specific details about the boy's childhood, except to suggest abuse. The boy was almost twenty, had been neglected by his father and mother and was now under the unfortunate influence of his elder brother Mattis. On the other hand, the recordings showed Andreas performing acts of his own volition. With evidence of this kind he could hardly blame his brother.

*

The evening was summery with low rays of sunshine appearing between high walls and turning people into dark silhouettes in the streets. A few shops were still open. Frølich wound his way past hordes of young people outside Oslo City, a shopping centre. Those with the most experience of prison identified him at once, and the groups dissolved as he passed. He crossed Biskop Gunnerus' gate and headed for Oslo Station. He counted maybe sixty junkies in the square called Plata: ageing drug addicts in wheelchairs and other shrunken, toothless rubber faces. A one-legged guy wearing a cap hobbled along on crutches, one trouser leg tied in a knot. Two slightly younger women with elasticated knee supports struggled to stay upright. He passed the bronze tiger in Jernbanetorget, its tail rubbed smooth, like its balls.

By the fountain on the seaward side stood a man in his twenties with his trousers around his knees openly injecting heroin into his thigh.

Frølich nodded to the man, who pulled his trousers up. They'd had their run-ins. His head changed its dangle position, indicating that he was planning to say something. Frølich got in first. 'Off you go, Walter. I'm skint!'

Walter 'dangled' off. Soon out of sight among the other junkies.

Frank Frølich leaned back against the fountain wall. The ground was strewn with used needles. Why had he thought he would find Andreas Langeland here?

He walked back and through the red-light area to Dronningens gate. Streetwalkers from Eastern Europe and West Africa hung around on the corners pretending they weren't streetwalkers from Eastern Europe and West Africa.

He spotted a police car on the corner of Rådhusgata. He waved. It was Abid Iqbal waving an arm out of the window. Abid was looking cool: three-day beard, dreads and seventies' sunglasses.

'How about a lift to the City Hall square?'

Abid reached back and opened the door. Frølich got in.

They caught the green wave in Rådhusgata, but before they reached Brasserie Hansken in Kontraskjæret, Abid received a message.

'Sorry, Frankie. Gotta turn. Can you jump off here?'

Frølich shook his head. 'I'll go with you. I was only checking to see if he was with the skateboarders in the centre. Don't think it's likely.'

Abid accelerated. Took a short cut through the tunnels in Henrik Ibsens gate.

'Where are you going?'

'To Mono.'

They stopped in Pløens gate, at the back of Youngstorget. A small group of youths were going their separate ways outside the entrance of the bar lower down.

Abid didn't move. Nor Frølich.

'Tell me if you think I can get out of the car without ruining everything,' he said.

'Let's just see what's happening.'

A figure crossed the street and exchanged a few words with two girls still standing outside the bar. They were wearing short skirts and had their legs crossed in smoker pose. Both shook their heads and turned their backs on the figure now heading towards the unmarked police car. 'He's mine,' said Abid.

'I'll wait a while,' Frølich said.

Abid looked at him.

'I know him,' Frølich said. 'What's he done?'

'He pushes cocaine at places like this – the Mono, Cosmopolite…'

The figure approached. A beanpole of a boy came up in the light from the low sun. He was wearing black clothes, leather jacket and jeans, had long hair dyed black and a little goatee. It was Janne Smith's son – Kristoffer.

Abid grabbed the door handle, but Frølich held him back. 'Please let him go.'

Abid freed his arm with an annoyed expression.

'Please,' Frølich insisted.

The boy passed them and Frølich followed him with his eyes. Both watched him around the corner and disappear from view down Møllegata.

Abid was not best pleased. 'You'd better have a bloody good explanation, Frankie.'

'I have.'

Frølich took his phone. Before he could dial Gunnarstranda's number, he was rung by his boss.

'Where are you?'

'City centre,' Frølich said. 'Youngstorget. I think we can say we have a little breakthrough in the investigation. Perhaps you could buckle up and meet me somewhere.'

'The psychologist killed Signe Strand,' replied Gunnarstranda. 'DNA match. But Erik Valeur isn't at home. If he killed Veronika as well, it could have happened in his office – in Hortengata. Meet us there.'

43

There was no warmth in the low evening sun any more. Sporadic gusts of wind blew away the heat that had been so oppressive earlier in the day. Children's laughter drifted between the light, rhythmic lapping of waves on the shore. The wind played in her hair. Lena gathered some strands in one hand and tried to put them behind one ear.

'I know what you're thinking,' he said.

She didn't answer. No one could know what she was thinking.

'You're wondering why I've visited you privately,' he said.

She looked up at him, still uncommunicative. They ambled along slowly. Wavelets licked over wet sand, which glistened when the water receded. The rocks were almost bare. Strips of beautiful marmorised stone undulated across the mountainside.

'What you told me about your boyfriend and the relationship you wanted to leave did something to me,' he said.

She undid her trainers and carried them in her hands. Her feet left faint prints in the sand.

He stopped.

She stopped, too.

At last he removed his sunglasses. 'I haven't been able to stop thinking about you, Lena.'

She met his gaze and at once felt undressed.

She swallowed and thought carefully before she chose her words: 'Why do you say that?'

Valeur looked down and smiled. 'I've been there myself. Once I hit someone I loved. It was a terrible thing to do. I've never suffered so much as I did afterwards, but I learned something, too.'

He started to walk again, without speaking. She stayed a distance of two strides behind him, wary of the heavy man who seemed engrossed in his own thoughts as he walked.

Suddenly he stopped, turned and said in an ice-cold voice: 'What are you doing?'

'Me?'

'I don't like you lagging behind.'

She met his cold eyes and looked away. Around her. The man was on edge, that much was obvious. There were people near by, though. There was nothing to fear, not for the moment. Nevertheless, he had to be pacified. But she had no idea how and chose silence as her strategy. She spotted a plane gliding soundlessly across the sky. Whether it was on its way up or down was impossible to know from this angle.

'I want you to understand this,' Valeur started in a gentler voice. He was standing very close to her now.

Instinctively, she wanted to back away. But she forced herself to stand still.

'I realised I'd neglected myself,' he continued. 'Yes, it sounds strange, I know. I hit a person I love ... and think I've neglected myself. But these were feelings I couldn't control, Lena. I had neglected my therapy. Had neglected to dive down inside myself – analyse *my* tensions, *my* feelings, *my* wounds.'

Lena watched the dry lips moving. Braced herself and met his eyes. They were ice-cold.

Then she understood. His dry lips and face were only a mask. Beneath this façade sat another person looking out at her. And, as if this stranger had understood what she was thinking, the steely gaze departed to leave a face full of reflection and searching.

She couldn't bear the nearness any more and had to walk.

Valeur walked too, still provocatively close to her.

There were a few resolute sun worshippers on blankets in the sand, wearing trunks or bikinis, bathers who didn't want to let the summer's day go until it was over. A little girl was eating a sandwich, shivering under a towel decorated with a portrait of Michael Jackson.

There was no one swimming any longer.

The man's unpleasant proximity was making her sweat. She had to clear her throat to make her voice carry. 'Shall we find a bench and sit down?' she asked, pointing to the path.

When they reached the gravel she had to slow down. The stones were hurting her feet. 'It's such a long time since I've walked barefoot,' she apologised.

Valeur walked right past the closest bench.

Lena hesitated.

He turned and pointed: 'Let's take that one.'

He grabbed her arm.

She tore it free.

They stood sizing each other up. There they were again, the ice-cold eyes, for a tiny second before his face softened and he said: 'Sorry, that was inconsiderate of me.'

She still didn't move. Held eye contact thinking: *this is a public place with witnesses. Relax.*

They started walking again. He didn't say a word. The silence poisoned the air around them; it became so dense and heavy that walking, breathing, became difficult.

They reached the edge of the forest. Valeur rushed towards a bench screened by tall bushes and two rocks.

He was walking two paces in front of her now.

The forest closed around them.

She found the pocket on her bumbag with her right hand, fumbled for the zip slider.

He walked faster. She also increased her speed. Where was the bloody zip?

She stopped, found it and opened the pocket. Her fingers wrapped around the phone.

Valeur turned. They exchanged glances.

He flicked his head. 'Come on!'

She shook her head.

'I said come on!'

She thought to herself: *you keep hold of the phone. You're trained. Nothing can go wrong, and you're near the goal now, very near.*

When he flicked his head a second time she looked down and walked towards him.

'It's frightening,' he said softly, tailing off into a mumble.

'Pardon?'

'It's frightening!' Valeur repeated in a loud, sharp voice, as though he were angry or aggrieved. She searched for his eyes without finding them while his voice continued to grate away. 'It's not the deception that's frightening. Being deceived is one side of the coin, betrayal always weighs heavy, but deep down everyone can see nothing can be done about the betrayal – it's done.'

'You don't need to shout,' Lena said.

'When the person you love deceives you it's not *your* responsibility,' he went on in the same sharp falsetto. 'It's the deceiver who makes the decisions.' She met his gaze. The eyes in the mask had changed character again. She knew she had to get away. As if he automatically sensed what she felt, he moderated his voice and carried on in a gentler pitch: 'Remember the man you want to leave is making his own decisions. But he couldn't have made these without you, Lena. You're part of his decision, the basis of his decision – have you thought about what that means?'

'No.' The hand holding her phone was clammy. She had her hand behind her back and she realised he must have noticed that long ago, but he hadn't made any comment.

Then he stopped and said: 'Now you'll see...'

He knelt down, pushed at a rock and looked up at her.

What is he doing?

His face smiled, but as before it wasn't a smile. It was the cruel stranger who was grinning with the lips of a mask.

'What frightened me about myself was the fury I struggled to control and how I wanted to punish Ragnhild. Well, I've worked on myself for long enough now. Of course, it was a projection. Ragnhild's betrayal was a repetition of my mother's betrayal of me.'

When he stopped talking, there was total silence.

Lena looked around her. They were completely alone in the forest. Grey and white tree trunks muted all sounds. The remains of the day's sunlight penetrated the foliage in narrow strips. Far away, between the trees, she saw the sea and behind it a dark mountainside where the sunshine glinted on windows like stars – as though a piece of sky had fallen to earth.

'Come here, Lena! Come on!'

She backed away from the kneeling figure.

At that second he stood up and yelled: 'What are you doing?'

He rushed towards her.

She spun around to make her escape.

The next second she saw her phone flying through the air as she screamed with pain.

She held her hand.

A white slash mark across the back of it. A stripe that turned red. *He cut me*, she managed to think before her head hit the ground.

The next moment he was pressing something against her face. She wanted to free herself but her body wouldn't obey.

His voice came from a long, long way away.

'I make the decisions now. Do you understand? You do what I tell you!'

44

Gunnarstranda sat in the car waiting for Frølich and the others. With closed eyes, he listened to Bobby Darin singing 'Fly Me to the Moon'. He liked Bobby Darin's version; Tove preferred Sinatra's. She even allowed herself to compare them, never having understood that Darin and Sinatra were two planets on different orbits. Liking one planet didn't mean you had to dislike the other. Gunnarstranda enjoyed both versions, but it was Bobby Darin's voice and drive that succeeded in lifting him into the absolutely timeless zone of complete calm. Consciousness moved with the notes as though following the melody in a weightless state.

Gunnarstranda still had his eyes closed when the locksmith knocked on the window. He gave a start.

*

Frølich turned into Hortengata as two forensic officers were coming through the door.

He jogged up the stairs. A door on the second floor was open.

The waiting room was small – and, not least, different. The interior was expensive. Two big wing chairs either side of a low table with a round top and crooked legs. Probably antique.

Frølich had to try one of the chairs. He sank down in bliss. A footstool shot out from under the seat as he leaned backward. He was unable to resist the temptation to try the stool and lifted both feet. Wonderful.

He had always wanted a chair like this. He would have to remember to ask the psychologist where he had bought it.

The magazines on the little table were *Mental Health* and a pile of well-thumbed comics from the seventies and eighties: *Asterix, Lucky Luke* and *Sprint*. Frølich's favourite was *Sprint*. He loved the unpredictability of the animal with the long tail.

Gunnarstranda poked his head in. 'And what are you doing?'

Frølich dropped the comic he'd picked up as if he had been burned, put his feet on the floor and stood up guiltily.

Valeur's office consisted, apart from the waiting room, of a small kitchen, an even smaller toilet and a big room with a sofa placed opposite a Stressless. Nothing else, no computer, no desk. Frølich went into the kitchen.

When Gunnarstranda received a phone call, Frølich turned and saw a filing cabinet in the corner. Four drawers. He made a beeline for it. The lowest drawer was empty. The next lowest was too. The two top drawers were full of hanging files.

'Leave it to us,' said the forensic officer, who looked up.

Frølich ignored him. He flicked through the files, didn't find what he was looking for and opened the next drawer.

Gunnarstranda put the phone in his pocket. 'Yttergjerde and the others are keeping an eye on the flat in Bærum. Valeur hasn't shown his face.'

Frølich didn't answer.

'But there's one thing I don't like,' Gunnarstranda continued. 'I can't get hold of Lena.'

'So? She's probably at aerobics or the cinema. She's free.'

Gunnarstranda tapped in a number and put the phone to his ear. It rang. He lowered his hand and sighed: 'She's not answering.' In a louder voice he said to the others:

'If Valeur killed Veronika Undset, he did it here. Bård, I want you to examine every wooden joint in the kitchen and toilet. Take off the mouldings and check every millimetre. If there was any blood spilled in this place, we'll find traces of it.'

To Frølich he said: 'Once again, what are you doing?'

Frølich looked up from the filing cabinet. 'Have you never asked yourself why Veronika chose Valeur in particular?'

'Do you know why?'

Frølich waved a patient file from the archive. 'I have an idea. You either choose a psychologist from the *Yellow Pages* or you have one recommended. If Valeur came via recommendation, it must have been through a patient here. That patient must be someone she knew. I have the name of a particular patient here. I think I know why she came here, and by God I think I know who killed her.'

Everyone in the room stopped what they were doing as if on command. They stared at him.

He pulled a face and pressed the file close to his chest. 'Just kidding!'

The men in white overalls snorted, turned away and continued with their work. Frølich motioned to Gunnarstranda.

They went out.

'Who?' Gunnarstranda asked, nodding towards the file Frølich was holding.

'I was going to tell you when you rang,' Frølich said. 'I was with Abid Iqbal. Who do you think we saw pushing cocaine to customers at Mono?'

*

Thirty minutes later Frølich parked a hundred metres from the house. He sat looking through the windscreen.

'So we're agreed, are we?' Gunnarstranda asked.

Frølich nodded and got out of the car. He walked the hundred metres and stopped by the gate. Heavy-metal music was pounding out through the walls. The basement windows were lit and a couple on the ground floor, too. Perhaps Kristoffer was alone at home. Frølich glanced over his shoulder. Gunnarstranda was standing by the car with his hands in his pockets. He nodded. Frølich went to the door and rang the bell. Nothing happened. He rang twice more before Gunnarstranda came through the garden gate. When he rang for the third time the music went quiet.

Frølich didn't want to be seen and stood by the wall at the side of the front door.

Gunnarstranda stood on the doorstep and prepared to play the stupid caller in a coat when he heard the latches of a window being opened.

Someone poked their head out.

It was impossible to make out any facial features. The roof light shone on his head from behind. He heard only the voice:

'What do you want?'

'Is Janne at home?' Gunnarstranda asked.

'No.'

'Are you Janne's boy?' Gunnarstranda asked, stepping backward so that he could be seen.

'Who are you?'

Frølich worked at the door.

Gunnarstranda coughed, and said: 'Hear you go to a psychologist in Tåsen.'

There was silence for a few seconds.

'Someone called Valeur,' Gunnarstranda said.

'Janne isn't at home and I've no idea where she is, so goodbye.'

'The golden goose has laid,' Gunnarstranda said quickly.

'What are you talking about?'

Frølich opened the door – as quietly as he could. A faint creak from a rusty hinge carried across the summer evening.

'The golden goose has laid,' Gunnarstranda repeated. 'You've won the lottery. Did you know?'

'Me? Win the lot—?' The last word disappeared with the boy as Frølich grabbed him.

'Ten years in clink,' Gunnarstranda said, walking towards the front door.

He stood in the doorway watching the boy struggling underneath Frølich. Thin and spindly and unusually angry. The two of them were a rolling tangle of arms and legs. He let them roll over to the wall before striding past, locating the staircase to the basement and going down. He sniffed the air. There was a vague smell of putrefaction. He looked around, digested the sight of the little hall. The concrete floor. A light outline on the concrete where there had once been a rug.

Two doors led into rooms. A large basement sitting room was furnished in adolescent Satan-worship style. Black walls, vampire-themed posters, kitschy figure sixes and a cross hanging upside down. A candle was burning on a low table inside a skull.

He lifted the skull and studied it. The candle tipped over. He blew it out. The skull appeared to be genuine. He banged a knuckle on the skull. *Jesus*, he thought. *What a hobby!*

The second door led into the bathroom. Inside there was an old-fashioned white bathtub on lion feet and an old washbasin on the wall. Blue tiles on the floor, white tiles on the walls.

When Frølich came in, Gunnarstranda was kneeling on the floor trying to lift the drain grille with his penknife. 'So he is alone here,' Frølich said. 'What are you doing?'

'Searching,' Gunnarstranda said. 'Could you go to the kitchen and see if you can find a plate?'

'A plate?'

'Yes, a plate.'

'What about the boy?'

'A plate, Frølich.'

Frølich went.

Gunnarstranda rolled up the sleeve of his right arm and stuck his hand down the drain.

Frølich was soon back with a big white porcelain plate.

From the drain Gunnarstranda pulled up a clump of wet, black gunge.

It reeked.

Frølich wrinkled his nose and grimaced.

Gunnarstranda dug down again. Another clump on the plate. When he stuck his hand down another time he met Frølich's eye and explained: 'If it was Kristoffer who scalded her he did it somewhere the water could run away.'

Gunnarstranda struggled to his feet and studied his catch on the plate. He rinsed his hands, took the biro from his breast pocket and prodded the black gunge with great interest.

'Bård and the others'll probably be a couple of hours at the psychologist's,' Frølich said to fill the silence.

'We don't need Bård,' Gunnarstranda said, straightening his back. Between thumb and index finger he held a tiny object.

'What is it?'

'As Marilyn sings so convincingly, "Diamonds are a girl's best friend". This is the diamond, Frølich. Veronika Undset's missing earring.'

45

A red-hot pain throbbed in her temples. There was something in her mouth and she had to vomit.

'Lie still!'

She obeyed, but had to have some air. She was hyperventilating. Couldn't get enough oxygen. Concentrated: breathe in, out, in, out, in. It was slow, but she was gaining control over her breathing. When the numb feeling in her skin went she could feel his hands over her body. It wasn't cloth she had in her mouth. It was a clump of sand and blood. She spat, opened her eyes. Tried to pull her legs from underneath her.

It was only now she noticed. She wasn't dressed. He had taken off her running gear.

'Don't look.'

She turned her head from where she heard his voice.

'Don't look, I said!'

The pain stung as the blow hit home. She fell back on her side. Barely aware that he was kicking her. Groaned only when all the air was forced out of her body. Her stomach and side were numb.

Breathed in … out … in … out.

She rolled onto her stomach and again tried to get up.

'Are you deaf or what? Don't look!'

This time she couldn't restrain an outburst and screamed with pain. Her back was ablaze. *What is he hitting me with?*

'Shut up, lie still and keep your eyes closed.'

Her left leg was trapped.

She jerked it. Metal against her ankle. He was tying her up. *He is not going to get his way.*

'Do you think I bought that story about the victim of abuse? Don't you think I know who you are? There's a picture of you in the paper, girl. Welcome to reality, Lena. Now you'll have to play with the bad boy in the class. Don't look, I told you!'

She passed out for a few seconds. When she came to her mouth was full of blood again. She was rolled over onto her stomach. She spat. Her left leg was still trapped. The weight of his body pressed down on her other calf.

Then she felt a hand between her thighs, hard fingers with nails that scratched. She wriggled like a snake. The pain burned and she screamed involuntarily as he shoved his fingers inside. *The bastard.*

She got more sand in her eyes. She thought: *don't lie still. If he moves I can free my leg. If he wants more he will* have *to move.*

The pain paralysed her groin and abdomen. But she didn't want to scream.

I'm stronger. I'm in better shape.

His weight shifted. It became more difficult to turn, harder to resist.

'That's the way, that's the way, theeeere we are …'

There. The weight of his body was gone. *Now or never!*

As quick as lightning, she rolled onto the leg that was trapped. Gathered all her strength in the foot that was free.

Missed.

As quick as lightning, she pulled back her foot.

She saw the outline of a figure, the body towering over her, big and naked.

She thrust out her foot.

Bullseye.

Her heel hit him smack in the crotch. He folded up and fell forward. She watched the fall as if in slow motion. Her free foot was a steel spring, retracted and shot out again. He hit his face on the way down. His head jerked back and up. There was a crunch. His head, arms and legs hit the ground like a corpse. He lay there, motionless. For a few seconds she thought she had killed him. No. Blood and slime were running from his mouth. His head moved. Blood between his teeth. He tried to struggle up onto all fours. *He is not going to get up again.* She kicked again and again. Lay on her side, still with one leg tied while the other foot kicked hard and rhythmically like a motorised sledgehammer. When he was quite still she started punching him. She hit him systematically, without stopping, as if this were her job. It wasn't the man she was hitting. She was hammering pain and frailty out of her body and consciousness, punishing herself and her lack of willpower. In the end she didn't hit to punish, she hit like a smithy over an anvil, to strengthen her spine. His body lay unmoving on the ground receiving blow after blow. She hit out until she was completely exhausted and lay on her stomach gasping for air. Until she could barely lift her hand.

When she had to rest the pains came. In her hand, foot, lower abdomen. She sat up. Her ankle was bleeding. He had tied her foot with wire. She loosened it. Crawled over his body, pressed her ear to the naked back and listened. His heart was beating. He was breathing. There was a gurgling noise. She twisted his head to the side. Grabbed his tongue to free the airway.

She crawled over to a rock, sat down on it and stared at the bundle of a man lying in front of her.

No light between the trees, but she could hear the sea. She got her bearings. Her clothes lay beside the rock, along with his.

He whimpered.

She jumped up. No. He was lying still.

She felt faint and nauseous. She sank to her knees, got up onto all fours and swallowed until the nausea went. Noticed the wound on the back of her hand was no longer bleeding. She remembered the pain, the mobile phone flying through the air. He must have had a knife hidden somewhere when he was kneeling. Where was it now?

She pulled the pile of clothes to her and dressed. Stared at the sleeve, the spattered blood. She ran her hand under her nose. More blood. She didn't care, searched his pockets, found the car keys and the knife. It was small. An open penknife with a blue steel blade. She weighed the knife in her hand. Eventually put it in her bumbag.

Afterwards she scrabbled around, still on all fours, looking for her phone – it looked too like a flat stone. She picked it up. Five unanswered calls, all from Gunnarstranda.

She put the phone in her pocket and walked back to the man lying motionless on the ground.

She picked up the wire he had used on her foot and stood with it in her hand thinking.

46

It was ten past four in the morning when Frank Frølich lifted the phone in the duty officer's room from its cradle and rang the home number of his friend Karl Anders Fransgård.

Frølich hadn't slept for more than twenty-four hours, but he wasn't tired. Adrenalin was coursing through his veins. He counted eight long rings before Karl Anders took the phone.

'Hi, KA. Frankie here. Can I talk to Janne?'

'Eh?'

Frølich couldn't be bothered to repeat himself.

Karl Anders stuttered a few vacuous phrases. There was the rustle of duvet and a whisper from the other end: 'It's for you.'

'Me?'

Karl Anders, somewhat impatient: 'Yes, it's Frankie. He's asking for you.'

'Hello?' The voice was alert – a good sign.

'Hi, Janne, I'm ringing because I know you a little,' Frølich said. 'At any rate I think I do. Listen, your son, Kristoffer, has been arrested. He's in custody. He's going to be charged with the murder of Veronika Undset. I can't say with any certainty whether that'll be the only charge.'

He paused to let her speak, but he wasn't interrupted. The line was still. He carried on: 'Kristoffer has reached the age of majority, which means that we in the police don't need to contact relatives. You won't be informed officially and you won't be able to make any demands or do anything else on behalf of your son. You have no visiting rights, either. On the other hand, you might be granted a visit if you come here now.'

Janne Smith was breathing heavily. Frølich let the silence continue to allow her to speak, but she didn't say a word.

'Come here now,' he repeated, in case she hadn't understood the first time.

Still silence.

'Kristoffer will be in custody at the station until his case comes up before the judge tomorrow,' Frølich went on. 'The police will ask for custody for four weeks with no rights to post or visitors. If the police request is granted, you won't be allowed to see him for four weeks – at least.'

He drew breath. Waited for a few seconds. Not a murmur.

'Incidentally, I failed to mention that your house is being examined by forensic officers at this moment. They will provide a warrant showing that they're entitled to do this if you ask them. They'll probably have finished by tomorrow morning.'

He fell silent again.

Waited.

There was a clatter as she put down the phone and broke off communication.

Frølich sat looking at the dead phone.

'What did she say?' Gunnarstranda asked.

Frølich swivelled back and forth.

'Well,' Gunnarstranda said impatiently, 'What did she say?'

'She's coming here now. She said that in this difficult situation the only thing she can do is give her son all the support she can muster,' Frølich answered, and got up.

47

It was in the brief period in the middle of the midsummer night, when it is actually dark, that the duty officer decided to take action after receiving an anonymous tip-off.

Two officers driving slowly between the shops in Karenslyst were instructed to head for Kongsskogen Forest, Bygdøy.

The squad car shot across the roundabout before Bygdøy. They had the road to themselves, accelerated up the hills to the royal estate of Kongsgården and passed it at great speed. As the driver turned off, the blue light shone against the deserted houses of the Folkemuseet and was reflected in black windows. The driver braked over the speed bumps, the full beam was lost in the darkness between the trees, then it shone across the road again and caught the yellow eyes of a solitary cat crouched at the edge of the road.

'Kongsskogen is pretty big,' the driver said.

The other officer didn't answer. Everyone knew the forest was big.

The driver turned into the car park, which was as deserted as the road they had just driven down. He stopped at the end and left the lights on. The cones of light from the headlamps picked out some tree trunks and became weaker as they went deeper. The two of them sat for some very long seconds staring silently into the darkness. It was the driver who broke the silence.

'I can't see anything, not a car, not a soul.'

The other officer didn't answer. It wasn't necessary. He couldn't see anything either.

The driver reported back over the radio that it must have been a false alarm.

'Are you in the car?' the duty officer asked.

The two of them exchanged glances. The driver said yes.

'Get out then! Start searching!'

When the driver opened the door the interior light came on. The officers saw their reflections in the windscreen.

Both hesitated. But in the end they grabbed torches and got out of the car. They trained together. Both hated losing when they competed against each other, whether it was in skiing, swimming or squash. Neither of them wished to articulate their anxiety or reservations. Neither of them wished to articulate the unease they both felt at stepping into the darkness. So they walked in silence, striding across the grass, each shining a torch. They maintained a distance of thirty metres between them.

Two torchlights shone between the trees. Neither of the men said a word. Neither of them wanted to reveal their nerves. For Christ's sake, this was a search. This was *routine* work.

The driver glanced to the right as his friend's torchlight came to a stop. He stopped too. He listened. He heard nothing. He said: 'Steffen, what's up?'

He received no answer.

At that moment his friend's torch went out.

The driver shone his own torch on where he had last seen the light. And saw only bushes and tree trunks.

A chill froze his spine. A claw took hold of his stomach. He breathed through an open mouth and forced himself to walk towards the place where his friend ought to have been.

The torchlight moved with the rhythm of his steps. The ground, the sky, the ground, the sky. He stopped, swivelled round a hundred and eighty degrees with the torch at a right angle to his body. Then the beam passed a face. 'Is that you?' he shouted, moving the torch to find the face. But there was no one there. *What the hell is this?*

'Steffen!' he yelled.

'Shh! Switch off your torch!'

It was Steffen's voice, but it came from somewhere behind him. The driver switched off his torch and saw a silhouette of his colleague in the darkness. 'I saw someone,' he hissed.

'Where?'

'Over there.' He shone the torch on the black trees.

'No,' Steffen whispered. 'The sound comes from over there.' He shone his torch in the other direction. 'Be quiet and listen.'

Then the driver heard running footsteps.

He switched on the torch.

A shadow flitted between the trees.

'Stop!' he shouted, setting off after the figure.

He ran with the torch beam flickering across the ground, the forest and the sky. His speed increased and he could hear someone panting. Heard running feet mixed with the sound of his own strides. Closer, closer…

At that moment his foot got entangled in something. He fell, his shoulder hit the ground and he rolled twice before his head thudded against the ground and the air was knocked out of his lungs. But he didn't feel it. All he thought about was the torch. He dropped it. He saw the light hovering before the torch hit the ground and rolled across the grass. It lay still, lighting up a triangle of grass a few metres away.

He crawled on all fours. Made a grab for it. It rose in the air. Someone lifted it up and turned it off.

It was pitch black. He said: 'Give me the torch.'

No answer. Then he was blinded by the light from the same torch. He yelled: 'Turn it off.'

The light went out.

The driver held his breath. It was utterly still. Not a sound to be heard. 'Steffen!' he screamed. 'Over here!'

'Where?' said a familiar voice. But it came from somewhere further away.

'Someone's taken my torch,' the driver shouted.

'Who?'

The driver didn't answer. He followed the movement of his friend's torch beam. It found a figure lying on the ground. A man with no clothes on. He was lying on his stomach.

The driver knelt down beside the man. 'Shine your torch here.'

The beam swept over the body. It bore clear signs of physical violence. The eyes were gummed up. The man was bleeding from the mouth and nose and there was severe bruising down his side, on his neck and over his face.

Steffen knelt down beside him.

'Whoever did this is close at hand,' the driver whispered. 'I dropped my torch. He took it.'

Steffen didn't answer. He shone his torch on a pile of clothes beside the lifeless man.

The pile consisted of rolled-up brown chinos, a checked flannel shirt and a light-coloured jacket.

The two officers stood up.

Steffen switched off his torch.

The summer night's dark hour was over. The grey feelers of a new day groped through the branches. The frugal light shrouded the outline of the man on the ground.

The driver lifted the jacket from the bundle of clothes. He rummaged through the pockets. Found a driving licence belonging to someone by the name of Erik Valeur. The driver knelt down. Despite the swellings to the man's face he was able to identify him as the owner of the licence.

'He's alive,' the driver said. 'We need an ambulance,' he added, studying the surroundings which were gradually revealed as the morning mist settled. Whoever had taken the torch was nowhere to be seen.

Steffen set off towards the car.

'The time is 05.30. Inspector Gunnarstranda is taking Janne Smith's statement.'

Gunnarstranda sat down on the chair and smiled at the woman sitting opposite him.

She looked back at him without saying anything.

'The police wish to take a statement from you because you're the best person to confirm or deny the recent activities of your son. You can start by telling us what you were doing and where you were on the day Veronika Undset was killed.'

The woman stared back at him in mute apathy.

'Janne Smith. Is that your name?'

She didn't answer.

'You're remaining silent. Does this mean you don't wish to make a statement?'

The woman was still silent, her gaze expressionless.

Gunnarstranda coughed and leaned across the table. 'We've spoken at length to your son – Kristoffer. He's given a statement which tallies to a significant degree with the facts and forensic evidence we have. Let me tell you what we've found so that you can stop me and adjust details as we go, OK?'

Janne Smith watched him without opening her mouth.

'At six a.m. on Saturday, 4 July Veronika was arrested outside her house,' Gunnarstranda started. 'She was arrested by Frank Frølich for being in possession of five grams of cocaine. She was fined, but only accepted the offence with great reservations. She claimed the drugs were not hers and she had no idea how they'd ended up in her bag. Do you know this story?'

The woman didn't answer.

'The next evening,' Gunnarstranda continued, 'still Saturday, 4 July, Karl Anders Fransgård had a party. Frølich was invited and you, as far as I'm informed, sat next to him. I'm sure you understand that the meeting between Frølich and Veronika was significant for both of them. It was less than twelve hours since they had parted company at the police station.

'After the party was over and all the guests had gone – when Veronika and her fiancé were alone in the room – she told him about the incident that morning when his friend Frølich had arrested her. She said it so that Fransgård would have the correct version from her, in other words, hear the truth from her lips before he was perhaps delivered a twisted version from Frølich. She also told him about the confiscation of the cocaine, but left out one important detail. The truth was that Veronika knew who really owned the drugs. The reason for this was that they were hidden in a gilt Zippo lighter which she recognised. It belongs to your son.'

'Kristoffer doesn't take drugs,' Janne Smith stated.

Gunnarstranda sent her a smile. He omitted to draw attention to the fact that she had broken her silence, choosing instead to comment:

'He may not, but Kristoffer deals in drugs even if he doesn't take them himself. He has, for example, been observed by undercover detectives selling drugs to others. He hangs around outside pubs and clubs. He's too young to be let in, but he has an understanding with some of the doormen. He's also been arrested on one occasion with eight doses of cocaine hidden in a Zippo ... did you know that?'

Janne Smith didn't answer.

'Well, our interest concerns Veronika Undset's last hours. Her confession to Karl Anders Fransgård on Saturday night ended in a quarrel. When he heard his fiancée was involved with drugs his conclusion was clear: he didn't want to have anything to do with her any more. He was frustrated and considered that she was leading a double life; she had secrets she wasn't sharing with him. The question he asked himself, and her, was: could he love, could he marry a woman who had so many sinister secrets? This frustration with his life and love led him to ring you on Sunday evening, didn't it?'

Janne Smith was silent. She interlaced her fingers and focused on Gunnarstranda.

'On Monday Veronika decided to have a showdown with your son. She knew where the lighter came from. She knew Kristoffer was a cocaine dealer. She'd seen him in action in town. She rang your son to meet him, but he refused to talk to her. She rang him no fewer than three times. In the end she made up her mind to visit him without making any previous arrangement.

'You'd gone to see Karl Anders Fransgård at his house. While you were with him Veronika Undset went to your house in Høvik. The door was opened by Kristoffer. He said you were out. She said that made no difference. It was him she wanted to speak to, not you. This was inconvenient for your son because at that moment he was busy packing and sorting doses to sell in town. But Veronika insisted and barged her way into the house. He wanted to take her upstairs to the sitting room, but she went downstairs, to his room. She was furious, you see. She confronted him over the lighter and the drugs and accused him of being selfish and thoughtless. She wanted to know why he'd put the lighter in her bag that Friday night. He told her it'd all been an accident.

'The previous Friday he'd come home after a trip to the city centre. One of our undercover officers, Abid Iqbal, had been watching your son for a long time and, as I said, had arrested him on one occasion. When Kristoffer saw him outside Cosmopolite he decided to lie low and went home. It was past midnight when he got back that Friday. Veronika and you were in the kitchen. A police car drove past the house before Kristoffer went in. The same car drove past another time when he was indoors. Kristoffer feared a police raid was in the offing. So he slipped the lighter into Veronika's shoulder bag. Assuming it wouldn't occur to the police to search his mother or his mother's friend. There was no raid that Friday evening and Kristoffer was thinking about retrieving his lighter, but Veronika had left with her bag before he could make a move. Then someone rang him, which the caller confirmed in his statement.'

Gunnarstranda paused.

Janne Smith was playing with her fingers, still with her mouth pinched shut.

'Your son's explanation of how his lighter ended up in her bag didn't improve Veronika's mood. She was very upset that Monday evening. She was under pressure herself, not least from the crisis in the relationship with her fiancé. She felt your son's selfishness and thoughtlessness were turning her life upside down. Veronika accused your son of intentionally wanting to destroy her relationship with Karl Anders Fransgård. She claimed that, you, his mother, were in love with him. In general, she said a lot of unpleasant things that angered your son.'

Gunnarstranda paused.

Janne Smith was staring at the table.

'The Monday evening when Veronika went to sort out your son she wouldn't accept any excuses from Kristoffer. She went to take out her anger on him and explain to him what the consequences of his self-centred behaviour were for others. She got nowhere. Your son wasn't interested in listening to her. After all, what could he do? The damage was done, and you can't turn back the clock. Veronika worked herself up into a fury, grabbed the drugs on the table, swept them onto the floor and stamped on them. She ended up chasing your son out of the room. In the corridor outside his bedroom they started fighting. Your son was holding a knife, which he sometimes used to chop up the cocaine. Kristoffer has told us it was a Stanley knife, which fits with the conclusions in our pathologist's autopsy report. Your son stabbed Veronika in the chest a number of times, until she shut up, as he put it.'

Gunnarstranda took a deep breath.

Janne Smith sat with her eyes closed, not moving.

'Would you like to continue the story from here?' he asked.

She didn't stir, as though she hadn't heard the question.

'Well,' Gunnarstranda said, 'then I'll go on with what your son said.

According to Kristoffer, he sat on the floor looking at Veronika's dead body. He also prayed to God. He had no idea what to do and cried most of the time. When you came home he was desperate and told you what had happened. In his statement to us he says that you two, on your initiative, carried Veronika into the bathroom in the cellar. There, between you, you undressed the body and put the blood-stained clothes in a carrier bag. He says you later poured several kettles of boiling-hot water over her stomach and nether regions, then rolled her up in some plastic you fetched from the garage. You taped up the package, carried the body into the garage together and put it in the boot of your car. You drove through the town until you found a conveniently placed skip to throw the body in. Afterwards you threw her clothes in a container for second-hand clothes – marked Unicef.

'According to Kristoffer, you then drove to Veronika's office. You let yourselves in with her keys. You checked the display on the office phone and saw she had rung your son's mobile several times earlier in the day. You took the phone with you. Your son's statement tallies with other statements and with what forensic officers found.'

Gunnarstranda lifted a blood-stained plastic bag onto the table. It was open. 'Among other things, this carrier bag,' he continued. 'It contains Veronika's clothes. The bag was seized by an officer who was shown the whereabouts of the container by Kristoffer last night. Your son's been charged with the wilful murder of Veronika Undset. The charge is based on a confession and a great deal of forensic evidence. Let me ask you now: is your son's description of your actions the complete truth?'

Janne Smith didn't react.

Gunnarstranda waited. It was so quiet in the interview room that he could hear himself swallow. At length he cleared his throat and said: 'Did you understand the question I asked?'

The woman was as motionless as before, staring at the table.

'Janne Smith. You'll be charged as an accessory to the wilful murder of Veronika Undset. At this juncture the police consider it was your son's actions that led to Veronika Undset's death, but you actively helped to hide the crime. It was your intention to obstruct the police investigation. You will also be charged with defiling a dead person's body. You scalded Veronika Undset's body so that police would think she'd been raped and killed by someone trying to hide the crime and their identity. Do you understand what I'm saying to you, yes or no?'

Janne Smith raised her head and looked at him through glazed eyes.

'Do you understand what will happen to you now? You'll be charged, arrested and held in custody.'

She nodded.

'I have one minor request,' Gunnarstranda said.

*

Janne Smith sat hunched with her forearms pressing against the table.

The picture on the TV captured both figures in the interview room. The camera was positioned at the corner of the ceiling to encompass both from above.

Kristoffer Smith sat in front of the screen with his eyes fixed on his mother and the policeman. He hadn't moved, either.

Frank Frølich leaned against the door and saw only Kristoffer's long hair resting against his thin, narrow back.

Frølich had no idea what to think, about the boy's back or anything else. He was inexpressibly tired, but looking at the TV screen gave him a sort of energy.

From the speakers beside the screen came a cough from Janne Smith. 'There's no point,' she said.

'Wouldn't you like to hear what I have to say first?'

'A request. What sort of request?'

'I'd like you to correct the summary of events you've just heard.'

'I don't understand what you mean.'

'I think you do, but it's your decision.'

The silence hung in the air of the interview room.

'What do you mean?' she asked.

'I would like you, for your own and for your son's sake, to correct the summary of events you've just heard.'

Frølich shifted position. Kristoffer Smith didn't move, his eyes focused on the screen.

At last Janne Smith cleared her throat. 'It's true we carried her into the bathroom, but I undressed her.'

'And your son?'

'I told him to go and boil some water.'

'And did he?'

'Yes.'

'And?'

'Nothing else.'

Gunnarstranda straightened his back. 'As I said, it's your decision.'

'What do you mean?'

'Tell me what happened when Kristoffer left the room?'

'Nothing happened.'

'You may as well tell me now,' Gunnarstranda said.

Her head still bowed, she didn't answer.

'Your son's statement is missing one essential detail which the prosecution and the judge will grind away at,' Gunnarstranda said. 'They won't leave it alone.'

'What?'

'You tell me – you know best.'

She raised her head. The two faces on the screen regarded each other at some length. Not a sound was heard. Finally, Janne cleared her throat and said: 'She stirred. Veronika, that is.'

Kristoffer Smith stood up. Frølich braced himself.

'She wasn't dead. After Kristoffer had left, she started whimpering. That plastic bag...' Janne Smith pointed to the bag of clothes on the table. 'It was in the corridor. I got it and put it over her head. Then I went to the garage and fetched a spade.'

Kristoffer slumped down onto the chair and turned to Frølich. The latter returned his gaze. 'Can you switch it off?' he said.

Frølich didn't answer. He wanted to know what happened.

'I kept hitting the bag until I was sure Veronika was dead.'

'But you didn't tell your son any of this?'

'No.'

'What did you do with her earring?'

Frølich never heard the answer. At that moment Kristoffer Smith was heading for the door.

49

She was sitting on the steps outside his door, asleep. Her head against the wall, her knees against the balustrade.

He looked at his watch. It would soon be seven in the morning. Five hours to the court session.

He bent down and placed a hand on her shoulder.

She gave a start and said: 'I fell asleep.'

'Did you come for your glasses?'

She shook her head.

He unlocked the door. Pushed it open. 'May I use the bathroom?' she whispered.

He nodded and waited in the sitting room until she returned.

'What is it?' he asked.

She hesitated. 'Can I sleep here?'

He realised this wasn't the right moment to hassle her, and said: 'I've only got a sofa. Well, you take the bed and I'll sleep on the sofa. I have to get up early tomorrow.' He looked at his watch. 'For tomorrow, read today.'

'Do you mean that?'

He nodded. Opened the bedroom door. 'It's absolutely fine, take the bed. I don't feel like changing the bedclothes, but if it's important, you'll find fresh bedding in the cupboard.' He opened the cupboard, took out a sleeping bag and was on his way back to the sitting room when she grabbed his hand. 'Stay here a little,' she said. 'Just for a little.'

They lay down on the duvet, both fully dressed. Her hair tickled and he shifted his head. Closed his eyes.

Frølich woke to bright rays of sunshine through the window. Sat up and drew the curtains fully. Looked at his watch. It was nine. Two more hours of sleep, he thought, minimum. He turned and met Iselin's eyes.

'It was the sun. Woke me up.'

He lay on his back and closed his eyes. Feeling her gaze on him. In the end he opened his eyes and looked straight into her face.

'Andreas is dead,' she whispered.

He stretched out his arm so that she could rest her head on it.

'He rang me, woke me up, it was two in the morning. He was driving. He told me what he'd decided to do. I told him not to. I think he put the phone on the seat so that I would hear the crash.'

Tears ran from her eyes down his arm.

Frølich pulled her closer. Her hair smelled of herb shampoo.

'It was out of town, on the R4. He crashed into a juggernaut,' she said. 'Rune, you met him, is a doctor in Akershus. He told me Andreas died on the way to hospital.'

Frank Frølich said nothing. There was nothing to say.

50

The heatwave was over. On the third day the rain fell from the heavens. Drops of water on windowpanes consumed each other and became streams. The rain formed puddles on the ground, which grew, extending into the lawns which were already saturated. Worms were forced to the surface where they tried in vain to flee, but were eaten by pitiless thrushes and white wagtails or just drowned in one of the puddles. The water gushed down kerbsides, widened as it met cascades from downpipes, found its way to manhole covers and drain grilles. Here and there, the drains couldn't cope. The water collected to form lakes in hollows and dips in the roads. Firefighters and water-company employees did what they could to clear the drains. Thunder and lightning knocked out substations and parts of the town were without electricity and in darkness.

Windscreen wipers bustled to and fro, to and fro. Frølich received a call from Gunnarstranda while he was driving. The old sourpuss wanted to talk about the Sivert Almeli case. It had been established that neither Valeur nor the Smiths had killed the man. Gunnarstranda was now busily examining Almeli's photos again, to see them with fresh eyes. He had some ideas he wanted to discuss.

Frølich looked at his watch. This wasn't a convenient moment. He had other issues to sort out – not least his resolution to reconnect severed bonds of friendship. It was pretty late already. Tersely, he said he would be back at work the following morning. He rang off and continued through the driving rain, south along Oslo Fjord, past the Sjursøya peninsula. Had to stop for traffic lights in the dip by Nedre

Bekkelaget and then turned off into Bekkelaget Harbour. To the left, towering cranes were lifting containers from piles that looked like toy building blocks. Frølich stopped the car in front of a white gate, buzzed the window down and surveyed the post with a panel of buttons. He noticed a camera mounted over the gate. Again he looked at his watch. The problem was that it was past office hours now. Should he ring? He decided not to and prepared to follow the instructions under the buttons. Then, without any warning, the gate slid open.

He waved to the camera, drove to the office building and parked in front. It was a two-storey brick construction. The windows were unlit. He sat in the car, unsure what to do. Outside, the rain was like a wall of water. On the ground, it flowed in torrents.

Then his nose detected a foul stench.

If you can divide smells into various layers, he thought, the way sounds can be divided into frequencies, this had to be the higher acoustic level of sewage – the one that warns you of the proximity of something you won't like.

Still in the car, with an involuntary grimace on his face, he took the key from the ignition and looked around for a yellowish-green mist or cloud hanging over the area, or at least a quivering in the atmosphere, some manifestation of this subterranean, anal bouquet that seeped in through parts of the car that weren't airtight, wrapping itself around every molecule of air, turning the ether into gas that filled both nostrils, progressed into the body and attacked the digestive tract, where it created an urge to throw up. But what he saw was the same as everywhere else in Oslo – clear air, thick with torrential rain.

The stench must have been caused by all the rain, he mused. Normally there wasn't this smell. The deluge over several days must have put the system under pressure.

There was a glimpse of blue over Ekeberg Ridge. Another peal of thunder rolled across. Frølich opened the car door and ran under the roof. The glass door in the entrance was locked.

Where was Karl Anders? He peered inside and caught sight of a staircase. Then he saw the Post-it. On the door handle.

I'm in the tunnel. KA.

Frølich undid his jacket, pulled it over his head and sprinted across the road that curved into the rock face. He was drenched in less than a minute, but it was too late to turn back. The tunnel opening was closer. His jeans were stuck to his thighs. He ran past two immense pipes more than a metre each in diameter. The pipes ended in the opening. He entered the tunnel. Stood gasping for breath. The two pipes roared like jet engines. They must have been part of the ventilation system. The stench had got stronger. Frølich continued up the incline leading into the mountain. The tunnel was as wide as a country road. The rock ceiling arched high above him. Water dripped from invisible holes in the blasted rock. The lighting became dimmer the further he went. Soon the road forked. Where could Karl Anders be?

A faint drone came from the tunnel on the left. The lighting there was better. He walked slowly inside and up the slope. At the top this road also forked. A narrower road had been blasted out to the right. Steep and dark, it led further into the mountain. Frølich chose the light and the downward slope. Rounding a bend, he saw a car he recognised. The road culminated in a large turning area. Karl Anders had parked his Volvo here.

He walked down the slope and came to a halt. Had to force himself not to back away. The smell was indescribable. It infiltrated both his nostrils. The air was so dense and foul it was almost impossible to move. Frankie held his breath. He kept swallowing.

An industrial plant extended deep into the mountain chamber. The tanks were covered with aluminium lids separated by bridges of mesh metal. From over by the rock face came the drone of enormous quantities of liquid being stirred by rotating screws and mysterious valves which splashed and thrashed under the metal cladding.

A movement from deep in the chamber revealed the presence of Karl Anders. He looked like a diver. Dressed in a yellow all-in-one rubber outfit with two diving cylinders on his back and a helmet with a headlight. He was standing on a platform and hosing himself down with clean water from a pipe that ran along the railing of one bridge.

Frølich waved to him and clambered up. There were green stripes of slime down Karl Anders's outfit and black stains on his face.

'Find what you were looking for?' Frølich asked, but could hear the joke fell flat.

Karl Anders sent him a chilly glare. He turned off the tap and unhitched the diving cylinders. 'Oslo has half a million inhabitants who go to the toilet and flush with water. They also have showers, up to several times a day, they wash the dishes, clothes, cars. And we haven't seen the like of the quantities of rain coming down now for years. Drainage, Frankie, when it comes to the crunch, is a question of logistics. Drainage is my profession. For me, this isn't about sewage but the art of engineering. There are two thousand two hundred kilometres of piping in this town. Two thousand two hundred kilometres. That's the length of Norway. We've programmed every single centimetre of piping into computer systems that make this structure quite unique. Think about it. Paris, New York and London have high levels of population, but the towns are flat. Oslo's a pot. We're talking falls and angles that cannot be compared with anywhere else in the world. We have computer systems that can simulate the effect of leaks from and into the pipes of any proportion you care to mention. The plant we have here can easily cope with the record downpours outside. This plant can turn your and my own personal shit into nearly pure water, which is transported into the Oslo Fjord at a depth of fifty metres. Before long we will have bathing-quality water in Bjørvika. The remaining sludge will be ploughed into the land as organic compost.

'What you're wrinkling your nose up at is fed into and treated by systems which lead the international community. Did you know, for example, that we're developing technology to reclaim biogas? Before very long the gas from your personal excreta will be helping to run more than a hundred gas-driven buses in Oslo. But you aren't interested in that, are you, Frankie? You've never been interested in anything apart from yourself. What do you want?'

'To talk.'

Without saying another word, Karl Anders turned his back on him and marched away.

Frølich followed. 'Surely you have time to answer a couple of questions?'

Karl Anders stopped and turned. Now they had an open tank on each side. Frølich looked down. The liquid in them was an unappetising greenish-brown.

'A couple of questions,' Karl Anders aped. 'You've destroyed my life, Frankie. The most stupid thing I ever did was to contact you after all these years. You came storming in and now I have nothing left.'

He turned his back again and marched off.

'And what do you mean by that?' Frølich shouted.

'What do I mean? Don't you understand anything? If you'd believed Veronika, none of this nastiness would have happened. You would've come to the party and met Veronika as a normal guy. She would be alive now.'

Karl Anders jumped down from the platform and continued with Frølich hard on his heels. They turned right and came into another mountain chamber. Here there was total silence. The water flowed into huge tanks like artificial lakes. The air was damp and cold, but there was very little smell. The enormous chamber was dimly lit by a few yellow floodlights on the wall. The water was reminiscent of quiet ponds in the moonlight, and beneath them you could hear the running of a stream.

'Veronika visited Kristoffer because she knew the boy and cared about him,' Frølich said to his friend's back. 'She was completely loyal. She knew who owned the cocaine when I searched her bag, but she kept her mouth shut. She kept her mouth shut to you as well. It was chance that she met me with the lighter in her bag. That sort of thing can happen any day – the Metro's two minutes late and you meet a stranger on the platform, you might even marry them. Life's full of such chance encounters. They're sprung on us all the time; we can't get away from them. What is significant is that Veronika decided to meet Kristoffer alone to clear the air. That is honest and fair. The person to blame is Kristoffer. He put the lighter in her bag, he stabbed her. I had nothing to do with that.'

'If you'd decided to let her go instead of arresting her that morning, none of this would've happened!' Karl Anders retorted. 'Veronika would've found the lighter in her bag and given it back to Kristoffer, and that would've been the end of it. Have you considered that?'

Karl Anders didn't wait for an answer: 'I don't think you've given this a thought. It would never occur to you to think a self-critical thought.'

He grabbed a long steel pole, which he rested on his shoulder. He walked back past Frølich. They trudged, one after the other, back to the noise and the stench.

They kept close to the rock face, walking across vibrating metal surfaces, until Karl Anders stopped. Without a word, he lifted a huge lid. It was hard to move. When the lid was free, a brownish-green liquid slopped over the metal. Frølich jumped back against the railing, but not quickly enough. The sewage went over his trainers.

Karl Anders grinned and shouted something over the noise. Frølich couldn't hear what it was. Karl Anders lowered his rubber-clad body into the sewage. He stood up to his waist prodding with the pole.

'Veronika didn't go to Kristoffer's to give him up to the police,' Frølich shouted. 'She kept mum about him, that's the whole point. She was loyal. But you weren't. When Veronika went to Kristoffer's house to have it out with him, you took his mother to yours. All that happened between you and Veronika was that she told you I'd given her a fine. That was all it took for you to desert her!'

Karl Anders shouted something back, but the din from the intake pipe drowned his words.

'What did you say?'

'I didn't desert her!' yelled Karl Anders over the noise.

'No? What do you think would've happened if Janne had been at home instead of in your bed when Veronika went over that night? Would she have ended up taking Veronika's life? Hardly. But it's stupid to think like that. Getting bogged down in hypotheses is a waste of time.'

'Nothing would've happened if you'd done things differently. Can't you get that into your head, Frankie? All your bad sides are still there. You destroy whatever you meet, you walk all over other people's property in your big boots, you trample them to pieces, you sneak around, you spy on people and stick your nose into their private matters. Now you've ruined my life. I don't want anything to do with you.'

Something was happening in the tank. A bang followed by an immensely protracted slurp echoed around the mountain chamber, and the dirty water ran away. Karl Anders climbed up and slid the top back into position.

'Do you know that people are fascinated by sewage, Frankie? People are wild about wading through shit. We arrange tours and call it the Sewage Safari. There are queues of people wanting to wade in the muck slopping about in the channels under Bankplassen. Businesses arrange guided tours in this plant. And women show the most interest. I give talks to attractive young women about the engineering behind sewage. They sit patiently listening until I've finished because they have so many questions they want to ask about shit. They're like children in the nursery playing doctors and nurses. They giggle and are overjoyed to be in a place where you can say bad words that are normally taboo. These evenings are every man's dream, Frankie. Is there any better pick-up spot? The girls squeal with delight when I tell them I put on my rubber outfit and wade up to my shoulders in the muck just because some ditz has thrown tampons down the toilet. They love hearing that. They tell me their own sinful secrets. But most of all they want to see the shit with their own eyes. Isn't it fascinating how beauty is always attracted to ugliness?'

Karl Anders spun around and walked right up to Frølich. 'But you're not interested in this. Say what you came here to say.'

'I have a beer can on the mantelpiece at home,' Frølich said. 'You left it when you came to visit me. Do you remember?'

Karl Anders didn't dignify him with an answer. He walked off. Frølich followed. They approached the opening to the chamber with the quiet water.

'You said you were with Janne when Veronika was killed. I asked her, but she lied. Janne betrayed you, Karl Anders. She lied to give herself and her son an alibi. That's why you were hauled in.'

'What's the beer can got to do with this?'

Karl Anders walked towards the wall.

'I've kept it. The point is that Veronika had a neighbour who was obsessed with her. You know the guy I'm talking about because it was you who gave us the tip-off. He photographed Veronika in secret. He kept an eye on her and followed her everywhere. The day after you were released he was murdered.'

The light went out.

Everything was thrown into total darkness. Frølich blinked in an attempt to remove the reflection of light from his retina.

Slowly his eyes adapted.

Frølich groped his way to the railing. 'Where are you?' he called out. 'Here.'

Frølich turned around. He saw nothing. The voice could as easily have come from above as behind him.

'Where?'

Karl Anders's hollow laughter rang out from goodness knows where. 'Yes, I know about the slimeball neighbour. He took pictures of Veronika and me while we were making love. Just imagine! I wanted to marry her! She knew, Frankie. She let me fuck her with the curtains open knowing the poor sod was sitting behind his window wanking while we were at it. Probably that turned her on. But did she tell me? Nope…' Karl Anders imitated her voice: '"Can we have the light on, Karl Anders?" Now I think about it, the guy was like you. He wanted to invade our private territory, mine and Veronika's, and she let him. But you haven't asked your question yet. Come on.'

Frølich groped his way towards the voice. 'Switch on the light,' he said.

'I can't. Everything here is automatic.'

'I don't believe you.'

Frølich moved forward with his hand on the rail.

'As I said, come on. What about the slimeball who was killed?'

'The man who killed this neighbour left his DNA. The beer can has your DNA on, Karl Anders.'

The noise appreciably lessened, but that didn't help. He had no idea where he was.

Frank Frølich pulled himself along the rail as he was talking. 'You knew who Almeli was, you knew where he lived, you thought he'd killed Veronika and you might've wanted to take revenge. Perhaps you only visited the guy to get the photos he'd taken of you and her. Perhaps something went wrong, I don't know. You went down to the cellar and killed Almeli there. Afterwards you went up to his flat and took the computer and camera. I know the beer can will prove this. But I'm ready to throw it away. I'd like you to confess.'

It was now so quiet that Karl Anders's laughter echoed off the walls in the darkness. 'You're even more fucking stupid than I thought,' he shouted. 'Is that what you think? That I killed the slimeball? They don't come any dafter than you. Yes, I might've wanted to kill him, but I'd never have been able to do it. And even you know that, if you wake up and use your brain.'

Frølich's eyes were beginning to get used to the darkness. He could see the figure five or six metres away. He said: 'I can see you.'

Immediately he was blinded by a bright beam. He closed both eyes. The light disappeared. He heard the sound of running feet. Had to blink the light out of his eyes. Now he couldn't see anything.

'Why did you do that?'

'Because I felt like it.'

Frølich couldn't tell where the voice was coming from. 'You mustn't forget I *know* what you're capable of, Karl Anders. Whenever I hear your name or look at the old class photos I remember the last night on Corsica. I blamed myself for years for what happened. For chickening out. But now I think a little differently. I've learned you can't turn back the clock. You can't do things for others. It was your idea to leg it that night. My mistake was to go with you. My decision. It's the most stupid thing I've ever done because I didn't touch the girl. It took me twenty bloody years to realise it wasn't *my* fault what *you* did to her. That's why I'm leaving it up to you to decide what to do with the beer can. If you can live with things like that, it's your business.'

'What are you talking about?'

'You know very well what I'm talking about!'

Frølich's eyes were used to the darkness again.

The figure he glimpsed moved away. He followed.

Karl Anders stopped.

Frølich stopped. The beam of light dazzled him again. He closed both eyes, tried to screen them with his hands, but all he saw was reflections.

'You talk as if you know what happened between me and her,' Karl Anders laughed. 'What do you know about it? She liked it, Frankie. She enjoyed every second. I went back there last year. Wondering whether she'd recognise me. I met her. She works in the same café. She's as attractive now as then. She's married with three kids. She serves the same food and the same coffee as twenty years ago. Her bloke, with his huge gut, sits at a table filling in lottery tickets. She lives a boring life in a boring place. And do you know what? She talked about that night as though Christmas Eve had come into her boring-as-shit life. I was the tall, blond guy she'd dreamed about for ever and who had come back for her after many years. Last summer the only thought in her brain was how to get me into bed, and here you are, snivelling and claiming I've done something to you. You've got no idea what you're talking about. You're a fucking loser. You were a zero the very first time I clapped my eyes on you!'

'You interrupted me,' Frølich said stiffly. He saw the other man move and stop. 'I've put Corsica behind me. I came here to talk about Sivert Almeli. So what do you say?'

The torchlight dazzled him again. Two brief seconds, but he was blinded.

'Sling your hook, Frankie!'

Frølich heard the sound of footsteps, but didn't move until his eyes were used to the darkness again.

Karl Anders wasn't there.

He groped his way through the pitch black not knowing where he was.

Then he felt how cold it was in there, inside the mountain. It was freezing cold. His teeth were chattering.

At that moment he received a blow to the back and fell. He put out his hands to protect himself, but it didn't help. His hands met metal. He couldn't protect his head. There was a bang to his temple and he passed out for a few seconds. When he came to, he was drenched in sewage. He stood up, but the sludge beneath gave way. He sank down. All he could think was he had shit on his hands, shit in his hair. He vomited. Brought up the contents of his stomach in one single heave. They splashed into the sewage. He found metal. Grabbed it and pulled himself up. It was an edge. Solid ground. He wriggled forward. Struggled to his knees, shook his head, groggy, and tried to stand. At the same time, he felt someone get a stranglehold around his neck and try to force him back under the sewage.

'It's your decision,' the voice hissed in his ear. 'You can either be flushed out fifty metres down in Oslo Fjord or ploughed into a field in Toten. Make-your-mind-up time!'

Panic concentrated the adrenalin in his body. He stood up. Wobbled, opened his eyes and saw a shadow swinging a pole. He ducked, but he wasn't quick enough. It felt like he had been shot. He fell like a sack of potatoes. Sewage oozed across his body. The pain numbed every muscle, but it kept his brain alive. Frølich summoned every ounce of strength in his body, rolled onto his side, found his footing and pulled himself out of the sludge.

'Does it make you feel any better knowing I killed the arsehole?' Karl Anders shouted. 'If so, I did it! That plonker with the comb-over was in her flat.'

Frølich tried to blink the liquid from his eyes.

'The slimeball and I watched the cop going through her underwear the same way the guy had been staring at Veronika. That was half the kick, Frankie, that no one could stop me. I cut the bastard's throat while you were mincing around like the twat you've always been.'

Frølich's vision returned. He kept blinking. In a flash he saw a shadow launch itself at him like a tiger. He fell on his back, in the sewage. The fingers that squeezed his throat were as hard and tough as Manila rope. He had to have air. Pushed his head up, but it was forced down again.

His hands were free. They groped Karl Anders's face. Found his eyes. He straightened his two forefingers and thrust with all the force he could muster. The hold around his neck loosened. Frølich came up and inhaled air.

Karl Anders was on all fours screaming. He was only a shadow, but that was enough. Frank Frølich interlaced his fingers to form a sledge-hammer fist and rotated like a discus thrower. Ninety kilos of flesh hit the target. Karl Anders fell onto his side. Frølich reached for the iron pole, found it and raised it above his head. He hit him. Raised the pole again. Hit him. Frølich screamed every time the pole hit home. He screamed twenty years of self-contempt out of his system. His head was empty. He just kept hitting – until the lean body beneath him no longer moved.

Deep down, he hadn't expected her to let him in.

She watched him coolly through the door opening for a few seconds before she noticed the bouquet of flowers. 'For me?'

Gunnarstranda nodded.

She opened the door fully and stepped aside. He thought: *diamonds may be a girl's best friend, but flowers open doors.*

'Lilies?' she asked.

He nodded. 'Martagon lilies. My own. Grow them at my cabin. I was there at the weekend.'

He sat down on the broad, white sofa and played with Tove's pendulum while Lena went into the kitchen. He heard her opening and closing cupboard doors. A tap ran. Through the doorway he could see her cutting the stalks and arranging the flowers in a vase. Eventually she came back and put the whole display on the table.

'Lovely,' she said, looking at his hands. 'What are you doing?'

'It's a pendulum,' he said, and showed her. 'Tove loves the esoteric, tarot and all that stuff. She maintains this screw has the answer to questions.' He wrapped the pendulum in his hand and winked at her. 'We have our hobby horses, Tove and I. Actually I'm happy it's nothing more serious than that. How are you doing?'

'OK,' she nodded. 'Back to work on Wednesday, I think.'

'How's the bike?'

Lena shot him a watchful glance.

Gunnarstranda grinned and dangled the pendulum.

She looked him in the eye. 'It's a total wreck. I'm really sorry to lose the bike, but at the same time immensely pleased I got away so lightly. Imagine, coming off your bike down a hill with alcohol in your blood. It's no joke.'

'Talking about drinking,' Gunnarstranda said with a smile, 'I take a little milk in my coffee.'

She got up. 'You thought you'd caught me there,' she said. 'But in fact I'd already put the coffee on when I was in the kitchen.'

One minute later she was back with two sizable mugs.

They drank.

Her eyes twinkled from over the coffee.

Gunnarstranda put his mug down. 'Now you don't need to cancel your sessions with your psychologist,' he said casually.

She looked down.

'His bike's definitely a wreck.'

She was unable to stifle a smile.

Gunnarstranda waved the pendulum again.

'Please,' she said with her eyes closed. 'Please stop that.'

'Lena.'

She opened her eyes.

'The flowers come from the bottom of my heart,' Gunnarstranda said. 'And I'm really looking forward to seeing you back at work. But you'll have to put up with being on the bench for a while.'

'Why?'

He waved the pendulum again. 'You were so lucky, Lena. Erik Valeur's completely off his chump, and you know that now. But it was a painful way to find out. Unprofessional. You should never have ended up in a wrestling match with the guy – I mean, fallen off your bike. You know as well as I do that the rat was about to fall into the trap. We would've got Valeur anyway, without wrecking a single bike or hurting anyone.'

He sipped his coffee.

She said nothing.

He put down the mug. 'If you want to be back in the team you have to show us you're not a loner, show us you're a team player, do you understand?'

'Have you asked the screw about that too?' she asked. 'If I understand?'

He grinned and lifted his mug again. 'Exceptionally good coffee,' he mumbled. 'I think I know how we can find a use for you, Lena.'

'You'd never say anything like that to Frølich.'

Gunnarstranda put down the mug and leaned back against the wall. 'Haven't you heard?' he said with downcast eyes.

'Heard what?'

'Don't you read the papers, either?'

'As little as possible, same as anyone with a certain need for dignity in their everyday life.'

'Frølich's done with the police, Lena.'

She eyed him with a deep frown. 'What do you mean?'

'He's been charged.'

'Charged?'

'He attacked his friend, Karl Anders Fransgård. Frølich's been charged with a non-regulation arrest and malicious assault in aggravated circumstances. Shame but that's the way it goes. One man's loss, another woman's gain. We need people.' He got up. 'So come back to work.'

She gawped. 'Frølich's been given the boot?'

'That's the long and short of it.' Gunnarstranda walked towards the door, opened it. Turned and looked at her. Waited until they had eye contact, then lifted a long, bony finger and pointed it at her. 'Get well soon, Lena. Properly well.'

She sat there, stunned.

Gunnarstranda closed the door quietly behind him and ambled down the stairs.